AF556057

7 DEADLY SINNERS

Debarati Mukhopadhyay is one of the most popular authors of contemporary Bengali literature. A young government officer by profession, she has written more than 20 bestselling novels including *Narach, Dakat Raja, Glanirbhabati Bharat, Shikhandi, Ishwar Jakhan Bandi* and *Aghore Ghumiye Shib.* Her corporate-world novel *Dasgupta Travels* was shortlisted for the Sahitya Akademi Yuva Puraskar in 2021. Many of her novels, such as *Narak Sanket, Ranrkahini* and *Shikhandi,* have been adapted for the silver screen. Debarati is a prolific writer and contributes regularly to Bengal's prominent literary magazines and journals. As an officer, bestselling author, travel enthusiast, amateur violinist and mother to an infant, Debarati is considered a youth icon. She also volunteers her time to guide government-job aspirants. A widely recognized public speaker, Debarati can be often found delivering motivational talks at educational seminars, conferences and in the halls of spiritual institutions.

7 DEADLY SINNERS

INDIA'S MOST FEARED MURDERERS

BESTSELLING BENGALI AUTHOR
DEBARATI MUKHOPADHYAY

RUPA

Published by
Rupa Publications India Pvt. Ltd 2024
7/16, Ansari Road, Daryaganj
New Delhi 110002

Sales centres:
Bengaluru Chennai
Hyderabad Jaipur Kathmandu
Kolkata Mumbai Prayagraj

Copyright © Debarati Mukhopadhyay 2024
Photographs courtesy: Debarati Mukhopadhyay/Wikipedia Commons
(unless mentioned otherwise)
Translated by Aritra Mukherjee

The copyright of the photographs vest with the respective photographer/copyright owner.

While every effort has been made to trace copyright holders and obtain permission, this has not been possible in all cases; any omissions brought to our attention will be remedied in future editions.

The views and opinions expressed in this book are the author's own and the facts are as reported by her which have been verified to the extent possible, and the publishers are not in any way liable for the same.

The book is based on court case materials and other reported facts, but some parts of the story are product of the author's imagination and have been dramatized.

All rights reserved.
No part of this publication may be reproduced, transmitted, or stored in a retrieval system, in any form or by any means, electronic, mechanical, photocopying, recording or otherwise, without the prior permission of the publisher.

P-ISBN: 978-93-90260-87-4
E-ISBN: 978-93-90260-47-8

First impression 2024

10 9 8 7 6 5 4 3 2 1

The moral right of the author has been asserted.

Printed in India

This book is sold subject to the condition that it shall not, by way of trade or otherwise, be lent, resold, hired out, or otherwise circulated, without the publisher's prior consent, in any form of binding or cover other than that in which it is published.

CONTENTS

Preface *vii*

1. By Disgrace of Godman: Mohanta–Elokeshi Case, 1873 1

2. King of Kumortuli: Khada Goonda Case, 1930 29

3. The Wrath of King, the Death of God: Bawla Murder Case, 1925 95

4. Dear Doctor Devil: Indumoti Ponkshe Murder Case, 1959 117

5. Fire Should Not Be Played With: Shamim Rahmani Case, 1960 145

6. The Witch and the Doctor: Vidya Jain Murder Case, 1973 163

7. Memories of the Malevolent Mistress: Troilokkyo Case, 1876 174

Bibliography 255

PREFACE

Seven stories, seven anecdotes, seven tales of gruesome yet captivating thrillers that are actually from the pages of history.

Time knows that 'true crime' was not a darling among Indian readers for the longest time. But if we look globally, people have never shied away from delving into true crime stories, where a true incident is packaged with thrill and romance for the people. The ingredients to retell a crime story for the audiences is simple—an excellent understanding of the criminal mindset.

These seven stories, cooked by me for your literary taste buds, are about real people like Elokeshi—a girl who was beheaded by her husband, yet he was hailed as a hero for punishing his wife. The story of Khada Goonda not only tells the story of a man with dual personality but also speaks of the miserable life of trollops in Calcutta under the Raj. There are stories of people like Bawla who became collateral damage, and there are stories of people like Shamim who killed because she was betrayed in love. There are also stories about the cruel and cunning world of kings and about those 'educated people' who treat women as napkins and are worse than rats and snakes.

For starters, you have stories of betrayal, pain and disgusting human beings. And for dessert, you have Troilokkotarini, the supposedly first female serial killer of India and her story of transformation from a poor brahmin village girl to one of the most notorious murderers in Indian history.

In 2018, my work, a superset of these stories, became quite a sensation in contemporary Bengali literature, and now thanks to Rupa Publications, my recipes have a revamp in English. These stories, based on true cases, span across a long period of time, from stories based in pre-independent India to stories based in post-independent India. I must accept that in this endeavor of mine, the knowledge from the archives of The National Library, Kolkata was really helpful.

So? Will these seven stories make the readers feel thrilled? Bored? Agitated? I really don't know! One may take a pen to write a scathing review, or they might just say 'wow!'

Will my seven recipes really smack the literary lips? I am waiting eagerly!

all gods in the Hindu religion, most of them were anything but pious and practiced things that were not befitting for a *sadhak*[3] of Shiva. For the last two-and-a-half centuries, many mohantas have been accused of supposed appropriation of temple funds and sexual harassment—The Elokeshi Murder Case is one such example.

There was a village named Kumrul, located on the outskirts of Tarkeshwar. The village was completely dependent on Tarkeshwar for all kinds of trade. Nilkamal Mukhopadhyay was a poor brahmin living in this village. He did not possess much land for agriculture and earned his living by doing odd jobs. He used to be the regular purohit of Harimohan Mukhopadhyay, a revered rich man of the village. But with the gradual decline in his health, he was relieved from the job, and soon life became difficult for him and his family.

When the first wife of Nilkamal Mukhopadhyay passed away, leaving behind their only daughter Elokeshi, Nilkamal married again. His second wife was Mandakini. Mandakini had a daughter named Muktokeshi. The poor brahmin Nilkamal was going through a tough time of financial nullity. Every day, he used to roam around for any source of earning.

At that time, the chief mohanta of Tarkeshwar temple was Madhab Chandra Giri, who was infamous for his promiscuous behaviour. Like many other women in villages around Tarkeshwar, Mandakini was also among the love interests of Madhab Giri. The fire was equally raging on both ends as many times, Mandakini went to Tarkeshwar to spend time with Madhab Giri under the pretense of going to the temple for puja. In return, she received rice, daal, fruits and,

---

[3]A sadhak, in Indian religions and traditions, is someone who follows a particular way of life designed to realize the goal of one's ultimate ideal, whether it is merging with one's eternal source, *brahman*, or realization of one's personal deity.

if she was lucky enough, clothes that were donated for puja at the temple. There was no way for poor Nilkamal to fulfil the needs of his wife. Hence, despite knowing everything, he chose to be silent on the matter.

Elokeshi, not getting any attention and care from her stepmother Mandakini, continued sustaining on bare minimum. However, as Elokeshi grew up, the entire Kumrul village was mesmerized by her charming grace. She had a braid that went beyond her waist, her face resembled the betel leaf and her eyes were beyond description in prose. Most of the people in her village were smitten by her beauty.

When Elokeshi was eight years and five months old, Nilkamal, in a lucky *muhurtam*[4] in 1867, married her off to an orphan brahmin man named Nabin Chandra Bandopadhyay by somehow gathering funds from his well-wishers. In those days, if a girl was unmarried after nine, people started looking at her strangely. Thus, there was no time for Nilkamal to waste, and he went for the most decent option available to save his reputation in the society.

Nabin worked at a printing press in Calcutta (now Kolkata). He had to stay at work for the whole day, and in a city like Calcutta, he did not gather enough courage and trust to leave Elokeshi alone at home. She was a simple village girl. Nabin thought it was highly probable that something unpleasant might happen to her if she was left alone at home.

Hence, Nabin decided to let his wife be at her father's place before leaving for Calcutta. But he did not have a good time being away from his wife. He never missed any holiday to visit Kumrul, and he brought new sarees, colourful bangles and new dolls for his wife every time he visisted.

---

[4]An auspicious day on which an important event, usually a wedding, can be held.

He also gave money to his mother-in-law as an allowance towards the expenditure of his wife. Lying alone in a rented room in a narrow lane of North Calcutta, he kept thinking of his wife all the time. He thought that he would bring her to Calcutta once he started earning a little more to afford a full-time female domestic worker in the house to keep a watch on her.

Five years passed like this, and Elokeshi passed her childhood days stepping into the delicate years of puberty. Her beauty won the race against her age and that attracted her husband to visit her like a bee keeping a watch on its its hive and queen. Soon, Nabin started visiting Kumrul every weekend. He used to count his days throughout the entire week to see the moon-like face of Elokeshi.

It was the month of March, but summer had already set in that year. After a tiring day, Elokeshi went to the pond for a bath. On every occasion, she usually took her little sister Muktokeshi with her, but on that day, she didn't call her. Muktokeshi was prone to catching cold, and if she took a dip in the pond at the odd time of afternoon, it would be inevitable for her to fall ill. Thus, Elokeshi decided to go alone and have a bath so that the cool evening breeze might comfort her by drying off her wet clothes.

When Elokeshi almost finished bathing in the pond, the sun was about to set, and the birds started flying in formations towards their nests. Elokeshi started her journey home in wet clothes. She was walking as silently as a cat through the muddy roads when she suddenly heard the sound of a horse. But as far as she knew, no horse was supposed to come here as the path was designated for the use of women only! Elokeshi tried to cover herself up as quickly as possible, but in a blink of an eye, the horse was almost behind her. The rider was none other than the mohanta of Tarkeshwar temple, Madhab Giri.

Madhab Giri was returning from a faraway town as there was a hearing in the court related to the temple on that day. The judgment was gradually inching against Madhab and that kept him agitated. Hence, to reach home quickly, he chose to take a shortcut through that narrow lane of Kumrul village. The horse was just about to run over Elokeshi when the quick hands of Madhab on its reins prevented it. The veteran debauchee was struck by a deluge of testosterone when he watched her.

That milky white complexion, that face resembling an artist's depiction of the moon—Madhab Giri was simply mesmerized by the enchanting belle. On the other hand, the look in Madhab Giri's eyes made Elokeshi uncomfortable, and she managed to run quickly towards her home.

Though Elokeshi tried hard to get out of Madhab Giri's radar, he, like a seasoned predator, found out everything about her. One day, Madhab Giri saw her entering her house and murmured to himself, 'She entered the house of Nilkamal, which means she is the stepdaughter of Mandakini.'

On the evening of that day, when Nilkamal arrived home after a long day of work, he started washing his feet with a dull face as he had not managed to earn more than a few pennies. Mandakini was about to serve him some dry puffed rice, when Kenaram, a trusted servant of Madhab Giri, arrived at the house. He said, 'O *bou*! Come quickly, Madhab Maharaj has summoned you. It seems he is in a very bad mood! Come quickly!'

Mandakini looked at her husband for a second and then hurried out of the house with Kenaram to see the mohanta. Nilkamal continued chewing the rice slowly. What was there for him to say anyway? For the past month, he had been almost broke. The money that Nabin had given to his wife was about to run out. In other words, Mandakini was running the family. Hence, he had no other option but to tolerate everything without any protest.

It was quite late when Mandakini returned home. Till the night fell, Nilkamal remained seated on the porch outside, but his daughters were fast asleep inside the room. The palanquin of Madhab Maharaj dropped his wife in front of the door in the dead of the night. Mandikini came up the porch without washing her hands or feet and removed the veil from her head. She said, 'Listen, what I just heard, if it goes accordingly, then it will not just remove our poverty but also will make us quite rich!'

Nilkamal was shocked after hearing everything from his wife. With a shaking hand, he touched his *poite*[5] and said, 'No, no! How is that even possible? Elokeshi is after all a Brahmin daughter and…shame! How will I even stand before Nabin!'

Mandakini was clearly agitated and annoyed by the refusal. She said, 'Huh! A man who does not have the capacity to earn a single penny is thinking about respect! You will lose your respect only if Nabin ever hears of it! I have already said to him that Elokeshi will not be available on the weekends.'

In the next moment, she lowered her voice and said, 'Do you think Madhab Maharaj will just let go? Will Elokeshi be able to escape? His men are all around not only in Kumrul but also in the entire Tarkeshwar. Perhaps, they are even keeping a watch on our house right now!'

'What if I ask Nabin to take her with him?' Nilkamal said in a faltering manner.

'Moron!' Mandakini sparked back as lowly as possible expressing her strong disagreement, 'Will Nabin take her flying out of here? Do you really think he will be able to

[5]A sacred thread worn by brahmins.

take her with him avoiding the spies of the mohanta? And, for one moment, why you are not even thinking of us! If they do not get her then have you thought what will happen to Mukto?'

Nilkamal became silent. Mandakini didn't say anything uncanny. Madhab Giri was an influential man after all. If he had decided to get Elokeshi then he would go to the ends of the earth to do that. Hence, Nilkamal didn't protest further.

On the day after, as per plan, Mandakini said to Elokeshi, 'Finish cooking as quickly as possible. We will visit Baba's shrine today.'

'Today? All of a sudden?' Elokeshi was surprised. She was feeling rather unwell and was planning to get some rest after work.

Mandakini looked fiercely at her stepdaughter and said, 'What sudden?! It has been five years and still you are unable to bear a child. You are about to turn 15! What are you thinking? If it continues like this, will Nabin take you to Calcutta with him? Rather, he will marry another woman. Come with me, we will offer puja to Baba Taraknath and then we will visit Madhab Maharaj. He will give you some medicine and even before a year you will become a mother!'

'Will Mukto not come with us?' Elokeshi looked at her little sister and said. She feared her stepmother a lot.

'No, Mukto will remain at home. She needs to give food to your father when he comes back home.'

Mandakini was becoming restless. Madhab Giri had promised that upon deliverance, he would gift her gold ornaments and lots of money. Madhab Giri had already sent two men to enquire whether Mandakini was coming with her elder daughter or not.

After the bath and breakfast, Mandakini helped Elokeshi to wear a new saree and tied a garland of jasmine into her braid. Nabin had given a bar of soap to Elokeshi that he had brought from Calcutta the last time he had visited. Mandakini used that to wash Elokeshi's face thoroughly, and then applied the cream that Nabin had bought for her. After that, they boarded a bullock cart and started towards Tarkeshwar.

After arriving at the mandir, they offered puja to Baba Taraknath. Then, Mandakini took her stepdaughter to the royal mansion of the mohanta. The sun was about to set. The young guards knew about Mandakini so they just smiled teasingly at her and opened the gates. After going through a few quarters of the mansion, Mandakini entered a small, dark room with Elokeshi.

Everything was planned beforehand and the guards of the mohanta locked the door from outside. Elokeshi, on seeing Madhab Giri above a big bed in the dark room, at the first glance, failed to recognize him. However, she soon understood who he was, and a scared Elokeshi stood cross-legged anxiously.

Mandakini covered her head with her saree and joined her hands, 'Baba! Please do something for my daughter before people start calling her infertile.'

Madhab Giri was smoking a hookah and lounging on his bed. He placed the hookah pipe on the holder and said, 'Don't worry, Baba's *prasadam* will bring a nice little baby boy in a year. What is your name, *maa*?'

Elokeshi almost curled up in fear and murmured her name, but Madhab Giri was not able to hear it. He was restless and signalled something to Mandakini with his eyes. Mandakini whispered to Elokeshi's ear, 'Baba will now give you some medicine. Take the name of Baba Taraknath and drink it.'

Elokeshi was feeling dizzy due to the thick smell of sulphur in the room, but she grabbed her stepmother's arm tightly and asked, 'Where are you going?'

'I am coming in a few minutes,' Mandakini hurriedly said these words and went outside. Elokeshi was clueless about what to do or say next. Hence, she chose to wrap herself as tightly as possible in her saree and stood still.

Madhab Giri looked at her lasciviously and said, 'Come here, maa! Sit by my side.'

Elokeshi stood still. She was not feeling good, and deep down, she desperately wanted to go home. But she was nothing but a poor, illiterate village girl with no idea of the road back to her home. When she remembered that there were two giant guards standing outside the door, her heart started pounding faster.

Madhab Giri did not wait any longer. He climbed down from the bed, took a small pot from the rack on the wall, and walked straight towards Elokeshi. He started caressing her soft cheeks and said, 'Take the name of Baba Taraknath and drink this water.' Elokeshi started feeling even dizzier, but she drank the water from the pot silently chanting the name of Lord Shiva. She realized that it was too sweet.

Madhab Giri pulled her gently towards himself and said, 'You're a nice girl.'

Elokeshi's head was spinning like a top. She struggled to utter the word 'Maa!' and then she fainted.

Elokeshi had no memory of how long she slept for, but the next morning she woke up to the chirping sounds of birds. When she opened her eyes and gathered herself, she realized that it was already morning. But she was not in her home's cheap bamboo bed at Kumrul. Rather, she was lying on a big four-poster made of mahogany.

'How did I end up here?' she wondered.

When she looked at herself, a chill went down her spine. She did not have even a single piece of thread on her body! Elokeshi shivered in fear and barely managed to collect her saree which was curled up on the floor, and wrapped it around herself. She almost felt like crying in grief and horror.

'How will I face the society now?' she said to herself.

She was not thinking straight. She managed to cover her up in some manner and as soon as she tried going out of the room, Mandakini caught her. She was waiting right outside the room. There was a huge gold necklace in her hand along with an expensive saree. Elokeshi started crying upon seeing her stepmother and said, 'Maa, I am finished! What…what shall I do now?'

Mandakini was already prepared for this outcome and tried to get a grip on the situation. She pulled out Elokeshi of the room and said, 'Shut up you shameless! Why are you crying? The Maharaj has given you this beautiful jewellery and a saree. He promised that on the next day, he will give two more bangles and a silver *kamarbandh.* Did your poor husband ever see these things? I am not even imagining him gifting these to you!'

But Elokeshi continued crying. The palanquin was waiting for them, and Mandakini, without continuing the conversation further, took her daughter and climbed into the palanquin. The bearers started walking towards Kumrul. Throughout the way, Elokeshi kept sitting almost in a vegetative state.

There was no evidence to show that Elokeshi was being forced to do that. Then onwards, she started living at Madhab Giri's house throughout the weekdays. Just on the weekends, his palanquin dropped her home. Soon, a lot of jewellery and expensive clothing came for Elokeshi. She was inherently beautiful. Upon that, the dazzling ornaments made her look like a queen.

Along with that, the social position of the poor brahmin Nilkamal gradually started improving. The almost crumpled house of Nilkamal grew into a lavish residence. Every

Saturday morning, Elokeshi used to come home and give her sister Muktokeshi some notes with the Queen's face inscribed on it. Nilkamal also remained in a jolly mood.

Though Nabin came to his in-laws house on weekends, he started noticing changes in Elokeshi's behaviour. Elokeshi was no more that simple and childish bride anymore. She had learnt the art of seduction in her gestures and words. The new sarees and jewellery invoked a deep curiosity in Nabin's mind. Nabin felt the disruption in his way of life but he remained so smitten by her charm that he was unable to express his doubts. With a growing splinter of doubt in his heart, he returned back to his tiny room in Calcutta every Sunday evening.

The days were going like this until one day. Though social media was not a thing then, rumours travelled through people, and in the transit, those were nurtured by imaginations, amendments and creativity. Such rumours reached Nabin in Calcutta after circulating through many amplifiers made of flesh and blood.

At first, Nabin could not believe what he was hearing. To check things out by himself, he reached Kumrul in the middle of the week without any prior intimation of his visit. He saw that his mother-in-law was cooking, and his father-in-law was massaging his body with oil and was preparing for a bath. It is needless to mention that both were shocked, as if they had seen a ghost, on seeing Nabin.

'Where is Elokeshi?' Nabin asked without even setting down the trunk he was carrying. For the last two nights, there was no sleep in his eyes. Whenever he tried to recall the innocent face of Elokeshi in his mind, he tried to convince himself that Elokeshi was still that simple girl. 'All the news is nothing but lies. It would be nothing less than sacrilege to even think anything dirty about my Elokeshi,' he said to himself.

Nilkamal was not prepared for Nabin's sudden visit. He was confused what to say to his son-in-law. Mandakini pulled the veil on her head and answered, 'Elokeshi has gone to the mandir, son. Freshen up, I will arrange something for you to eat.' Nabin generally maintained a calm demeanor, but when provoked, he would transform into an unstoppable beast. He did not pay any heed to the request of his mother-in-law and asked, 'Which mandir?'

Mandakini swallowed an empty gulp and said, 'The mandir of Baba Taraknath.'

Without wasting a moment, Nabin rushed towards Tarkeshwar temple. If he could get a palanquin on the road then it would be good, but the unavailability would not be a deterrent. He would reach the mandir on foot if necessary. After about three hours, Nabin came back, enraged, from the temple. Elokeshi was anywhere but at the mandir.

Burning in the fire of rage, when he stepped into his in-laws' house, he saw Elokeshi in front of him. In the meantime, Mandakini had managed to send an emergency message to Madhab Giri and brought her home as quickly as possible. Nabin took his wife into a room and locked it from inside. Turning towards Elokeshi, he straightaway asked, 'What about these rumors I am hearing about you?'

Elokeshi didn't have an answer to his question; she just rested her chin on the headboard of the bed, sobbing silently. Though she was living the life of a queen, the man standing in front of her, her loving husband, committed no sin to endure all the trouble. Everyone knew, including Elokeshi, that the man was madly in love with her.

Nabin became vulnerable on seeing his wife crying like that. He was silent for a while thinking what to say in a situation like that, as he thought his allegation perhaps hurt his wife to the core. At the end, he said, 'Let us go to Calcutta tomorrow.'

Elokeshi stopped crying and looked up at her husband with teary eyes. She just gave a brief reply in a soft voice, 'Let's go.'

But the fate of human beings is not completely decided by them. Mandikini, standing at a distance, was eavesdropping on the conversation. The last word from Elokeshi sent shivers down her spine. She desperately ran back to her husband Nilkamal and said, 'Go to Tarkeshwar right now and tell Madhab Giri everything in detail. Nabin may elope with his wife tomorrow morning to Calcutta.'

Nilkamal felt like a zombie, devoid of any sense of self-respect and love towards his own daughter. Still, he garnered just enough strength to utter the next words, 'If she goes, let her go! Nabin will take his own wife, how can we—'

Mandakini did not let her husband finish and started shouting at him, 'This idiocy of yours is the real reason for the condition of our family! Do you really think that Madhab Giri is just going to let us roam about freely if Elokeshi runs away? All the rage of the mohanta will be diverted towards us. He will destroy us, perhaps burn us to death! Then where will I go with Mukto?' Mandakini took a quick breath and continued, 'Just go now, right away, and tell everything! Let us do our duty and let mohanta decide the rest.'

When Madhab Giri got to know everything from Nilkamal, he was enraged. 'How dare he elopes with my mistress right in front of my eyes!' He ordered his servants then and there: 'Inform all the palanquin bearers and bullock cart owners that tomorrow Nabin Banerjee must not leave even with an ant let alone his wife!'

Such was the influence of Madhab Giri that the announcement spread across all the lanes and corners around Tarkeshwar like wildfire. Men were deployed by

Madhab Giri in every nook and corner to stop Nabin and Elokeshi.

On the other hand, Nabin and Elokeshi stayed up for almost the whole night. Since Nabin questioned her character in the afternoon, Elokeshi had not stopped sobbing for a moment. Nabin was clueless about how to handle the crisis. The only thing that continued to ring a bell inside his head was the philosophy that he must stand by his wife as a friend beyond all protocols of a marital relationship. He didn't utter a word and continued to comfort his wife by running his fingers through her hair.

The night had passed, and the sun was upon that fateful day of 27 May 1873. With the first light of dawn, Elokeshi busied herself collecting the small items she intended to take with her, while Nabin ventured out in search of a palanquin. Elokeshi kept a gloomy appearance on her face. Let alone her stepmother and stepsister, she didn't even utter a word in front of her father. She was desperately waiting for the moment when the train would leave the Sheoraphuli station whistling off towards Calcutta, taking her away from that dungeon.

But what an incredible day it was! Not just in Kumrul, but when Nabin almost reached Tarkeshwar on foot, he was unable to spot a single palanquin or a bullock cart. Nabin continued roaming around anxiously. The cool morning sun soon climbed up the sky unleashing its full power on a sultry day of May. The blazing heat almost extracted the life out of him. Even after a long search, he failed to find any mode of transport and returned home with a heavy heart.

Elokeshi was ready to go. Upon seeing Nabin, she eagerly asked, 'Shall we start?'

Nabin did not reply back to her. He just asked his father-in-law, 'Do you have any idea where all the palanquins are?'

Nilkamal just played back the answer he was programmed for, 'I have no idea.'

It did not take much time for Nabin to understand that someone in the house did not want him and Elokeshi to be together. He was about to lose patience, but he maintained his composure and went outside a second time to find a bullock cart at least.

Later, Nabin did find some carts but no one agreed to be hired. Nabin tried to lure them by promising a fare four times the standard rate, but they remained steady on their stand. On top of that, as instructed by Madhab Giri, they started mocking Nabin: 'Showing off attitude with the money earned by the mohanta's whore eh? Don't you feel like dying to make your wife do such…' An enraged yet helpless Nabin returned back home.

On the other hand, Elokeshi thought that perhaps the transporters were on strike, and hence, Nabin failed to arrange something. She soon realized that they would not be able to leave Kumrul that day. So, she sat down to cut a fish and cook a meal for her husband.

Nabin was burning with rage since he had heard the words of the cart drivers and seen everything else that was happening. He stormed into the kitchen, and seeing the bonti in front of him, picked it up and delivered a sharp blow to Elokeshi with it. Within a moment, Elokeshi's head rolled on the floor towards the heap of fish scales.

Even before anyone could have made any sense of the matter, everything was finished. Nabin went with the blood-dripping bonti to the office of the district magistrate of Hugli. He surrendered, saying, 'Saheb, I have killed my wife. Please punish me!'

This is the nerve-wracking story behind the famous Elokeshi Murder Case of 1873. This has been the plot of many movies and plays. Many artworks on clay dishes, called *pawt* in Bengali, were drawn based on this story. But it does not end here.

Though Nabin surrendered in front of the district magistrate, driven by the trance and heat of the moment, when the case was raised in the district court, he started denying all the charges against him. 'I did not kill Elokeshi. I don't know who killed her!' were his words. Not just that, he filed a case against Madhab Giri alleging that he raped Elokeshi. Besides, he also filed cases against Kenaram, the trusted aide of Madhab Giri, and his father-in-law Nilkamal Mukhopadhyay.

Interestingly, just six days after the death of Elokeshi, the otherwise healthy and fit Mandakini died under suspicious circumstances. The lawyer appointed by Nabin argued that to remove the possibility of any possible interrogation of the witness, men of mohanta killed her and made it look like suicide.

During that time, almost all newspapers in Bengal and across India were busy extrapolating and reporting the details of the case. It was quite a popular and enticing story for a time when housewives were believed to be the avatar of *sati*. Even thousands gathered around the court on the days of the hearing.

Though according to the language of the law, in this case, the victim was Elokeshi and the criminal was Nabin, the general population of the country became biased towards Nabin because for the society, a husband forgiving her wife after knowing everything was nothing less than god.

The entire rage of the public fell on Madhab Giri, and people termed him as a scoundrel who deserved only to be hanged. In this case, considered to be one of the most studied legal cases of British India, the public prosecutor was

Mr Ishwar Chandra Mitra, and the lawyer on the defense was the reputed barrister Mr Umesh Chandra Banerjee, who later became the first elected president of the Indian National Congress.

Nilkamal, under oath, gave the statement that Nabin came home on the morning of 27 May 1873, and on that day, Nilkamal was at Tarkeshwar for attending an invitation at mohanta's home. When he returned, he saw Nabin, Elokeshi and all other family members at his house. He also said that nobody else in his family, apart from him, had ever visited the mohanta's home in the past two years.

Nabin, standing on the right side witness box of the judge, screamed, 'Lie! He is lying, My Lord!' It's an absolute lie! When I reached Kumrul, he was in the house and Elokeshi was not present.' The Judge ordered Nabin to stop, and ordered Nilkamal to continue his statement. Nilkamal said that he left for work at dawn and he had no idea what happened after that.

On the other hand, the neighbour of Nilkamal, Harinarayan Bhattacharya, and a few others, supported the theory that Nilkamal's house was nothing more than a brothel, and Mandakini and Elokeshi were no less than sex workers. The public prosecutor Ishwar Chandra Mitra said 'Then Nabin's accusation does not hold any stand, My Lord. Elokeshi was a prostitute in reality. How can one accuse an honorable man like Madhab Giri of raping a girl who sold her body willfully? Whatever the mohanta has done, though not fitting for a man of his stature, has done it after fully paying for the service.'

The little sister-in-law of Nabin, Muktokeshi, said, '*Jamaibabu* [Nabin] came out from the kitchen with the bonti and said, "I have beheaded your sister."'

The veteran defense lawyer Umesh Chandra Banerjee raised a question, 'Can we trust her statement? I believe she is being forced to lie either under threat or by being bribed. It is to be noted, My Lord, that Muktokeshi is wearing earrings that are quite expensive. I would like to ask, how can a poor brahmin like Nilkamal provide her with such an ornament? If not, then who gave it to her? Who is paying for the expenses of this case? Why, on the morning of 27 May 1873, did the mohanta stopped all the modes of transport in and around Tarkeshwar?'

Though Umesh Chandra Banerjee tried to dazzle the lawyer with some counter arguments, it was not really a cakewalk for him to prove that his client Nabin was innocent. Nabin, although denied all accusations in court, himself committed his crime in front of a high-ranking government official on the day of the incident, a typical trait of a crime of passion. The *chowkidar* of the village, Ramdhan, sepoy Manik Kha and the deputy magistrate of Hugli Mr Kedarnath Das, also heard Nabin telling the district magistrate that he had killed his wife himself.

Umesh Chandra Banerjee tried to play the insanity card: 'It is obvious for any man to be driven mad if he comes to know about the infidelity of his wife. My client has killed Elokeshi but is not in a healthy state of mind. My Lord, I would like to plea for considering that as temporary insanity of my client.'

After the debate of this remarkable case, Judge H.T. Princep asked the jury to give its verdict. In those days, the system of jury was prevalent in India where a few jury members used to give the verdict after prolonged debate and reasoning, and the judge used to sign on the judgment making it legal at the end. This system continued in India even after Independence and lasted till 1960. The famous case that supposedly brought the end of the jury system in India was *Commander K.M. Nanavati v. The State of Maharashtra* in 1959, which was later fictionalized as a Bollywood movie.

During that time, not only the courtyard in front of the Hugli District Court but also the roads beyond it were crowded with thousands of general citizens. Everyone was curious to know whether Nabin would be proven innocent or not. After a prolonged reasoning, the jury panel gave the verdict that Nabin was not guilty since he killed his wife under a momentary episode of insanity, not in cold blood. In a matter of moments, the huge crowd waiting outside burst in joy. Everyone started chanting the name of Nabin and everyone demanded the arrest of the mohanta.

But that joy did not last long due to the final verdict of the judge. Judge Princep was not convinced by the verdict of the jury and later the case was raised to Calcutta High Court. The public prosecutor was Jagadananda Mukhopadhyay and the defense was the same, the veteran Umesh Chandra Banerjee. But this time, the verdict was the opposite. The judges declared that even if the accused Nabin Chandra Banerjee was temporarily insane, it never implied that he could take the law in his hands. Thus, the final verdict declared Nabin guilty of murder and he was charged under Section 302 of the Indian Penal Code (IPC), with the punishment of imprisonment for life.

On the other hand, based on Nabin's complaint at the Hugli District Court, an arrest warrant was issued for Madhab Giri. After absconding for over two months, Madhab Giri surrendered himself to the law. However, after that, Madhab Giri did not respond to anything, as if he had lost his power of speech.

When the Hugli District Court ruled against Madhab Giri with a huge sum as a penalty and a long imprisonment, he appealed to the Calcutta High Court. The lawyers appointed by the mohanta raised the point how Nabin, an accused, could complain against the mohanta. They also emphasized that there was no proof of Madhab Giri raping Elokeshi.

Meanwhile, the case prolonged to unexpected turns. Nilkamal passed away. For the autocratic nature of mohanta, there was no dearth of his enemies in Tarkeshwar; they were the ones who kept the case running. A former employee of Madhab Giri stated that Elokeshi was not a sex worker. She was forced to come to the mohanta by her stepmother, and the mohanta intoxicated her before raping her. Another man named Umacharan said, 'This is not the first time the mohanta is doing such a thing. He has raped other women of the village before.' A villager named Rameshwar said, 'One day, when I went to the mohanta's house, I saw that Elokeshi was curled up in fear and her stepmother was pushing her towards the mohanta.'

Though the lawyers and barristers appointed by the mohanta tried to take advantage of all the loopholes of law, all their efforts went to waste. The chief judge declared that Madhab Giri had to pay a hefty penalty and was subjected to three years of life in prison. There was a wave of joy in the public on hearing the news of the mohanta's punishment after a long legal battle.

Later, this story has been portrayed in Kalighat's pawt art and in picture books published by many publishing houses in Calcutta. Some of them depict Nabin just arriving at his in-laws' home; in some, the episode of Mandakini taking Elokeshi to the mohanta is drawn; and some others carry the gruesome scene of Nabin chopping off his wife's head. Three elements of this case became the talk of the town—rape, murder and the court proceedings. There have also been 19 hit plays performed based on the story.

For mohantas of Tarkeshwar, Madhab Giri was not the last to be caught in such shameful and criminal activity. Later on, mohanta Satish Giri was also found guilty for being involved in such sexual scandals. The daily *Bengalee* printed that Elokeshi's father could be classified as a human being who stooped lower than the mohanta by selling off his daughter for his own well-being. The English daily *Englishman* also printed the story and the case details in numerous issues for a long time. The historic book about Tarkeshwar named *Tarak Mangal* by Kedarnath Sarkar also speaks of this heart-wrenching story.

Till today, one can feel the agony and rage of Nabin in the old lanes of Tarkeshwar. This is a tale of love, lust and liaison that ended with loath and liquidation. One can still hear cries of pain from the historic objects scattered around the historic town of Tarkeshwar.

A Kalighat painting depicting Mandikini introducing Elokesi to Madhab Giri

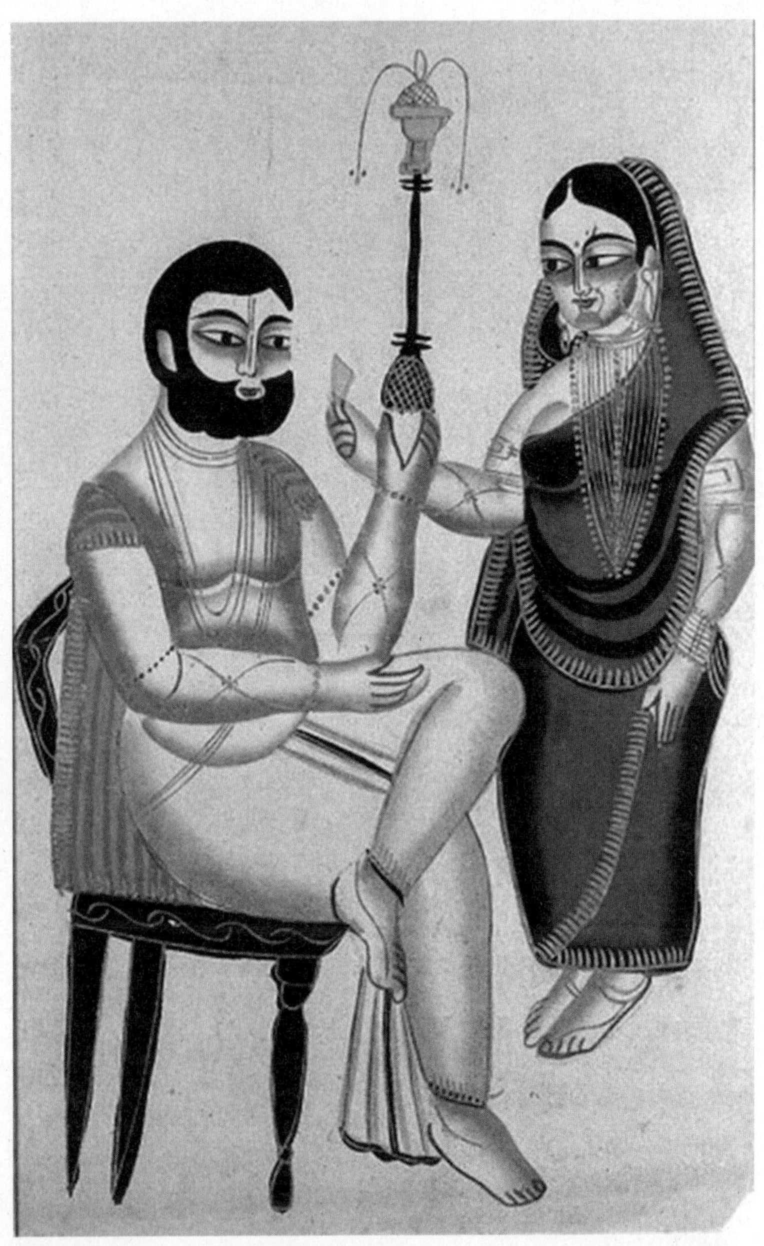

A Kalighat painting depicting Elokeshi offering a betel leaf to Madhab Giri

A Kalighat painting depicting Madhab Giri trying to intoxicate Elokeshi

A Kalighat painting of the moment when Nabin beheads his wife Elokeshi with a bonti

A Kalighat painting of the moment after Elokeshi's murder

A Kalighat painting depicting the trial of Madhab Giri

KING OF KUMORTULI:
KHADA GOONDA CASE, 1930

Two convicted murders, 20 suspected. Seventy-five cases of theft, robbery and extortions. Numerous instances of escape from the traps of British police. Arranging for the marriages of numerous orphaned girls. Giving food to homeless widows. Saving sex workers who were forced to enter the trade. Providing patronage to various orphanages.

These are the deeds of one man who ruled North Calcutta for quite some time 100 years ago, a man whose name terrified many rich people—Khada Goonda. A dual personality like him even amused the police commissioner of Calcutta, Charles Tegart. He supposedly stated that a person like Khada Goonda, who could ruthlessly murder people and still get love and affection from the public, was quite rare to find. Khada was popularly known as the 'King of Kumortuli'. To discover more about the thrilling stories of Khada Goonda, we have to travel back in time to the era when the Union Jack was still waving upon India.

The year was 1936. Back then, everyone was confident of the upcoming independence. The forty-ninth annual conference of Indian National Congress (INC) was organized in the city of Lucknow and the then president of INC had just nullified the newly sanctioned Government of India Act, 1935. The reason cited was the non-inclusion of Indians in the process of framing it. Netaji Subhas Chandra Bose was busy trying to eradicate the British from the Indian soil with military action and was roaming around Europe to form alliances with the leaders of Axis powers.

Meanwhile, the temporary floating bridge connecting Howrah Station and Harrison Road had been disassembled. Braithwaite, Burn & Jessop Construction Company was jointly awarded the tender to construct an engineering marvel of its time—a cantilever bridge without any pillars, today known as the majestic Howrah Bridge.

Around that time, Rabindranath Tagore was trying to tackle the financial crunch at Visva-Bharati by travelling around India with his team of dancers that performed and raised money. Pained by the troubles of such a personality at such an old age, Mahatma Gandhi also tried to arrange for funds to help Tagore.

On 5 September, when Calcutta woke up, there was some commotion on Balaram Majumdar Street, right beside the artisans' district of Calcutta—Kumortuli. The word *'kumor'* means clay artists, and *'tuli'* is another Bengali term for locality. Hearing the commotion, many early morning pedestrians and local residents arrived at the scene. Only a few days remained for Durga Puja celebrations to begin, and the area was quite busy. Many artisans, who had been working overtime, also clustered around to enquire the reason behind the commotion.

In those times, every road used to have a narrow passage running parallel to it for manual scavengers to use. Like every other day, Mohan, a scavenger working for the Calcutta Municipal Corporation, went inside a narrow lane behind a three-storeyed building on Balaram Majumdar Street to perform his cleaning duties. What he saw there horrified him to the core. A corpse with a missing head was packed inside a service duct at the back of the building. Mohan's hands, carrying the broom and bucket, started shaking. He could not call for help either. The place was like a canyon with tall buildings preventing the entry of sunlight. The walls did not have any windows and shouting in such a place was not going to do anything other than creating a damped reverberation.

Mohan hurried to the main road and started shouting at the top of his voice, 'Mu—Mu—Murder! Murder! Where is everybody?! Someone please come!' Within five minutes, there was a small crowd. From the morning customers of tea stalls to artisans holding paintbrushes, everybody in the crowd was stunned by the sheer gruesomeness of the scene. Mohan was running on the street in panic, trying to cool off his nerves. He had seen numerous headless cats and dogs but never a headless man!

Around that time, Binoy Kumar Ray, an overseer of the Corporation, was patrolling the area. His job was to monitor that every scavenger was doing their job properly. Naturally, he halted to look into the matter. At first glimpse of his boss, Mohan ran towards him and explained what the pandemonium was all about. He led him to the exact spot to show the chilling scene. Ray was taken aback, but he controlled his emotions and acted as required. Even though the crowd was busy exploring the possibilities that led to this event, he hurried to the nearby Shyampukur Police Station; after all, one of his subordinate scavengers had discovered the crime. Hence, it was his responsibility to report the incident. Additionally, the officer-in-charge at Shyampukur Police Station, Panchanan Ghosal, was his friend.

Right after the report was filed, Inspector Ghosal, along with Inspector Sunil Kumar Ray, rushed to the spot accompanied by a team of constables and hawaldars. The officers were also stunned after initial examination of the place. Inspector Ray said with utter amazement in his voice, 'Can you imagine the cruelty of the act, Mr Ghosal! It is difficult for someone to execute such a task if he does not have extreme anger against the victim. If you observe the cut around the neck, it is evident that the person is an experienced killer.'

Ghosal was investigating the narrow lane with microscopic precision. The lane was sandwiched between two parallel blocks of buildings. Though it was walled by multi-storeyed buildings on both sides, none of them had any doors opening to the lane. Hence, there was no way anyone could step into that lane from any of the houses. The lane seemed to be infinitely long, like a tunnel leading to a dark end. He asked Mohan, 'How long is this lane?'

A trembling Mohan replied to the inspector, 'Sahib, this lane continues till Shobhabazar Street.'

Ghosal then focused on the dead body. The house, where the corpse was packed, was quite old and huge. The lack of maintenance resulted in the growth of trees through its walls. The roots of the banyan tree had penetrated the unplastered brick wall deeply. The foliage formed a blinding canopy resulting in a place where anything could be easily hidden. The service duct, which wrapped the remains, was bounded by many such roots of the banyan tree clinging to the wall.

One thing became absolutely certain to both officers: the way the body was stuffed four feet above the ground in the narrow duct, proved that multiple people were involved in the act. The body seemed quite heavy, and the place was too narrow for a single person to manoeuvre such a heavy payload.

A few minutes later, the police photographer, fingerprint expert and planmaker reached the spot. However, due to the lack of adequate illumination, the photographer was unable to get a proper photograph. But this problem was also solved. Moni, the nephew of Gopeshwar Pal, one of the celebrated artists of Kumortuli, was a part of the crowd that wanted to know more about that unprecedented event. When he heard that the photographer was unable to complete his job due to the lack of proper lighting, he called his uncle, Pal, and both of them quickly sketched the whole scene with photographic accuracy and then gave it to the inspectors.

In the meantime, the news of this murder spread across the city. People, whose relatives or friends were missing for the last few days, started contacting the police with the suspicion that the victim might be known to them. But the corpse was headless, so nobody was able to recognize it.

Fortunately, the two police officers who were investigating the case were two assets of the Calcutta Police. Ghosal was a star cop who later became the deputy inspector general of Calcutta Police. He apprehended numerous shrewd criminals during his illustrious career. Besides, he is supposedly the first Indian who did his doctoral research on criminal psychology. He was also an extremely talented author who penned many books and used to be a member of the literary congregation attended by Rabindranath Tagore.

On the other hand, Ray was a gifted criminal investigator. He was able to discern the time of death and many other minute details by simply observing a cadaver. Even before the police physician arrived on the scene, Ray scanned the corpse, and judging the stiffness of the muscles and the clotting of blood, he stated: 'Panchanan babu, this man was killed approximately 10 hours ago, that is, around 9.00 p.m.

The body was laid on its back on the road. Ghosal gazed at it and said, 'From the size and built, it can be said that the age of the victim is around 27. There is also a poite around the neck; he can be a Bengali, Madrasi, Odiya, anything! How do we find out who he is?'

Ray, after surveying every fold of skin and cloth, said, 'Look! The whole body has a dense cover of body hair.

There is a tattoo of a flower on the lower portion of the left hand.' He summoned the fingerprint expert and said, 'Paresh, please take a print of all the digits of both hands. Let us see if that matches any of the criminal records we already have.'

Paresh quickly started his job. He first cleaned the hands and then applied some ink on the fingertips of the dead man. After that, he carefully pressed them against a sheet of paper.

The sun almost reached the zenith before all procedures were completed, but during primary investigation, the corpse could not be identified. An interrogation of the local residents also proved futile. After the dead body was sent for post-mortem, Ghosal and Ray went back to the Shyampukur Police Station.

Several questions were hovering the minds of Inspectors Ghosal and Ray: who was responsible for such a gruesome murder in the city of Calcutta? Who was the victim? These questions were driving them crazy. As with most police departments all over the world, Calcutta Police also maintained a network of informers. Shyampukur Police Station also had some, but even they were unable to shed any light on this murder.

Ultimately the post-mortem report was delivered. Inspector Ray was correct: the post-mortem report clearly stated that the victim was aged around 27 and the murder was committed around eight or nine the previous night. The person was stabbed multiple times first and the head was cut off later, while he was still breathing. After getting the report, Inspectors Ghosal and Ray started the investigation with full steam.

The post-mortem report revealed that the murderer even slashed the veins of the feet, maybe after cutting off the head. The way the body was mutilated proved that the murder was not committed just to kill but to make him suffer. Was it a crime of passion? Was he killed by his competitor in the race of love? Or was he just an astray young man who got himself embroiled in some chaos at the nearby red-light district and was slaughtered for it?

These were some of the many premises based on which the investigation was trying to proceed. However, even after investigating everything, the inspectors eventually came back to square one. But they were indomitable, and they again started following routine investigation protocols in and around the areas surrounding the crime scene.

One day, Ghosal reached Chitpur and met a man who came running to him and said, 'Sir! I knew Pagla!'

'Who is Pagla? Who are you? What's your name?' Ghosal, with raised eyebrows, shot a load of queries to the man.

'Sir, my name is Ambika,' the man scratched his head and continued, 'The man who was found dead was called Pagla. I knew him. I talked to him even before the day his body was discovered.'

Inspector Ghosal quickly brought Ambika to the police station for interrogation. Ambika said that he had been roaming around Balaram Majumdar Street on the day the corpse had been discovered but had not been able to gather the courage to go and face the police. He had feared he would be accused falsely. But now, he had the courage because he had heard from various sources that the officers investigating the case were not those who falsely framed an innocent person into an accused in a case.

Ambika's voice was shaking as he said, 'Pagla was actually the local name of Atul babu. He used to be a music tutor in our area. He also played the tabla. There were numerous girls in Sonagachi who used to be his students. On the evening of 4 September, when I was coming home, I had seen Pagla chatting with Manindra babu outside his home. I had also halted there for a few minutes to join the adda.'

'Who is Manindra babu? Is he also a pimp, or is he a fixed client of someone?' Ghosal interrupted him.

'No, no, he is not a pimp. He is a resident of this area and readily helps people of the area in times of need. He is also a wrestler and has his own team.'

'Okay, continue.'

'We had been chatting when some goons surrounded Pagla and started threatening him. Their leader, Khoka, had suddenly pointed his finger towards Pagla and said, "The name is Khoka. Heard that, right?! I will not just kill you but also cut off your nose." Pagla had been shaking in fear. He had kneeled down, grabbed Khoka's feet and said, "Please let me go. I will never ever go near that girl, I promise by the name of Goddess Kali!"' Ambika stopped talking and took a deep breath.

'Then?'

'Manindra babu had also pleaded with the gang leader to forgive Pagla. Then the gang had left us and walked away. Pagla had been mute with shock. Manindra babu had tried to boost his morale and requested me to accompany Pagla out of the locality. Pagla and I had just proceeded some distance along the Garanhata Street when suddenly Khoka and another fair-skinned man pounced upon Pagla. Khoka had grabbed Pagla by his neck and instructed the other person to call a taxi.'

Ghosal observed that even after a few days of the incident, when Ambika was describing his experience, his face showed clear signs of anxiety and terror.

'When they had grabbed Pagla like that, I had run away out of fear. The fair-skinned man had tried to stop me but Khoka had not shown any interest in me. I had run to meet Manindra babu in order to narrate the whole episode. While I had been running away, I had looked back once and saw that they had been joined by some other goons. They had packed him in a taxi, which took off along Garanhata Street.'

'Do you remember the taxi number?' Ray was sitting across the table when he asked.

During the interrogation, Ghosal spotted that Ambika had the habit of biting off his tongue when he felt remorseful. When Ray asked the question, he did the same and said, 'No, Sir! At that time, I had only been focused on saving my life. I forgot to note down the number.'

The officers relaxed a little. Finally, they got a lead. Now, they had to interrogate this person called Manindra babu. Inspector Ghosal noted all the information he got and then started the routine questions, 'Okay, this man, whom you are calling Pagla, this Atul Babu—what more do you know about him?'

Ambika was now less anxious and replied, 'Sir, as I said, Atul babu used to teach music and tabla to various girls in our locality. He was a nice person as far as I know. I never heard about him getting into any problems.'

Suddenly something struck Inspector Ghosal. 'How were you able to recognize the body of Pagla that day when we found the corpse? The head was missing!'

'It doesn't matter, Sir! Pagla was a heavy drinker. He was frequently found lying around drains in the Sonagachi area, drunk to the brim. He had characteristic dense layer of body hair and a flower tattoo on his left hand, which is easily recognizable. I am confident that it's Pagla's body. I can vouch that many girls of Sonagachi will also recognize the body even without a head!' Ambika replied with utmost confidence. After that, Ghosal and Ray allowed Ambika to leave and left for Sonagachi to interrogate Manindra Pal.

Ambika had already said that Manindra Pal was a

recognized wrestler living in the Sonagachi area. He even had his own team and ring there. That information helped the inspectors locate Manindra. After a brief interrogation and cross-checking, it was found that Manindra Pal knew the same chain of events as Ambika. Apart from the already collected information, some more points were added by Manindra. He said, 'When the goonda Khoka had been threatening Pagla, I had tried to pacify him and said that Pagla would not go again, but Khoka glowered at me with red eyes and said, "Not go again?! He went to Molina's room yesterday! His days are numbered."'

Manindra Pal paused for a moment and said, 'I am a revered person in this area. I don't know whether it was out of respect or something else, but Khoka had gone away. But after some time, Ambika had come running back and told me that they had kidnapped Pagla.'

Ray asked, 'Was Pagla in love with somebody? Do you have any idea?'

Manindra pal nodded his head and said, 'Atul belonged to a good family. Their ancestral home is in Jessore, and his brother is a physician. But Atul got distracted during his teenage years and landed in this place. He was an introvert and never talked much. That's why people called him Pagla. But I never observed any flaw in him. Actually, even if the girls in this area are sex workers, they respected him as their music teacher. Pagla was a nice person who never disturbed anybody.'

'Who's Molina? Is she a resident of this place?'

'Yes, Molina is a prostitute in this area. Recently, she was cast in a film. She lives in a house at Imam Baksh Lane.' Manindra Pal paused for a moment and looked at the floor. Then, with a lowered voice and raised eyebrows, he continued, 'It is possible that Pagla fell in love with her. But I don't see anything wrong in it.'

Ghosal asked, 'Did you know this man—Khoka—before this incident?'

'As far as I know, Khoka is an escaped convict. He is trying to evade the police and he can be seen in this area around the night.'

'Does he visit any specific person?'

Inspectors, I must say that I don't know much about the girls here,' Manindra Pal smiled to wash off the obvious idea, and continued, 'But me, along with the boys of my team, tries our best to help them whenever possible. When people try to cheat the girls by not paying them and try to do things forcibly, my boys and I teach them a lesson. That is why I am a respected person in this area. I heard from the local girls that before getting kidnapped, Pagla tried to hide at Naki Bina's place. However, out of the fear of Khoka, not only did she refuse but also instructed her domestic worker to drive him off. But now she may not confess all this out of fear of the police.'

'Who is Naki Bina?'

'She is a resident of this area. Her nose is very sharp. Hence, everyone in this area calls her Naki Bina!' Manindra babu guessed what the next question could be. Even before they asked, he said, 'Her address is 2, Nilmoni Street.'

The two officers came back to the police station and talked among themselves. Till then, they knew that Khoka knew two girls from that area, Molina and Naki Bina, and Khoka threatened Pagla because of her closeness to Molina. Pagla had known about the threat to his life and tried to save himself by taking refuge at Naki Bina's home.

Next day, Ray came to the police station and said with a tensed voice, 'If Khoka is an escaped convict, then we must have his records. But I enquired about it in the archives yesterday and no such entry was found.'

Ghosal replied, 'Surely he used another name.'

'Yes, that is possible. And that's why we need to interrogate these two girls as soon as possible. Time is running out!'

The address 2, Nilmoni Street held a mansion with an astounding facade. It was a fact that, at that time, almost all the houses in the Sonagachi area were multi-storeyed with adequate facilities and handsome architecture. If someone took a walk through that area during those times, one would be saluted by the many tall buildings that were present in almost all lanes of the region.

However, the mansion was not only the largest among them but also the epitome of luxury, boasting superior finishing, impeccable architecture and an overall commanding presence. It soared above the rest with its intricate artwork that beautifully complemented the brick red hue of the walls. The floors were adorned with high-quality marble, and a driveway through the porch on one side was currently occupied by a parked car.

A number of bird cages of various sizes were oscillating in the wind, hanging from the second-floor balcony. Almost every cage was glowing with colourful birds, both local and imported. The atmosphere was filled with their chirps. It was evident that Naki Bina earned an enviable amount of money. A mild and pleasing feminine voice could be heard coming somewhere from the second level:

Jodi cholele murarei, tyeje brojopuri
Brojonari kotha rekhe jao
Jibon upay bole dao.

If Murari choose to leave his home,
Where will his love survive,
What will be the purpose of life?

Inspector Ray was a music aficionado and was impressed by the voice. He closed his eyes while listening to the song, 'Marvellous! What a sweet voice! Can you tell me whose composition this is, Panchanan babu?'

Ghosal smiled and answered in a calm voice, 'I am not at all an expert of music, Sunil babu.'

'This is a famous *kabigan*[6] of Haru Thakur!'

'Who is that?' asked Ghosal.

Ray thought that it was unusual for anybody to not have heard the name of such a talented artist. He said, 'That's really odd. You haven't heard of Haru Thakur? Harekrishna Dighari was a famous *kabiyal* (wandering poet singer). He composed many such beautiful kabigaans.'

'Okay.'

'Wow!' Ray again closed his eyes and said, 'She is a true artist. Such dedication, such skills!'

'Shall we go inside to witness the dedication more closely?'

Ray got the sarcasm, and without wasting any more time, he proceeded towards the main door.

Many people were walking on the street. They might have been writers, lawyers or even teachers, but in the red-light district, their identity was one—clients.

Ray and Ghosal were dressed that day like clients. They were both wearing expensive sets of Santipuri dhoti and panjabi, and had put ample amounts of seductive perfume. Both were holding teak wood walking sticks and were chewing on Benarasi paan. The moment they stepped in,

---

[6]Kabigan is a form of Bengali folk performance wherein folk poets sing and perform. This was popular in nineteenth century Bengal, which includes the Indian state of West Bengal and Bangladesh. The mythological themes from both Hindu and Muslims religious texts were commonly used for kabigan.

two servants came running toward them with folded hands, 'Please come, babu! Please come in…'

Without any further instructions, the two servants escorted them to a huge drawing room in the first level of the house. The floor was covered in soft mats in a ring, for the people to sit. There were tabla and tanpura in one of the corners. After the two inspectors took their seats, one of the servants brought two chilled glasses of refreshing drinks and said, 'Please make yourselves comfortable and have some drinks.'

Inspectors Ray and Ghosal drank the glasses empty. After cleaning their lips with their palms, Ghosal said, 'We are coming from Burdwan, quite far, you know! Is this the residence of the celebrated Naki Bina?'

'Yes, babu,' said one of the servants.

Ghosal said, 'We have heard a lot about her fame, so we were not able to restrain ourselves from meeting her. I think we will be able to meet her, right?'

'Definitely, babu! You have come here all the way from Burdwan. There is no way you will return without meeting her! But you will have to wait a little. A zamindar babu is here.' The servants continued trying hard to keep them engaged.

Holding out a 10-rupee note, Ray said, 'It is alright! You take this and bring two paans for us. You can keep the change.' He continued scanning the room and said, 'I heard that last week there was some problem here. Some men came and kidnapped that Pagla master. Is this true?'

The price of two paans was at most four annas, which meant that he would have the change of nine rupees and twelve annas! The huge amount of tip made the servant ready to do everything for them. He started swinging the *pankha*[7] as fast as possible to comfort the godly babus.

---

[7]A type of fan used since the early sixth century BC.

However, that last question from Ray surprised him. He said, 'How do you know about Pagla master babu?'

'We are coming to this place for the first time but we. are aware about everything,' Ray said.

'What can I say, babu.' The servant pulled a sad face. 'That day, when I had been cooking in the kitchen on the second floor, I had heard loud voices coming from downstairs. I had come down running and seen Pagla master, the babu who used to play tabla, had been grabbing our mistress by the feet and crying, "Bina, please save me! They are going to cut me into pieces!" On the other hand, eight-to-nine muscular men had already barged into the room and had been staring furiously at Pagla master.'

'Did Pagla master come regularly here?' asked Ghosal. 'I saw him many times at Basanti's place too.'

'That is normal, babu! Pagla master used to teach music to many women here. He used to blabber a lot, but he was a nice person. He had no greed for money and was happy with whatever he got. He also loved our mistress, but on that day, she didn't save him. Rather, she had stood still and those men had dragged him away in a taxi.' The servant sighed, 'Then I heard the news that Pagla master had been murdered!'

'Who are you blabbering to, Bise?' said a woman around 24 years old as she entered the room. She looked beautiful and her sharp nose distinctly reiterated her prefix; she was indeed Naki Bina.

Bina raised her eyebrows and was about to say something when Ray interrupted her. He stood up and said in a deep voice, 'Namaskar! We are from Shyampukur Police Station. I think you are aware about the murder of music teacher Atul Ghosh. On the night of 4 September, he had come to your place, right? Why did you turn him away?'

The servant named Bise was stunned after he heard the

identity of the supposedly new customers. He looked at his mistress with terror and guilt in his eyes. He never thought of the possibility that the police could infiltrate Naki Bina's house disguised as clients.

Bina was shocked but didn't express it. When she had been entering the room, she had overheard some of the words by Bise, and extrapolated the rest with her intelligence. From the overall scenario, she had reached the conclusion that it was useless to deny anything.

She answered in a calmed and composed voice, 'How could I let him stay, Sir? There is no one in this locality that lives long after going against Khoka babu. If I would have let Pagla master stay that night, then Khoka babu would have killed me ruthlessly.'

Ghosal asked, 'Where does Khoka live?'

'Is he a man to stay in one place, Sir! I really have no idea where he is. He comes to this locality sometimes, stays at Molina's place and disappears, leaving no trace. Recently, Molina started acting in films. Hence, she remained busy and, therefore, Khoka babu has not been around that frequently.'

There was no time to waste, as someone could have informed Molina about the ongoing operation before the inspectors could get to her. The girls of Sonagachi were definitely not pea-brained. A little callousness on the investigators' part might have resulted in a blunder. Hence, after rushing out of Bina's house, the two inspectors almost ran all the way to 32, Imam Baksh Lane, where Molina lived.

But Molina was not home, and all the servants in her house were terrified. Someone had threatened them so effectively that even after interrogating for a long time, no details were divulged from their end.

While both officers were trying their best to extract at least some information from the servants, Panchu, a police informant, barged in and informed them, 'Sir, don't waste time on these people. Molina's mother has already packed her bags and is about to escape through the back door to meet her daughter!' The two officers didn't waste a moment and rushed to the back door. Panchu was absolutely correct. On being apprehended by the two inspectors, Molina's mother sat down shivering with fear. The lady didn't seem like an experienced criminal and gave in easily to police pressure.

Ghosal said in a bold and angry voice, 'I see you are escaping with Molina's jewellery, eh? Arrest this woman immediately. A little time in the dark room will make her start singing!'

The middle-aged woman almost became white with fear. She started crying loudly, 'What are you saying, sahib? Molina is my daughter, I was just going out to deliver clothes and jewellery and you thought I was a thief?! O Maa Kali, save me!'

Ghosal maintained his authoritarian attitude. 'Molina is your daughter? Who are you lying to? Are you a fool?!'

The woman then stopped wailing and pretending. She understood that the officers had done some homework. 'No sahib, she is not my blood, but I raised her from childhood. I introduced her to prostitution. Without this Sarojini Dasi, was there any way for her to be this famous in this span of time. I picked her up from the footpath. I may not have borne her, but I am her mother!'

'Okay,' Ghosal dialed down his anger a bit, 'So where is your daughter right now? Will you take us there?'

Sarojini said, 'Why not, sahib? My daughter is currently at my other house in Uttarpara. Today morning, she told me to bring her goods. Hence, I am here.'

The officers quickly planned their course of action. It was extremely necessary to unearth the real name of Khoka. Ray returned back to the police station with the constables. On the other hand, Ghosal went to Uttarpara with Sarojini.

During the journey, he was able to get some more information from Sarojini by playing the 'friendly cop' card. She was not aware of any exclusive client of her daughter but claimed that a man had dropped Molina off at her Uttarpara home. She was confident that she could recognize him if she saw him again. She believed that he was quite rich and paid Molina handsomely, as for the last few months, Molina had doubled Sarojini's pocket money.

Ghosal inquired, 'Do you know anybody named Pagla?'

'That music teacher, right? Sure, Sir! Whenever I would come here, I would see him playing the tabla. He is a great artist, but I have not seen him recently at all,' answered Sarojini.

It didn't take much time to reach Sarojini's house at Uttarpara. Molina was inside. She was not anxious. Rather, she was relaxed and thinking deeply about something while sitting on a chair. Molina was really beautiful. Her complexion resembled the color of fresh turmeric. Her eyes were symmetrical and her eyebrows were like an intricately crafted bow. Her figure was slim and she was taller than the average Bengali girl. She was sitting cross-legged and singing,

'Sei lo, bhaatare sukh holo na
Gola dhore goliye dibi dekhiye rosher goli
Koto byata guun geye berabe goli goli...

If your man leaves you thirsty, my baby,
Shove him once in these lanes of love,
And your fire will burn forever, my dove.'

The sudden arrival of her mother with a man, dressed as a typical admirer of her beauty, shocked her. She had not expected a man with her mother that morning. She shouted in a high-pitched voice, 'Ma, you brought a babu from Sonagachi to this place?! Have you gone mad? If Khoka babu comes to know about this, he will murder both of us! You know—'

Ghosal interrupted her, displayed his identity card, and said, 'I am a police officer. I need some information regarding Khoka from you. Please tell the truth, else you will face the consequences.'

'Police?!' She stood up and asked in a weak voice, 'Wh—What do you want to know?'

'Who is Khoka? What is his relationship with you?' Ghosal asked brusquely.

Molina said, 'He is my babu, my exclusive client. I have been his mistress for six months.'

'What is his profession?'

'I don't know, Sir. He comes sometime and disappears. He never said anything about himself, nor did I ask. Previously, I needed to work throughout the month to earn a decent amount of money. But after I met him, he pays more than what I earned earlier. I have to work only for a few days in a month! I am happy with this. What he does, where he lives—it's none of my concern.'

Ghosal started looking at her suspiciously. It was difficult to gauge whether Molina was telling the truth. The only way to know for sure was repetitive questioning with different levels of complexity. If any discrepancy occurred, then she would be caught red-handed.

'How much does Khoka pay you?'

'Twelve hundred!' Molina sounded proud when she uttered the sum of money, 'Even in films, they don't pay me more than ₹15 a day. But here, I earn ₹40 a day just sitting around. Khoka babu is exceptional!'

'That I can see, but what about Pagla master?' Ghosal observed a sudden spark in Molina's eyes as he completed his question.

She quickly tried to retain her composure and said,

'You are talking about my music teacher Atul babu, right? He was a nice guy. He used to teach me tabla and that's all I know.'

'Do you know that your Khoka babu is on the run after murdering your tutor Pagla?' Ghosal asked to invoke some reaction from Molina.

Molina stared at Ghosal after listening to the news, her eyes wide and her lips trembling in disbelief. She just said, 'What are you saying, Sir? Pagla master is dead?!' Then she covered her face with her hands, and after an almost inaudible shout, she fell on the floor.

Sarojini shouted, 'My god! What happened, Molu? Are you alright?'

Ghosal was a bit ceptical about the whole incident. He never expected that reaction from Molina as he had been confident that Molina had been involved in the whole case. But whether she fainted to evade further questioning or whether it was a genuine reaction—Ghosal couldn't tell.

After some time, Molina regained her senses. Right after opening her eyes, she sat upon the floor. Her eyes were overflowing with tears like a waterfall, and her whole face was wet. She covered her angel-like face with her soft palms and cried silently, shaking with sobs from time to time.

Both Ghosal and Sarojini were unable to understand the situation. Sarojini said, 'Why are you crying like this for Pagla's death? I know he was a nice person, but I can't understand why you are crying so much for him!'

Molina didn't utter a word. Her eyes reddened with grief. She said in a choked voice, 'Sir, please catch Khoka babu. He must not escape! If someone kills a person like Pagla, he must rot in hell!' Just a few minutes ago, Molina had been a proud admirer of Khoka, but the tables had turned suddenly.

Ghosal said, 'Calm down, Molina. First, tell me everything that you know.' He continued in a friendlier voice, 'Was Khoka not happy about the fact that you liked Pagla?'

Molina, still crying, said, 'I am a whore, Sir. I do not enjoy the freedom of liking anybody. I was a fixed girl for Khoka babu. Can anyone withstand his girl being friendly with someone else? But believe me, Sir, Pagla was not that kind of a person. He didn't even try anything immoral when we were alone. He really loved me!'

'Pagla was murdered on the night of 4 September. Did Khoka babu visit you after that?'

Molina then controlled her sobbing and said, 'On the dawn of 5 September, Khoka babu suddenly came to my house in Imam Baksh Lane. He barged in and said, "Molu, get ready." I asked, "Ready? Why?" Khoka babu said that he was going to some faraway place for a few days. Then I asked, "Why should I get ready? It is not like you are taking me with you." He looked at me with fiery eyes and said, "In my absence, do you crave to lure other babus with your charm? Talked like a typical whore! I will not let that happen. Pack quickly, I will drop you off at your mother's place and then leave."'

Molina took a deep breath, and continued, 'He came here, dropped me and left. And after that he has not come back. I never suspected anything. Now, I understand that he left me here so that I cannot get the news of the murder of Pagla!'

Ghosal asked, 'Was anybody with him when he left?'

Molina coiled her pallu around her fingers and said, 'No, Sir. He was alone that day. But a day before that, somebody was with him.'

'A day before Pagla was murdered? Khoka came to you on that day, too?!' Ghosal seemed curious and amazed.

'Yes, Sir!' Molina paused a bit to remember the events,

and then said, 'On the night of 4 September, I had been in my room practising music when Kali came. Kali was an accomplice of Khoka babu. Kali had ordered me to accompany him, as Khoka babu had said so. I had not resisted; after all, Khoka babu was paying me a handsome amount of money every month. At that moment, I would have even gone to hell if Khoka babu had ordered. Hence, I got ready and left with Kali. To my astonishment, Kali had guided me through the narrow lanes of Sonagachi to Usha's house. Usha is another sex worker like me. She is an amateur and gathered some money to buy a house recently. I had been shocked and angered. I am Molina of Imam Baksh Lane. I do not pay heed to many kings and zamindars; they come running to me. And there was me, at the house of a girl who is not worth even half as much as me. That was nothing short of an insult. But I just kept calm and waited until Khoka babu came with his friend Keshto babu.'

'What was the time?'

Molina paused for a while and said, 'It should be around ten, because I remember hearing the bells of Armani Church.'

Ghosal had not expected this amount of information from her. He understood that even if Molina was a girl who sold pleasure for money, she actually loved Pagla. That could be the only explainable reason behind her overzealous attitude in solving the case.

'Then?' he continued the interrogation.

'I had seen that the blue shirt of Khoka babu was stained with red in some places. When I had enquired about it, he dodged the topic saying that those were paan stains. I never imagined that those were blood stains, the blood of my Pagla!' Suddenly, Molina's voice cracked. She covered her mouth with her pallu, cried a little to vent her sudden surge of grief, and then continued, 'Then he went out with

Keshto babu. When he came back, it was about two in the night. Khoka babu had a shower. I had smelled the perfumed oil in his hair. He had even changed the stained blue shirt with a freshly ironed grey one.'

'Was Keshto with him when he returned?' asked Ghosal.

Molina nodded her head, 'No, Sir! At that time, he had been accompanied by Bhupen babu, Usha's fixed client. After that, they drank and enjoyed themselves for the whole night. Next morning, Khoka babu had said that an arrest warrant had been issued against him and he had to remain underground for a few days. I have already told you what followed. We left in a rush; hence I missed bringing many essential things. Therefore, I asked my mother to bring my things; after all, I have no idea how long I have to stay here, as I am only allowed to leave on Khoka babu's orders.'

When Ghosal had hired a taxi to travel so far to Uttarpara from Calcutta, he had never imagined that the journey would yield such results. He was more than satisfied. He didn't waste any more time and he, along with Molina, started his journey back to Calcutta in the same taxi to raid Usha's residence. Before entering Sonagachi, Ray and three other constables boarded the taxi from Shyampukur Police Station.

The team reached Usha's residence, and started their investigation. Luckily, Bhupen babu was right there. Bupen babu was about 45 years old and was wearing a white dhoti and panjabi. He was arrested and interrogated on the spot, but the information didn't add anything useful to what Molina had already described. Usha attempted to resist, but she was silenced with the threat of potential arrest for obstructing public servants doing their job.

On being questioned, Bhupen started sobbing. 'Sir! Please let me go! I—I am a gentleman. I have a jute business. I live beside Darmahata. I have a family!'

Usha, who was standing right there, suddenly came

and embraced Bhupen, 'Please let him go, Sir! My babu is nothing less than a god!'

Ghosal quickly got to the point, 'How did you meet Khoka?'

Bhupen controlled his emotions and replied, 'Sir, I stay here for a few days now and then. I am fed up with the daily complaints and quarrels back home. Usha gives me the peace I need. I met Khoka babu and his friends, Keshto, Gopi, Subol and Kali—in this locality. During the evenings, I used to feel bored here. Hence, I used to have a chat with them in the Blackquire Square Park that is close by. Sometimes, after the chat, I used to invite them for dinner here.'

'On the night of 4 September, when Khoka came here with Molina, were you here?' asked Ghosal.

'Fourth?' Bhupen started scratching his head.

Suddenly Molina stepped in, 'That night when I came here! Have you lost your mind?'

Bhupen said, 'Oh! Actually when I come here, I forget everything except Usha and wine. But yes, the night before 4 September, Habunath Goonda was apprehended. That event made quite some noise, I remember.'

Ghosal thought for a second about the authenticity of Bhupen's statement. Indeed, after an immense amount of effort, on the night of 3 September, the police were able to apprehend the infamous Habunath Goonda of Howrah. The news had caused a ripple throughout the city.

Bhupen continued, 'On that day, we had been drinking at the Blackquire Square Park till the dead of the night. I had been so drunk that I had fallen asleep right there. After waking up, I had come back here to see that Khoka, Kali, Kesto and the two girls were having a meeting.'

After wrapping up the interrogation, the two inspectors came back to the police station. But then, something strange happened. Sub-inspector Achintya Sanyal of Shyampukur Police Station was sent to the Lalbazar headquarters for retrieving existing information regarding Khoka. He called up Ghosal and Ray from the headquarters and said, 'Sir! There is no record of anyone with the name Khoka, but on the night of 5 September, a drunkard was causing commotion just beside Imam Baksh Lane. The men from Bottala Police Station apprehended him. His name is Gopi.'

Ray combed through all the records at his office, desperately searching for any clue or piece of information. To Achintya, he said, 'Don't waste time on some stupid drunkard now! I told you to enquire about Khoka, he is an escaped convi—'

Ghosal interrupted inspector Ray, 'Wait, wait! Sunil babu, I think Gopi is actually Khoka's gang member. Bhupen mentioned Gopi's name once while talking about Khoka's friends.'

There was a pause. Achintya was waiting on the other end of the wire. He took that cue to step in, 'Sir, this Gopi confessed in a drunken state to being Khada Goonda's accomplice.

Ghosal and Ray both stared at each other with eyes wide open.

'Khada? Is he talking about the infamous Khada?!'

On the way back from Sonagachi, Molina was dropped off at her Imam Baksh Lane residence. Two disguised police agents were stationed near Molina's house. If Khoka tried to contact her in the dead of the night, then these two would attack him. Bhupen had already been brought to Shyampukur Police Station and was in jail. Bhupen knew Gopi. Hence, the two inspectors took Bhupen along and they rushed towards Bottala Police Station.

The two officers were brimming with excitement in the vehicle. Ray said, 'That dangerous Khada Goonda! He is pretending to be Khoka! Don't you agree, Panchanan babu?'

'Absolutely!' Ghosal expressed his consensus. Actually, right from the beginning, the method, the precision of cutting off the head and other details convinced me that this was not a novice criminal's job. But Sunil babu, I never imagined that this could be the work of Khada!'

After World War I, the prices of everyday commodities in Calcutta underwent inflation, and with the surge in prices, there was a proportional rise in the number of criminal activities. After Charles Tegart took office as the twelfth commissioner of Calcutta Police in 1923, he pledged to deal with the notorious criminals in a strict manner. It was then that the Goondas Act, 1923 was passed.

According to this Act, if any criminal was declared as a goonda, that person could be expelled from the entire Bengal province for an indefinite period of time. If any goonda tried to infiltrate into Bengal through illegal routes, he was bound to be apprehended. It cannot be denied that the British government abused this Act to tag revolutionaries as goondas and put them in jail. But it is also a fact that this law mitigated the amount of criminal activities in Calcutta by a considerable margin. During that time, the most notorious criminal of North Calcutta was named Khada Goonda.

Khada was a wanted criminal. The police once caught him, and he was in custody for a brief period of time. But the police had to let him go because of lack of evidence. After that, the police were not able to catch him again. Khada was intelligent and brave, and his skill of improvisation was enviable. However, for the downtrodden people, he was a messiah. For instance, there is a story that circulated widely:

after looting a wealthy individual, he supposedly spent all the money to fund the marriage of a helpless widow's daughter. Another rumour spoke of him adopting a group of orphans in a village after their parents succumbed to cholera. When people tried to cheat the girls at Sonagachi, Khada Goonda extracted their money from the people who cheated them. It didn't matter how dangerous the cheater was, Khada was a step ahead in bringing them on track. These were the various reasons why many people gave him shelter and never informed the police about his whereabouts.

It was natural for such a name to be at the apex of the list of legendary lawbreakers, and when the Goondas Act came into effect, the police got the authority to arrest Khada just for the crime of being in Bengal—no other evidence was needed to file a case against him! But the Calcutta Police only realized how daunting a task it was to catch Khada Goonda in 1934. In that year, a police constable, Dewadat Tiwari, luckily saw Khada Goonda in one of the narrow lanes of the city. He was well accustomed to the physical description and face of Khada due to an old case against him. When Tiwari realized that under the provisions of the Goondas Act it was forbidden for Khada to be in Bengal but he was still roaming about freely on the streets, he started pursuing him at once.

But Khada's sixth sense was nothing less than that of a cat. Realizing that he was being tailed, he suddenly changed the pace of walking, and when the moment was right, he started running. Constable Tiwari followed him, but after being led into a maze of narrow lanes, when the constable, was completely clueless about the map, he pounced on him from a gap. He drove his knife through the constable, but luckily, it missed his heart. With no further delay, Khada disappeared from the area and Tiwari ended lying in one of the dark alleys, bleeding and unconscious.

For the heroic act, Constable Tiwari was awarded with a bravery medal. However, Khada remained loose out in the wild. It seemed as if he disappeared from the city without leaving any breadcrumbs. Later, many criminal acts took place that involved Khada, but before the police could arrive at the crime scene, Khada would escape. He remained as elusive as djinn. This cat-and-house game continued for a year, and in the middle of 1935, the police got a solid tip about his whereabouts. This time, Shivcharan, a police informant, brought the news to Ghosal.

Shivcharan used to be a petty thief. Tired of getting caught every time and living a rodent-like life, he ultimately gave up on thievery and became an informer for the police. He used to earn a decent tip whenever he gave crucial information to the police. One fine morning, he came to Ghosal and said, 'Sir! This time the news is solid! Khada is not just living a relaxed life in the city but has rented a room in Kripanath Lane under a false name.'

'If this news is found to be true, Shivcharan, you are going to get a big prize!' Ghosal replied in an elated voice. However, Shivcharan did not seem excited. Rubbing his palms together, he replied, 'It doesn't matter how much money you give me, I will not go close to that house! I will just point it from a distance. After that, it is your team's responsibility. If Khada comes to know that I have revealed where he lives, I am dead for sure!'

But it didn't matter how much Shivcharan tried to dodge the reaper, fate had something else in store for him. Though Shivcharan pointed towards the house from a distance, due to sheer bad luck, right at that moment, Khada came out of the house. When he saw Shivcharan just by Ghosal's side, everything became clear to him. Ghosal tried to grasp him with his well laid out team, but Khada got hold of a bicycle lying a few feet away from the door and escaped.

On the very next day, Shivcharan's corpse was discovered on the porch of a house in Kumortuli. A long knife had been shoved into his rib cage, with only the wooden handle poking out of the chest. There was no confusion in guessing whose act it was. Witnessing the end result of being a good samaritan to the police, nobody in the area agreed to be a witness. Witnessing the end result of being a good samaritan to the police, nobody in the area agreed to be a witness.

But there was a person named Baren babu, who visited the police station and informed that there was a boy named Bidhi in his locality. Bidhi had been eating puri at a sweetmeat shop in Kumortuli when he had seen Shivcharan eating jalebi just by his side. At that moment, Khada had come out like a ghost, and in a flash, driven a knife through Shivcharan's chest. He didn't even get the time to realize what was coming, let alone trying to escape. The shopkeeper and Bidhi had been known to Khada. Hence, no harm had come to them.

The police asked, 'Where is this Bidhi? Take us to his home.'

Bidhi somehow guessed that Baren babu had visited the police station. Hence, before the police could get to him, he went underground for the next few months. Due to the dearth of witnesses and the unimportant stature of the victim in society, the case was buried deep in a stack of old papers.

After that incident, Khada again came to limelight. He made a run for it after robbing a zamindar residing at Kumortuli. He had stolen jewellery worth thousands of rupees. Along with that, he took a loaded revolver from the safe. When the investigation of the robbery case was in full swing, a young and brave officer of Calcutta Police spotted Khada in a boat in the middle of the Hugli River. They were both crossing the river on the same boat. Though there was no backup, the officer attempted to catch Khada by himself. But in a jiffy, Khada dived into the river and swam his way to freedom.

Till police got the lead that Khada was involved in the robbery, the case had not got its due importance. But as soon as it was revealed that the mastermind behind the heist was none other than Khada, the case suddenly got a meteoric upgrade. It suddenly became a heavyweight case. Top officers from the headquarters at Lalbazar started following the case closely. This incident in the middle of the river gave a new momentum to the manhunt, and apprehending Khada became the top priority of entire Lalbazar.

Gopi, a close associate of Khada, was detained by the police for roaming around in the street while being drunk. It was not a crime severe enough to put anyone behind the bars. Though Bhupen was called in to recognize Gopi, and he did so with ease, the police had to extract the information quickly from Gopi as there was no valid reason to keep him detained for too long. The police tried all the textbook methods to grill Gopi, but he evaded them continuously.

Then Ghosal said, 'Let us try one thing. In order to find out a cunning criminal, the best way is to find his weak point. Khada kept Molina as her mistress for a large sum of money and then fell in love with her. Perhaps this love was the reason behind the murder of Pagla. The way he beheaded him indicates anger instead of self-preservation. I think we should use Molina as a bait and keep strict surveillance on her home. This can ultimately lead us to Khada.'

'But Sir, the house is already under surveillance,' replied a young investigating officer, 'There are two constables, in disguise stationed around the house of Molina at Imam Baksh Lane.'

'Yes, I know that,' Ghosal answered, 'but if Khada comes

to meet his lover, he will come in the dead of night. Let those two constables be there, but I will be lurking around the house from tonight. If I see an opportunity, I will attempt to catch him right away.'

Ray, not very happy with the plan, said, 'But won't this be too much, Panchanan babu? You and only two constables? You know how dangerous a person Khada is. I think it will be better if the constable just calls us in and we raid the house with full force.'

'No!' Ghosal defended his idea. 'We cannot get hold of Khada like that, Sunil babu. I was an officer in two investigations against him. You have no idea how clever he is. There is nothing to fear. Khada is not an unknown entity to me. I will go, and that's final.'

That night, as per the plan, Ghosal, along with two constables, took shelter in a dark corner near Molina's house in Imam Baksh Lane. And for obvious reasons, they did not inform Molina about the operation. There was a lot of calculation behind that plan. As per the description of their relationship stated by Molina, it was evident that Khada was quite possessive about her. He had kept Molina, away from danger, at Uttarpara before he went underground. The police believed that if he heard that his mistress had resumed residing in the middle of Sonagachi all by herself, it was highly probable that he would try to visit her at least once.

The first night was uneventful. On the second night, the lanes of Sonagachi, especially Imam Baksh Lane, were bustling with sex workers and their customers. The asbestos rooms in the distance were lit up, with the girls standing in front of them. Gradually, as business picked up, the doors were being shut one by one. There was a lot of noise in the streets. In a dark corner, where Ghosal was hiding, the sound of music slithered in to break the monotony. Someone was singing in a house that was by the side. The accompaniment of tabla and sarangi relaxed the otherwise tense mood, and Ghosal became a little inattentive to his surroundings.

It was around 2.00 a.m. when, suddenly, they heard a dreadful cry from the first floor of Molina's house, 'Help! Save me! Help!' In a moment, the lane in front of her house became busy with people running around. Everyone was saying the same thing in terrified voice: 'Khoka has returned!'

The second officer of Bottala Police Station, Asirul Haque, was present in that area as a part of his daily patrol duty. He and Ghosal rushed towards Molina's house at once, but they were not able to change the course of fate. As soon as they entered Molina's house, a man jumped from the first-floor balcony with a pistol in his hand. Right after landing like a cat, he started firing randomly to create a panic.

Within few minutes, the officer-in-charge of Bottala Police Station, Jatindra Mukherjee, arrived with his police force. Ray from Shyampukur Police Station also arrived later. They combed meticulously through the entire block, but they were not able to find a trace of Khada—as if the man had vapourized.

Molina was shivering with fear in her room. A strong rope and a bottle of chloroform were lying a few feet away from her. Khada probably guessed that Molina would not come with him willingly at that time. But just like a possessive boyfriend, he had planned to override the free will of his love. He thought of making her unconscious and then transporting her to the dark lane behind the house, with the help of the rope. Subal and Kali would then put an unconscious Molina in a taxi, and Khada would then climb down, join them and escape. He had kept his accomplices, Subal and Kali, waiting in the lane, and he climbed into the room using the pipe.

But things didn't go as per plan. Khada never realized that Molina was going to make a fuss and cry out like she did. The sudden change in situation made him use his weapon to divert the attention of the cops, and he escaped, leaving Molina behind. The bottle of chloroform was carefully collected as evidence by the police.

Once Molina woke up, Ghosal asked her, 'Are you angry with him for killing Pagla?'

Molina replied, 'That is one of the reasons. But the primary reason was that I almost lost my independence. Women like me never get a husband, never raise a family and never experience the love of a man who values us beyond our bodies. Everyone in this world sees us as meatbags and nothing more. However, despite this, we can be the master of our own wishes. I don't want to lose this freedom for any sum of money.'

Many tantalizing facts had been discovered while interrogating Gopi. But that had not been an easy task. It was revealed that many relatives of Khada were residing at 10, Kripanath Lane, the same house where Shivcharan identified Khada around a year ago. It was also discovered that Khada visited his relatives often. Ghosal didn't waste a second. He raided the residence with the entire police force.

Ghosal was aware that Khada was famous among the sex workers for his philanthropy and messiah-like attitude. Whenever they were in any kind of financial turmoil, it was Khada who protected them. That was the reason why nobody in the sex workers' community of Sonagachi ever testified against Khada. But there were women who didn't have good relations with Khada. After a lot of convincing, one of them spoke up, under sheer duress and terror, that Khada lived in one of the 'twin rooms'. In the other one lived two old men: the father and the uncle of Khada. That was all she said. Ghosal understood that Khada, pretending to be Khoka, had been living in that area for a long time.

After searching, a blood-stained dhoti, panjabi and underwear were found in his room. On each of the clothing items, the letter 'S' was embroidered meticulously. Ghosal said with a sense of suspense to Ray, 'Tell me, Sunil babu, do we know the real name of Khada?'

Ray, while searching for something on the floor with a hunter's concentration, said in a low voice: 'This floor has been dug out, Panchanan babu. Is it possible that he has hidden the head of Pagla down here?'

Within a few minutes, the entire mud-floor of the room was excavated by the constables. Though Pagla's head was not found, what was found was nothing short of treasure. Huge piles of jewels, ornaments and cash were unearthed from Khada's room.

When the news broke out, the place brimmed with crowds trying to get a glimpse of the discovery. Two constables were placed just to manage the crowd. Among the crowd, there was an old woman with a tilak on her forehead. She said that on 4 September, around midnight, Khada returned to his house with a big knife in his hand. She had also watched him washing his clothes around midnight by the side of the well.

After a while, a young man said, 'That night was a full moon night, saheb. When we saw Khada babu in the locality, we started rolling down our shutters. While returning home, I saw that the bucket in which Khada babu soaked his clothes was filled with blood-red water. I swear by Maa Kali, I am telling the truth!'

Just beside the blood-soaked clothes of Khada, a laundry slip was found. The slip had the brand logo of Mathuram Laundry in Maniktala Street. The date, 5 September 1936, was inscribed on it. It was evident that something was given to the laundry on that date for washing.

Ray continued his investigation in that room, and

Ghosal reached the laundry to inquire about the slip. The clothes that he recovered after producing the slip were all embroidered with the letter 'S'. Though the clothes were washed, some red flecks were still clinging to the threads of the letter. By that time, Ray had already found an eye witness from the slum area of Kripanath Lane. The man was named Deben. His testimony later proved to be one of the turning points in solving the Pagla Murder Case.

Deben said that on 4 September, around half an hour before midnight, Khada had been smoking a beedi, sitting on the porch outside his room. He had observed that Khada was barefoot. He had been wearing a blue shirt and white dhoti. His confidant Keshto had also been standing beside him.

Deben had been shocked when he discovered that there were huge splotches of blood all over Khada's shirt and dhoti. Apart from that, Khada had been carrying a huge knife. After a while, Khada had entered his room. Deben tried to peep inside but Kesho started engaging with him so that Deben was unable to see inside Khada's house.

When Khada had come out after some time, his hair had been wet and he had been wearing a grey shirt. It had been evident that he took a bath and washed his clothes in the middle of the night. Other than that, the strong smell of *ittar* (perfume) had filled the air around him. When Khada had seen that Deben was staring at him with a lot of questions in his eyes, he just came forward, took out a revolver, threatened Deben, and then whistled calmly walking towards Shobhabazar Street.

Deben also said something astounding, 'Khada is my schoolmate, Sir! Khada, Keshto, Haripada and I, all went to the Oriental Seminary School.'

'My god!' Ray murmured, 'Khada was a student in the school where Rabindranath Tagore studied! Terrific!'

Deben said, 'When we reached higher classes, most of us

left studies due to poverty, but Khada and Kesto continued. Haripada and I now reside here. Both of us have a small shop and we are still friends.'

Ghosal asked, 'But what about Khada and Keshto?'

'Forget friendship, they don't even talk to us properly. The terror of Khada is so intimidating that it is becoming difficult to reside here with each passing day.'

Upon hearing everything Deben said, Ghosal contacted the once childhood friend of Khada who resided in the same locality, Haripada Sarkar. His business was booming and he owned a much bigger shop. It was evident that Haripada was much luckier and more skillful when it came to trade and business. He said, 'Saheb, I feel ashamed to say that Khada and I were schoolmates. He has made the lives of all the residents of this locality hell. But everyone fears death, so nobody dares to do anything. If you guarantee my safety by providing me an armed guard, only then will I help you, else I cannot!'

His conditions were agreed to. Haridapa babu knew Khada from tip to toe, and he started accompanying the police in raids where the probability of finding him was higher.

Ten days passed like this, and then someone tipped the police station that Khada was seen on the narrow lane by Balaram Majumder Street, the same place where the headless corpse of Pagla was discovered. Haripada was not there in the police station that day. Hearing the information, Ghosal and Ray rushed to the place with two armed sepoys. Reaching there, they found out that Khada came to visit the old venue of his kill. He also paid a visit to the homes of that old woman with tilak in the forehead and the young man, and threatened them that he would kill them mercilessly. A huge team of constables and officers mopped the entire area, not leaving a single corner. But as usual, Khada was not there.

The search started late in the night. It was almost dawn and everybody was tired of the repetitive failures. Suddenly, another tip came in that Khada was spotted at a slum in Howrah. Washing sleep off their eyes, Ghosal and Ray rushed towards Howrah in the police jeep.

When they reached the exact room in which Khada was supposed to be found, they barged through the door without any warning and found a man lying on a charpoy bed. On seeing him, one of the constables, who knew Khada by face, suddenly shouted, 'Sir! Tha—That is Khada..right there!'

Upon hearing that, Ghosal and Ray took out their revolvers, pointed them towards the man and pushed the constable out of the room. Everyone knew of the ferocity and fitness of Khada. Hence, everyone expected a magnificent showdown. But nothing like that happened. Without any fancy gymnastics, Khada calmly surrendered to the police. He was taken to Shyampukur Police Station.

The entire force of Calcutta Police was filled with excitement with this easy conclusion of such a hair-raising story. The officers of all neighbouring police stations arrived at Shyampukur Police Station and congratulated them: 'Bravo Panchanan babu! Bravo Sunil babu! You two are gems of our force!'

Though everyone was rejoicing, Ghosal was not happy. It was very odd for someone like Khada to give in without any resistance. This was a big anomaly and something seemed off. When all the other officers were listening to the tales of the daring raid from Ray, standing in a circle around his table, Ghosal was busy crawling through the files to get the recorded description of Khada Goonda. He found it at last:

Name: Khada Goonda
Age: 35
Height: 5'8"

Complexion: Fair
Physical description: Fit and muscular build
Special note(s): A tattoo on his left arm depicting a snake around a coconut tree, a rose and a line inscribed at the bottom, 'Dear Khada'.

Ghosal drove through the excited crowd of policemen, entered the lock-up and started examining the arrested man. Everything was matching the recorded description: the tattoo, the complexion and the height. The criminal records also had a blurry photograph of Khada and that also matched with the man. Still swimming in the sea of doubt as he came out of the lock-up, he saw Haripada entering the police station. On hearing that police had apprehended Khada Goonda, he had come to identify him.

Ghosal guided Haripada babu to the lock-up. On hearing that the childhood friend of Khada Goonda was here, the other policemen also gathered around to get a glimpse of him. When Haripada looked at the man in the lock-up, he walked back few steps in fear. The reputation of Khada Goonda was so dreadful that even his childhood friend did not dare to be close to him.

Asirul Haque was standing in the crowd. He tried to ease his fear by playfully asking, '*Moshai*? Why are you so afraid of your classmate?'

Everyone started laughing.

'When that classmate is none other than Khada Goonda, there is a reason to be feared, Sir!' Haripada babu was looking at the man without a blink in his eyes. With a faint smile he said, 'But now I am not scared anymore, as the man sitting here is not Khada!'

'What are you saying, moshai!' The jolly atmosphere of the entire police station suddenly turned gloomy. Everyone rushed towards the lock-up: 'This man is not Khada?!'

'No, but he resembles Khada very closely. He is Sudhir, the doppelganger of Khada. He has close resemblance to Khada in terms of physical appearance, but Khada looks a little different. Sudhir is used by Khada to fool the police.' Haripada babu paused for a moment and continued, 'If he was the real Khada, then, by now, at least two of you would already have been dead!'

Ghosal came forward and said, 'I doubted this from the very beginning. Khada is not a person who would surrender so easily. It was really hard to believe.'

Haripada babu said, 'It is not so easy to get Khada, Sir! Till the time he was studying with me at the Oriental Seminary, Khada topped the class in almost everything, from studies to sports. He is both intelligent and daring.'

'Khada used to be the topper in Oriental Seminary?' Jatin Mukherjee of Bottala Police Station asked with surprise, 'Then how did he turn into such a terrifying criminal?'

Haripada babu said, 'The one thing that Khada had from the beginning was exceptional bravery. Due to this, he was a bit reckless and got involved in many things; some were good some were bad. Right from the school days, Khada, Keshto, Gopi and a few others formed a gang. At first, the motto of that gang was to fight for India's Independence. They took an oath to loot the rich and help the poor. However, as they got acquainted with criminal minds, they eventually became a usual robbery gang. Everybody in our locality guesses that they are responsible for at least 30 murders!

'How many members are there in Khada's gang right now?' asked Ray.

Haripada babu answered, 'Probably 70 to 80 members. They not only rob the rich but also rob trains in Bihar and Orissa. They are so ruthless that if someone tries to confront them, they kill them without any hesitation!'

Everyone was listening tacitly. Ghosal asked, 'Well, Haripada babu, can you tell us where Khada actually lives? We searched everywhere, from Kripanath Lane to Molina's house, but still he is on the run!'

Haripada babu smiled sarcastically and said, 'Khada is a remarkable character, Sir. He has connections in both the upper and lower strata of the society. He disappears without any trace quite often, and then the responsibility of his reign is bestowed upon Keshto and Gopi. Often, he completely transforms himself into a suited-booted gentleman, and lives among the elites of the society. I have also heard that he is a member of some of the most respectable clubs in the city. Sometimes, he roams around in an English attire, playing golf and snooker with known industrialists and businessmen of the city. You will find him with a pipe in his mouth and a tumbler of scotch in his hand in those times. He often delivers speechs at social gatherings and meetings too. While you are desperately trying to find him in the dirty lanes of Sonagachi, he might be playing tennis in the Calcutta Club or the Rotary!'

'What?!' Ray was visibly astounded, 'This is nothing but a dual personality, moshai!'

Haripada babu continued, 'Not just that. Once he had an affair with Nila, the beautiful daughter of a high court judge. It so happened that without having any clue about the real Khada, he was spellbound by his gentlemanly behaviour and etiquettes and was almost desperate to make him his son-in-law! When Khada understood that things were getting out of hand, he broke up the relation.

After spending few days like this, he will be found roaming around in a torn lungi and vest, in the red-light district of the city. Then, he will again start living with criminals in dirty hideouts.'

Ghosal looked at Ray with a frown, and the other

officers also got busy discussing among themselves about the incredible life of Khada.

'Is he a man or some magician!' said Ghosal.

As the police got to know more about Khada, the dream of catching Khada was becoming dimmer with time. Ghosal cleared his throat and asked, 'Tell me Haripada babu, how did you get to know Sudhir, the doppelganger of Khada?'

'One day, I found them together at the Blackquire Square Park. On that day, for some reason, Khada was in a jolly mood. On seeing me, he told about his tactic of using Sudhir to fool the law enforcement. At first, Sudhir did not have all the tattoos like Khada. Khada forced him to get them done,' said Haripada babu.

'What?! Then Khada was never in prison?'

'No, Sir. The photo of the man that you have in the police records is not of Khada's; it is of Sudhir's!'

Many days passed by. The news had spread that Khoka was none other than Khada himself. The entire Calcutta police force was trying to get hold of Khada with all its might. Sonagachi and Kumortuli were infested with moles. Those informers sometimes reported that on some days, Khada arranged the marriage of a sex worker's daughter or he smashed the face of some customer who tried to physically harm a sex worker. The police had rushed to the spot with every piece of information, but it yielded no result. Khada remained free. He had sometimes used makeup and other ways to dodge the officers every single time. Khada had visited that narrow service lane in Balaram Majumder Street many times. No one knew of his unnatural affinity towards that place. The police had also rushed on getting such news, but as usual, he was not found.

Ghosal and Ray had released Sudhir, the doppelganger

of Khada, after discussion between themselves. If Khada was arrested, then the court might ask why the police kept Sudhir in custody in spite of knowing that he was innocent. Khada might use that as a tool to turn the tide of his case, if he was ever tried. With those scenarios in mind, they decided to take that step.

At first, local citizens used to inform the police, even if they were white with fear, whenever they saw Khada. After the series of failures of the police, they also started believing that it was impossible to get hold of Khada. After that, even if they saw Khada in a dark corner of some lane, they closed their eyes and prayed to god silently.

However, after a few days, an incident happened that was shocking and terrifying, yet awe-inspiring. On that night, Ghosal was at the Shyampukur Police Station, getting ready for his patrolling duty. In those times, every police station did not possess its own vehicle. Officers used to do their rounds in taxis or rickshaws. Upon getting ready, Ghosal ordered a sepoy, 'Oye Ramlal, call a rickshaw! It's time for a round.'

While the sepoy Ramlal was away to get hold of a rickshaw, Gopal Banerjee suddenly slammed through the door. He was a lawyer practising at Bankshall Court. He had defended an accused in a recent case of mugging. He had come to the police station to appeal for the bail of the accused.

Ghosal was a little disappointed with the behaviour of Banerjee. He knew that for that certain case, the accused was not eligible for bail. But despite being a lawyer, Banerjee seemed to disagree with that. For the last few days, he had been coming to the police station and just wasting the time of police. He said, 'What's the matter, Banerjee babu?'

Banerjee smiled cunningly, 'What else Ghosal, I am here for the bail of my client and—'

Ghosal replied calmly, 'I have told you a hundred times that in this case, the accused is not eligible for bail. As a lawyer, you should know that very clearly. I have no idea why you are just wasting my time every day. Why are you being such a bugger, huh?' The bitter conversation lasted for few minutes among the two. Banerjee was behaving like an annoying defense lawyer and Ghosal was adamant on his stand. In the meantime, Ramlal had already informed Ghosal two times, 'Babu, the rickshaw is here.'

But the debate lasted till one in the night. Ghosal gave up his plans of going on a round and remained seated in a disgruntled mood in his chair, and Banerjee left the police station murmuring in disappointment when he failed to achieve his goal. The rickshaw that was standing outside the police station for Ghosal was instead hired by Banerjee to return home.

Half an hour later, Banerjee again rushed into the police station, but this time, his expressions were different. Ghosal was documenting something in the register at that time. He looked up to see that the fair face of Banerjee was blood red and he was gasping for breath like a fish taken out of water. Trying hard to breathe, he said, 'Pa—Panchanan babu! You have lu—luckily survived today!'

Ghosal realized that there was something wrong. He stood up and helped Banerjee to sit and gave him a glass of water. Then he tried to calm him down and said, 'Try to relax Gopal babu, have some water…Breathe deeply…relax.'

Banerjee settled to normalcy after a few minutes. In a spooky voice he said, 'You—you have survived today Sir… by god's grace, Sir…by god's grace! For returning home, I hired the rickshaw meant for you. The rickshawala had a cloth wrapped around his head. He didn't see me, I didn't see him. After going through Shyambazar, when I asked him to take a turn towards my lane, he turned back and gazed at me with suspicion in his eyes. I did not understand why he did so, but when I reached home and proceeded to pay him his fare, he nodded his head and said, "You need not pay the fare Gopal babu. Remember my face very carefully, my name is Khada. Tell Panchanan Ghosal that he missed death today as you took the ride in his place. But tell him not to worry, his days are almost over!" Then, he laughed insanely and disappeared with his rickshaw.' Banerjee's voice was trembling with fear.

On hearing about the incident, everyone in the police station became tense Ghosal had been the officer-in-charge of many investigations against Khada, right from catching Sudhir, to interrogating Molina after bringing her from her Uttarpara hideout. He was also involved in preventing Khada from escaping that night with unconscious Molina. In multiple incidents, he had stood as a wall between Khada and his goals. Hence, Ghosal was at the top of Khada's hitlist.

Ray advised, 'I think you should be away from the city for a couple of days, Panchanan babu.'

'*Dhus*!' Ghosal dismissed the idea jokingly, 'A service in police means that one has to be fearless, moshai! Let us see how far this Khada can take it!'

The next day, an informer brought the news that Khada was conspiring to kill Ghosal by breaking into his residence through the window. As soon as that information reached the north section commissioner of Calcutta Police, M. Norton Jones, he issued the order of immediate installation of grills on the windows of his residence.

A time came when the fear of Khada reached a point where all the officers, including Ghosal, started wearing bulletproof vests while raiding an area. They also started the mandatory use of metal helmets and always carried loaded revolvers. Gears like bulletproof vests and helmets were usually kept at Lalbazar headquarters for raiding the hideouts of armed revolutionaries. However, with a special office order, those were issued to the policemen involved in the Khada Goonda case.

Fifteen days passed by, and then another incident took place. On that day, Ghosal and Ray were having a discussion in the police station. Sipping on tea, Ghosal said, 'Think for once, Sunil babu. We are so desperately searching for Khada and company, but none of us have any clear idea how they look. But they know us. This is what makes this case more complicated.'

'That is true. The pending cases are completely on halt because of this Khada. The routine works are also disrupted. How long will it go like this?!' Ray finished his words, and just when he was about to take a sip of his tea, Putiram entered.

Putiram was a very trusted informer. When he used to be a thief, he took the art of pickpocketing to a whole new level. He won a dare with his friends by successfully picking the wallet of the officer-in-charge at Bottala Police Station! Putiram had also proved to be a very useful asset in the field for the police. Recently, he had been ordered to concentrate on the search of Khada and keep all other tasks at pause. That is why, the moment he entered, both officers looked towards him inquisitively.

Putiram said, 'Sir! Khada is here! Come right now! This time, the tip is solid.'

Ghosal and Ray kept their cups on the table and started preparing to leave in a moment. While arranging their gear, one of them asked, 'Where? Imam Baksh Lane? Molina?'

'No, Sir!' Putiram shook his head, 'There is a famous girl named Kamala living at Chitpur road. She has earned a lot of money in a very short time. She also bought a three-storeyed house. On the second floor of that house, Khada is due to receive felicitations from many prostitutes in the area for his kind heartedness. Along side that, there will be a huge party, food, dance, wine and everything else. I ran as fast as possible the moment I got the news!'

When Ghosal and Ray almost ran to that three-storeyed house and climbed to the second floor, they saw that the door was closed. The officers could hear the sound of songs and *ghungroo*[8]. On the instruction of Ghosal, some constables broke the door by slamming it hard with their guns in a matter of seconds. They had also brought along Haripada babu to recognize the real Khada. What happened after that was nothing less than cinematic. Everyone saw that a man jumped out of the window, at least 30 feet above the ground. Haripada babu shouted: 'There! That is Khada, Sir! Do something! Fire! Fire!' But even before the officers could have taken aim and pulled the trigger, Khada was out of the scene.

The felicitation party turned into chaos. Few girls who were sitting with garlands in their hair and wearing glimmering dresses started running erratically, and some of them even started crying. When all the people in that area arrived at the road below, they remained open-mouthed in awe. They were expecting the broken dead body of Khada, but they were not able to spot even a single drop of blood! A paan vendor was shivering in his stall just nearby. Ghosal babu and team rushed to him and saw red marks of palm on the cheeks of that poor man.

'I was just getting out of my stall when I saw a man landing on the footpath just like a cat. He jumped up in a second like nothing happened to him. He walked straight to me, slapped me hard and said, "Give me a cigarette right now!" I—I had recognized Khada Goonda by that time and started praying for my life. Khada Goonda is not human

---

[8]A musical anklet tied to the feet of Indian classical dancers.

Sir! He—he is a ghost, otherwise how can one survive even after jumping like that! Taking the cigarette, he slapped me again and said, "Who will light it, you f****r!" Then he took the matchbox and lit his cigarette. Taking a deep puff, he took my cycle and sprinted off in a second.' The paan vendor kept shivering throughout the time while he spoke.

The entire area was combed meticulously that day. The girls who kept their doors shut, claiming they had a customer inside, had their doors slammed open, and their rooms were thoroughly searched. But Khada had successfully escaped. Kamala Dasi, the girl in whose house the felicitation was arranged, along with few other girls, were taken into custody. But even through intense interrogation, no useful information could be extracted from them.

Khada appeared again on the radar in two weeks' time. And this time, the news was so ridiculous that Ghosal and Ray didn't want to believe it. The informer who brought the news was named Chhoku. 'If I am lying, you can cut my ears, *huzur*! Chhoku never gives a false tip. I am telling the truth, Khada babu is at Shantiniketan! He is residing in the guest house there and roaming freely!' said Chhoku.

Ghosal looked at Ray cluelessly. The latter was also flummoxed. Was that even possible? Was Khada really residing in the guest house designated for VIPs at Shantiniketan?!

Though both the officers were not at all convinced of the news, Haripada babu, who was sitting right next to them, said, 'Nothing is impossible for Khada. I have told you before that he has quite some influence in the upper echelons of society.' Thus, they all started preparing for a trip to Bolpur. That time too, Ghosal insisted to be in the team in spite of being in the top of Khada's hitlist.

However, right before the day they were about to embark, an order came from Deputy Commissioner Jones, 'Under no circumstancse should the atmosphere of the Shantiniketan ashram be disturbed. Rabindranath Tagore is at the ashram. Even if Khada is found, he must be apprehended outside the perimeter of the ashram. There is no scope of using any firearms inside the ashram premises.' Ghosal and team were in a fix. It was already impossible to catch a daredevil like Khada, and on top of that, there were so many constraints on operational protocols. It seemed impossible to draw out Khada from the ashram.

Besides that, Ghosal's mood was also a little gloomy. He loved writing, and few of his works had been published in some local magazines. He had a dormant dream that one day, he would meet Tagore at Shantiniketan to touch his feet and get his blessings. He was about to visit Shantiniketan for the first time in his life, but he had no scope to avail such an opportunity as he would be busy in something far removed from the world of novels and stories.

Though Ghosal left Calcutta with a heavy heart, he left no stones unturned in his attempt to meet Asia's first Nobel laureate. He reached Bolpur with the Haripada babu and lodged at the Commoners Guest House at Shantiniketan. They disguised themselves as casual tourists. Then he started investigating the entire area and became so busy in his mission that he didn't even carve out time to visit the ashram.

His efforts bore fruit at the end of the third day. He found Khada dressed in a white dhoti and panjabi, with books in his hands and a canvas satchel hanging from his shoulder in the lanes in front of Uttarayan, the retreat of Tagore in Shantiniketan. But as soon as Ghosal approached him, he dissolved in the crowd and, as usual, there was no trace of him thereafter. After that, even with the tremeadous efforts of Ghosal and the local police, Khada could not be traced, not just in Shantiniketan but the entire town of Bolpur.

Ghosal returned to Calcutta after yet another failure. But he did not belong to the breed who gave up midway. Instead of sitting idle, depressed and heartbroken, he restarted the search with a new zeal. He started looking into the details of the case files again.

Then he decided to recall the two constables who were deployed near the house of Molina. Instead, he placed an undercover armed policeman near the house. Khada stepped into the trap laid for him. He had grown desperate to meet Molina, the girl for whom he murdered Pagla by mercilessly beheading him out of jealousy. But fearing the depth of the laid-out trap, he sent his trusted companion Keshto to her home to meet her instead. Keshto was caught by the police on 22 September 1936. The search for Khada ultimately had a solid lead. It was like severing the right arm of Khada.

Khada was a seasoned criminal, but Keshto was not like him. He belonged to an educated brahmin family but bad acquaintances had turned him into a criminal in his early age. Khada was actually proud of his activities. He boasted of his deeds like they were some achievements, but Keshto was the complete opposite. He often regretted his deeds and felt like a stain on the name and honour of his family.

Though the police believed that third-degree torture was the only way to break Keshto, Ghosal played it differently as soon as he discovered this angle of Keshto's personality. He instead ordered to arrange for good food and bedding for his stay in the lock-up. Keshto knew that he was at the top of the wanted list of police due to his affiliation with Khada. He also knew that the police were going to grill him right after he was arrested. But he was reasonably stunned by this completely stark treatment.

Ghosal said in a very calm voice, 'Keshto, I know you have ended up here because of fate, but you belong to such a revered family. Even if you don't open up to me, I will not force you.' Then he ordered the constable standing next to him, 'What is this! Why is he in cuffs? Immediately open them!'

When a human being is full with food after starvation, they usually lose the sharpness of their brain. Ghosal knew those theories, and thus he first fed Keshto with high-calorie foods after a day of starving him. Keshto was already startled. Still, he was on alert, taking the police's generosity as some form of conspiracy.

Ghosal then ordered a sepoy, 'Bring my easy chair from my quarter!'

He then requested Keshto to lay down on that in a relaxed mood. He knew that was going to make him sleepy and more vulnerable to interrogation.

Things happened as planned. With a stomach full of heavy food and a soft recliner chair to lay on, Keshto started to lose himself. After the heavy dinner, Ghosal started chatting with him like he was a friend who met him after a long time. He started enquiring about things that had no relevance to Khada—his parents, his siblings, his hobbies and many more such topics. Then, slowly, Keshto started to blurt out everything about Khada,

'Khada is very cruel, Sir. If he determines to kill someone, there is no way he can get out alive. Let us take the case of Pagla master. Khada knew that Pagla was in love with Molina but he didn't pay much heed to that. But when he discovered Pagla in Molina's room that night, he was tempted like a tiger and started slapping Pagla repeatedly. Pagla was a fool, not a courageous person at all, but before leaving, he threatened Khada, "You are a wanted convict and still you dare to hit me? I will go right now to the police and they will take you in!" Though we all knew that Pagla didn't have the guts to do what he said, coincidentally, just after that, Molina's house was raided by the Bottala Police

Station force twice. Khada suspected that Pagla might have developed the courage to do what he said and he made up his mind to kill Pagla.

'On the night of 4 September, we captured Pagla, boarded a taxi and reached the ghats. When we grabbed him, Satya Gowala and Haru Gosai saw us, as Pagla was making too much noise. When we reached the ghats, Khada ordered Pagla to go and take a bath in the Ganga. Pagla did what he was told without protesting. At that time, Gauriya got up at the ghat after a swim. He dealt in stolen items. He first stood with us, but when he realized that someone was going to be killed the spot, he slipped away. Khada was quite enraged by his behaviour.'

Keshto paused to take a sip of water, and then he continued, 'Where was I? Oh yes! Then Khada took Pagla to a nearby Kalbhairabh Shiv Mandir. He ordered Pagla to pray in that temple and drink the *charanamrit*[9] from there. Pagla did as he was told. Then he was taken to the service lanes of Balaram Majumdar Street. Khada took out his most beloved knife and asked Pagla, "Do you have any last wish?" Pagla, instead of trying to cry for help, blew up his chest and said, "I want to see Molina one last time!" Hearing that, Khada's patience ran out and he grasped Pagla by his throat. Then, he stabled him through his heart three times in quick succession. Khada has a lot of knowledge of human anatomy. He has read many books on the subject. Hence, he knows the right place to deliver the blow so that the victim does not get a chance to survive.

'After that, Khada and I went to his house at Kripanath

[9]Charanamrit is a sacred concoction with deep-rooted significance in Hindu rituals and ceremonies. Composed of five essential ingredients—milk, yogurt, honey, ghee (clarified butter) and ripe bananas—it represents the unity of the five elements and is offered to deities during puja or worship.

Bose Lane. We met Deben there. Khada removed his blood-stained clothes and took a bath. But then, for some reason, he took me and went back to that service lane behind Balaram Majumdar Street. He found Pagla's body and cut the veins and muscles of his feet, and in one single blow, chopped off his head.

'Then we took the severed head in a jute bag and reached the river. Khada threw the bag into the dark water of Ganga, quite far from the bank. A man saw us and asked, "What did you throw?" Khada replied, "A dead cat!"'

Ghosal, Ray and the rest of the personnel at the police station were listening to the uncontrolled blabbering of Keshto with pin-drop silence. Keshto was in a trance, thanks to the knowledge of human physiology and psychology mastered by had Ghosal. Nobody estimated that Ghosal's technique would work like magic.

When Keshto stopped, Ghosal said with empathy, 'I am really sorry to hear that such a good man like you had to go through such experiences for Khada. A man who can kill a nice fellow like Pagla so ruthlessly can easily rape and torture the poor girls of Sonagachi. God knows how many!'

'No, Sir!' Keshto protested, 'In this matter, Khada is not just disciplined himself but he is also very strict with others. Khada protects thousands of prostitutes living in Sonagachi, Ram Bagan, Nather Bagan, Imambari Lane and Champatala. He always tells us to protect them with all our might and not even think of causing them any harm. He says they are our only friends in this world. When the police chase us through the narrow lanes like dogs, they are the ones who gives us shelter. They give us a place to hide, food to eat and bed to rest. They become our temporary mothers for that time.'

'Understood,' Ghosal babu took a pause and then asked calmly, 'Where is Khada right now?'

'He is at Deoghar, Sir!' Keshto said while carefully observing a lizard on the wall trying to eat a fly few inches away from it.

'Deoghar?' Everyone was shocked. When the entire Calcutta Police was searching for him in the city and suburbs, he was roaming around in far-off Deoghar!

'Yes, Sir,' Keshto smiled as the lizard ate the fly, 'Khada has rented a big palace in Deoghar, and he has established himself as the 'King of Kumortuli' there. He is living a royal life with lots of servants there. He is feeding hundreds of poor and inviting the social elites of the city for dinner almost everyday. He also chats a lot with government officials there. He throws parties every now and then. I know he has earned a lot of reputation in only a few days. I was there as his dewan, but suddenly Khada wished to bring his queen, Molina, to the palace. That is why I came here, to take her to Deoghar, but you caught me. Panchanan babu, don't even think of going there. Khada is angry with you; you will also end up like Pagla if you go there.'

The night almost turned into dawn as Keshto kept on speaking. By sunrise, he had curled up like a baby and was deep asleep in the recliner.

Ghosal, Ray and the rest came to the room next to that and sat with awe. What Keshto just told them was beyond belief.

Ray said, 'My goodness! King of Kumortuli? How many more tricks does this Khada have up his sleeves?'

Ghosal was in some other deep thought. Without answering Ray, he ordered the sepoy standing next to him, 'Madhu, go and cuff Keshto, and put him in the lock-up. He has spilled everything. When he is awake, he will remember what he has said in a trance and then it will be difficult to handle him.'

Ghosal was correct. Right after Keshto woke up in the lock-up, he started shouting and cursing. He remembered how the police had tricked him to reveal the secrets of Khada and how he had failed the trust of Khada. Regretful, he banged his head on the walls of the cell.

His behaviour made Ray nervous and he didn't take the chance of keeping him in the lock-up of the police station anymore. He immediately transferred him to the jail.

⁂

At last, it was time to take down the boss, and the officer who volunteered to be the lone wolf in this fight was none other than the pride of Calcutta Police, the brave-hearted Ghosal. Keeping aside the fear for all of his family and friends and without caring about his life, he embarked on a journey to Deoghar. He did not take any force or team with him, as he knew that Khada was clever enough to be alarmed by any anomaly.

After a lot of requests and bargain, Khada's classmate Haripada babu agreed to go with Ghosal after he was assured complete police protection for the next six months. Deben was also requested, but he had got married recently and he did not want any probability of his wife ending up as a widow.

One problem in the plan was that if they boarded the train from Howrah station, then other members of Khada's gang would get some information. To avoid that, Ghosal and Haripada babu hired a car to Naihati. Then they crossed a bridge and hired another car to reach Asansol via the Grand Trunk Road. Then they boarded the train from Asansol to Deoghar.

Ghosal was wearing a peshwari cap and a silk kamiz. He was also wearing kohl. It was impossible for anyone to identify him as Bengali, let alone a police inspector. Though he was smoking cigars in a relaxed mood to further strengthen his character, deep inside, he was extremely anxious regarding the next few days.

The train reached Deoghar the next morning. Right after getting down from the train, Ghosal rented a room and told Haripada babu to stay there. Then, he removed his makeup and started his work. Every second counted. Though Keshto was in jail, other members of the gang were scattered around Calcutta. The news of Ghosal's absence from the city could easily reach there, and all the efforts would again go to waste. Ghosal boarded a rickshaw and ordered, 'Take me to Bilasi town.'

Keshto had given the address of the palace in Bilasi town in trance. Ghosal had been to Deoghar before and in that context, he knew that Bilasi was the cleanest and most beautiful locality of the city. The roads were wide, and huge trees arched over them, providing shade. The roads were also lined with bungalows that looked like they came out of a fairy tale. He knew that the place was occupied only by the elites of the city.

Just as he had reached Bilasi, it had started raining. Ghosal had no umbrella with him, so he quickly took shelter in the shade of the watchman's room beside the gate of a huge mansion.

The magnificent gate was designed to look like the wings of a bird. A red carpeted path was visible inside it through the green lawn, and continued for atleast 500 feet, ending at a circular fountain. The huge porch or *gari baranda* was adjacent to it.

Ghosal was near the gate, waiting for the rain to stop, and there were few other people who were standing just like him. Among them, there was a local schoolteacher, a Bengali man named Ramkrishna Batabyal. Ghosal introduced himself as a tourist. He said that he was a clerk at a business firm in Calcutta and came here with his family for a holiday. He went out to buy some stuff and got caught in the rain.

Ramkrishna babu said that he had in Deoghar for the past three generations. He kept talking about how his grandfather had left a small village by the side of Hugli River, come to Deoghar for a job and then settled there by buying a plot and ultimately building his own house. He said that his busy schedule had prevented him from visiting his ancestral village in the past few years.

Ghosal kept listening to him, and after a while, in a very low voice, asked the schoolteacher, '*Mastermoshai,* from the time I came here, I have been hearing that a Bengali king has come to Bilasi. Do you know anything about it?'

Ramkrishna babu was a little surprised. He said, 'My god! You don't know? The King of Kumortuli is staying here! What a kind-hearted man he is. I have no count of how many poor people are being fed by him everyday. Apart from that, distribution of clothes and other things are also done by him.'

'Where is he staying?' Ghosal almost whispered as he asked, 'Do you know?'

The schoolteacher smiled, 'You are asking about his residence standing right next to the gate? This is the mansion you are looking for.'

For a second, Ghosal's heart stopped. He had not paid much attention to the house at first. Beside the gate, a stone was inscribed in clear and bold English letters, 'King of Kumortuli'.

The schoolteacher kept on speaking, 'Wait for few more minutes. As the clock strikes 10, the king will come out in his car. He distributes money among the poor standing by the side of the road. What a kind-hearted man!'

Ghosal was thunderstruck. Being such an experienced cop himself, he never realized that he had come right to the lion's den all by himself. He took leave from Ramkrishna babu and started walking briskly. The latter called after him, 'O moshai! Where are you going? Let the rain stop at least!'

But Ghosal paid no heed to his words and continued walking. With long steps and drenched clothes, he walked towards the police station. His brain seemed to have frozen, and he had no idea how to catch that cunning devil all by himself.

By the grace of god, he found that the officer-in-charge of the local police station was also a Bengali named Suresh babu. He became quite excited when he met Ghosal, and he said, 'I have been hearing since yesterday that some officer lines Calcutta has come here for some investigation. Can you elaborate on the matter? Our Bilasi is a very peaceful area!'

Ghosal smiled but didn't say anything. Though Suresh babu was the officer-in-charge, he was one of Khada's fans as Khada successfully managed to capture the attention of local government officials there by throwing regular parties. Ghosal said, 'A murderer has escaped from Kumortuli, I have come here in search of him.'

'Oh! Is that so?' said Suresh babu. 'The King of Kumortuli is present here. Though I must say he does not care about a petty police officer like me but he is on good terms with my boss. By the order of my boss, I was even stationed at his gate for his security for two days! If you need any information, I can enquire from his servants.'

'No, no! Do not tell anyone!' Ghosal dissolved the idea immediately and continued, 'Can you provide me with men when needed?'

'Why are you even asking, Sir! I will help you with everything I can.'

Ghosal was in deep contemplation after getting out of

the police station. The way Khada had hypnotized everyone there made it difficult for him to trust anyone.

After some time, he set out for one of his relatives' house in Deoghar, Rabindranath Bandopadhyay. He was the deputy magistrate of Deoghar. Ghosal thought that he was the only one who could be trusted. If Haripada babu had not accompanied him, then perhaps he would have taken shelter at Rabindranath's place.

Rabindranath was thunderstruck after hearing everything: 'What are you saying, Panchanan?! The King of Kumortuli also invited me, but I was busy with something else.'

Ghosal said, 'As you can understand by now, Robin da, he is a dangerous man to say the least. Considering the way he has everybody under his spell here, I am doubtful about whom to trust. Can you give any idea how to arrest him?'

Rabindranath thought for a while and said, 'Do one thing. Finish your lunch here after freshening up. Meanwhile, I will talk to the sub-divisional officer saheb. This area falls under the Dumka commissionerate. I will convince him to send his force here from Dumka.'

Ghosal was a little relieved, 'Good plan, Robin da! When the force is here, we will raid the bungalow in the middle of the night and apprehend Khada. Please go talk to him.'

While Rabindranath left in his car, Ghosal took out his service revolver and kept it under the care of his sister-in-law, Rabindranath's wife. Then he ordered the orderly of the house to inform Haripada babu about everything and also instructed him to bring the latter with him. Then he took a shower to destress.

His sister-in-law asked, 'Shall I serve lunch now, Ghosal?'

'No boudi, let Robin da come, we will eat together.' Ghosal said, Meanwhile, let me take a quick stroll.'

Deoghar city is on the Chota Nagpur Plateau by the side of Mayurakshi River. Whether the clean air or the abundance of greenery, the city is a well-known destination for people wishing to spend days in the lap of nature. Ghosal decided that as he had come till Deoghar, he might as well visit the Baidyanath Temple and take home the prasadam from there. However, his priority was his mission, so he doubted whether he could carve out enough time to earn some blessings. He had never even dreamt of the situation that Khada had created for himself there.

During their train journey to Deoghar, Haripada babu told some remarkable facts about Khada. There were at least 10 poor families in Calcutta whose expenses were borne by Khada every month. He used to donate hefty sums to some of the ashrams in Birbhum. He mingled around with the upper echelons of the society and remained quite influential in those circles. Haripada babu had also told him about the subtle differences between Khada and his doppelganger Sudhir so that Ghosal didn't face any difficulty in recognizing Khada.

Ghosal was walking casually while reminiscing the words of Haripada babu. However, all of a sudden, he was stupefied when he saw someone standing a few yards away from him in front of a laundry shop counter—it was none other than Khada. He was wearing an expensive, green silk panjabi. His silky flock of hair was waving in the gentle breeze. His eyes had a clear shade of pride mixed with hilarity. Ghosal double-checked the man by looking at him from several angles. He was sure that it was not Sudhir.

When Ghosal saw Khada, Khada also locked his gaze with him and froze for a few seconds. Then he walked up straight to Ghosal and put his hand in the right pocket of his panjabi. Ghosal's hand also went to his right pocket in reflex, but it was empty. He had forgotten to take his weapon from his boudi while going out! A chill went down his spine.

Ghosal had never been compromised in such a way ever in his career. But he was not someone to succumb to fear easily. He kept his eyes locked on Khada and pretended confidently like there was a revolver holstered in his right pocket. He kept his fingers inside in such a way that it looked like a barrel protruding in his pocket. Khada smiled mockingly and said, 'Well, well, who do we have here? It seems that the pride of Calcutta Police Panchanan Ghosal moshai has blessed Deoghar with his footsteps! How are you doing, Sir?'

Ghosal kept his mouth shut and kept his eyes glued to Khada.

Khada said, 'Sir, I have my hand on my revolver the same way you do. If you shoot I will shoot, if I die, you will die too. So, let us think of something else. Let us both move back peacefully and nobody will know anything. In that way, both of us get to keep our lives and reputations. What do you say?'

Ghosal was about to say something but suddenly there was a doubt in his mind. From the case history of Khada, it could be inferred that he never lost any chance to go for a kill when he confronted his enemy; he just got the job done and moved over the body. Why was Khada talking so much then? There could be only one explanation—he too was unarmed! Ghosal called a dangerous bluff, and he moved straight towards Khada. The latter became still and then said in a threatening manner, '*Khabardar*! Don't take one step forward or else I'll shoot, Panchanan babu!' Ghosal didn't pay heed to the warning and pounced on Khada.

Ghosal's guess turned out right—Khada was also unarmed like him. And with the way he was dodging the attacks, it could be seen that the long habit of using weapons had blunted his hand-to-hand combat skills. The fist fight continued, and at one point Khada pushed Ghosal to words a drain by the side of the road. Ghosal also pulled at Khada's feet and dragged him into the drain. The two fought like crocodiles in shallow water and the narrow drain. Oddly, the road was empty. The few who passed by at a distance turned a blind eye when they smelled trouble.

The fight went on and on; neither was ready to give up until his muscles gave up. By some stroke of luck, two sepoys were walking by doing their rounds at one time. Surprisingly, one of the sepoys came running forward and started hitting Ghosal instead! '*Badmash! Raja babu ko thusat ho?* (You criminal! How dare you trouble our honourable king?)' Luckily, the other sepoy recognized Ghosal as he had seen him talking to Suresh babu, a few hours ago at the police station. He sensed some anomaly and rushed to call police officers. Coincidentally, right then, Suresh babu had been coming towards Rabindranath's residence with Constable Dilawar Khan to discuss something with Ghosal. When he saw Ghosal in that situation, he extrapolated the rest of the story. Khada was grabbed from two sides by Suresh babu and Dilawar. Ghosal was about to give up, but the backup arrived right when it was needed. And that is how the terror of North Calcutta, the wanted dacoit who robbed trains on the tracks of Bengal, Bihar and Orissa, the ill-famed Khada Goonda, was trapped in the chains of law.

When Khada realized that his game was over and there was no card left in his hand to play anymore, he started laughing like a maniac. 'Congratulations, Panchanan babu! What a fortunate man you are! For the first time in my life, I went out unarmed, and that is the reason you are still breathing. Otherwise, no enemy of Khada has ever survived for more than 13 seconds. You know, that is the maximum flight time of a hen! What to say, Panchanan babu... Actually, when I woke up this morning after keeping my dagger and the pistol inside my steel trunk, I discovered that the washer had not brought my clothes. I can't explain how angry I became! I was so angered that I walked out to the laundry by myself and then we met! You are lucky!'

By that time, Suresh babu had brought cuffs and ropes from the police station nearby. Miraculously, at that time, Rabindranath appeared from a van with 10 armed constables.

Khada looked at Ghosal with curiosity and levity in his eyes when Suresh babu was tying up the rope around his waist. 'Are you sure Panchanan babu that I am Khada? Look carefully—am I not the duplicate of Khada, Sudhir? The man who you, arrested before? Then it will be a great shame for you, inspector! Ha ha ha!'

By that time, Haripada babu had also arrived at the scene. He nodded his head and said, 'There is no doubt this time. This face, these eyes, these can belong to none other than Khada, especially that chilling laughter.'

The smiling face of Khada suddenly turned dark. 'It was duty for Panchanan babu but I will not let you live Haripada scoundrel! Wait till I come out. Start the countdown of your life!'

From the rented mansion of the 'King of Kumortuli', a dagger with an ivory handle and a vintage Remington Model 1888 was recovered. Along with that, 12 diamond studded necklaces and ₹17,000 in cash was also recovered.

On arriving at the police station, Ghosal asked Khada, 'Didn't you feel remorse after killing an innocent man like Pagla so ruthlessly?'

'Why should I feel sorry?' Khada asked with raised eyebrows. 'Do you people regret killing a mosquito? When a mosquito bites you, you kill it. In the same way, Pagla tried to bite me, I killed him! Panchanan babu, only the fittest have the right to survive.'

Suresh babu asked, 'Don't you fear god? You are going to pay for your sins in your afterlife, you know that right?'

'God?!' Khada laughed. 'I am ready to believe all ideas on this planet but three—ghosts, god and love! Trust me, this life is all we have. There was no past before birth, there will be no future after death. And love? That is the most bogus idea ever! Otherwise Molina would not have fallen for that f*****g *tabalchi* (tabla player)!'

'There may be no past or future, but there is karma. For all that you have done, you are going to be hanged,' Suresh babu said.

'I know, I know!' Khada said, shrugging his shoulders. 'Do you think I am afraid of death? I have no regrets in my life! I have done whatever I wished in my life. I have lived every moment of it. I have not kept my fantasies buried in the fear of afterlife like you guys! However, there is a regret that I have.'

'What?'

'Sometimes, I despise the work that do. I feel bad about myself. During those times, I escape to mingle among the gentlemen. During one of those times, I married a girl in Chandernagore. I have kept ₹50,000 ripped with her and said that when I die, don't mourn for me; live your life, enjoy every moment after you hear that I am no more. But you know what I fear? I fear that she will not enjoy life when I am hanged. Rather, she will live the life of a widow, wear white and become vegetarian.' For a moment there was something sparkling in the corner of Khada's eyes, 'And I feel sorry for some families, whose expenses are borne by me. Lets stop talking aboiut this!'

Before leaving Deoghar, Ghosal wired Inspector Ray: 'KHADA ARRESTED—NO CASUALTIES.'

The name Khada Goonda became synonymous with terror in the City of Joy at that time. People were afraid to stop out of their homes after dark; rich people marrying off their daughters were always on their toes and were scared of the probability that Khada and his gang might rob all the jewellery. Apart from that, the general fear of getting killed was always there.

That is why, when Khada Goonda, also branded as a 'public enemy' by the news outlets, was arrested and the news became public, many ordinary citizens gathered around the police station. Among them were famous people too, like poets, artists and businessmen. Everybody hailed the heroic deeds of Ghoshal and the other bravehearts of Calcutta Police.

The jewellery and ornaments worth lakhs of rupees and thousands of rupees in cash recovered from the house at Kripanath Bose Lane and the rented mansion in Deoghar were gathered together. All of the jewellery was robbed from various rich families in and around the city, so to identify their rightful owners, they were displayed in an exhibition.

Those few poor families who survived on the financial aid of Khada were fished out. For them, he was no less than god. Hence, when they heard that their god is going to be prosecuted and probably hanged, they started mourning like they lost a member of their family.

❧

In total, 75 cases of theft and robbery were filed against Khada. Apart from that, the charges of murder of Pagla and Shivcharan were also filed against him. However, on hearing the figures, Khada laughed out loud and informed Ghosal that he had killed atleast 20 other people apart from that! He was proud of the fact that he had actually lost the count! But as those cases do not have any evidence, they were ineligible to be considered as legal weapons against him.

At last, the case of Khada Goonda was raised in the

court. The judge was magistrate I.S. Mukhopadhyay. The members of the standing council were the M.M. Basu and solicitor S. Choudhury. The honourable court of justice gave a sentence of 75 years of imprisonment for the 75 cases of theft and robbery. The jail became the new home of Khada. After that, the trials for the murder cases were initiated.

So huge was the chargesheet of this case that the typed pages together weighed almost 8 kg! In total, 16 witnesses recorded their testimonials and the total counts of exhibits were 135. The hearings continued for 31 days and, finally, M. Khandkar sentenced Khada to death for the murder of two people.

There is a rumour that after the sentence was awarded, Khada, standing in the witness box, first congratulated Khandkar and the jury members. Then, proudly smiling and his head held high, he walked to the van without any nuisance. When a defense counsellor tried to meet him after the judgment, he said, 'I am on this planet for only a few days; I am going to be hanged soon. Can you please request Panchanan babu to meet me once? It is very important.'

Ghosal went to jail to meet the most worthy and challenging opponent he had ever faced in his service history. But on that day, for some reason, Khada was very gloomy and depressed. He said, 'Can you please come on any other day, Ghosal moshai? I am really in a terrible mood today!'

But after that, Ghosal was unable to carve out time for the meet. On 31 July 1937, at 6.00 a.m., Khada was instructed to have a bath. He wore a clean dress and an expensive scent after that. Then he asked the sepoy in front of his cell, 'Can you please bring me some flowers?'

It is said that the dying wish of a man sentenced to death is always kept, if possible. On this occasion too, there was no exception. When the flowers were brought, Khada himself made a garland out of that and wore it around his neck. Then he said, 'Yes, now take me wherever you want!'

The officer-in-charge of Alipur Police Station, Hemanta Gupta, was present in the execution chamber. Standing in front of the gallows, Khada said, 'Do you know how Ghosal moshai is doing these days?'

Gupta answered, trying to keep his awe concealed, 'He is doing good.'

Khada said while smiling, 'Tell him that the King of Kumortuli, Khada, will remember him even in the afterlife, if there is something like that.'

Khada Goonda is no more. In the pages of history, the spine-chilling deeds of Khada were buried. But even if Khada is no more, the service lane in which Khada chopped off the head of Pagla, behind Balaram Majumdar Street, still exists. Over time, the lane has earned a name—'*gola kata gali* (the lane of beheading)!'

THE WRATH OF KING, THE DEATH OF GOD: BAWLA MURDER CASE, 1925

A murder by firing a shot—a case that shook British India to the core. It shook the status of all the heads of princely states of the country at that time. The story begins is the city of Bombay (now Mumbai) almost a century ago. The date was 12 January 1925. The respected member of the elite Memon family, a famous Muslim family of those days, Abdul Qadir Bawla, went for a ride in his convertible with the love of his life a few hours before sunset. The huge car was running towards the suspension bridge on Gibbs Road after coming out of the Kemps Corner in the Malabar Hill region of Bombay. There was no reason to hurry. Bawla saheb had instructed his driver from the very beginning, '*Dheere chalo, bohot khubsurat mausam hai aaj* (Go slowly, the weather is beautiful today).'

Bawla was one of the premier businessmen of Bombay. Though he carried the royal blood, his social stature was earned with his own sweat and blood. In just a few years, he had grown his family business at least few times more than what it was before. This young fellow had become one of the most respected citizens of the city not just for his wealth and opulence but also due to his philanthropy and kind-heartedness. He had never denied his role as a responsible citizen of the country, and that led to his meteoric rise in the society.

His busy life was composed of mainly three things—his business, management of his wealth and social activities. But even for a busy man, it was not unnatural to sometimes have the urge to be free and romantic. The beautiful sceneries of Malabar Hills were not able to draw his attention, as his eyes were transfixed on the beautiful lady who was sitting by his side.

His manager Mathews was sitting in the back seat of the car. When Bawla shaheb realized that he and his love were not alone in the vehicle, he tried to control his emotions. But emotions are strange things—one doesn't control them, they control one instead. Bawla saheb tried to divert his thoughts for a while, but he soon gave up on preserving his demeanour and looked to his right.

'Can god create such a beautiful thing?'

To his side was Mumtaz Begum. It is said that Mumtaz, the wife of Shah Jahan, was a beauty beyond any earthly description, but Bawla saheb firmly believed that the Mumtaz sitting to his right was even more enchanting than her. It didn't matter how dark and scandalous the lady's past was. After all, a lotus blooms in mud only.

Going against all odds, Bawla saheb had decided that he was going to marry Mumtaz and give her the due respect in society as his wife. But Mumtaz was yet to know the dormant wish in the heart of the man sitting on her left. If she came to know of it, then perhaps her pink cheeks would turn red blushing with love and her dark eyes would probably be wet with the happy tears of exuberance and thankfulness. Her love for Bawla saheb would probably flow beyond the threshold of social decorum.

Mathews cleared his throat and asked, 'Huzur, will you get down at the bridge?' Bawla saheb was so enamored by Mumtaz that he didn't respond to Mathews. The chilly breeze brushed against them, causing them to sense the evening cold and blouring Mumtaz's locks of hair across her face. He was humming a tune and was about to sing some lines when a red Maxwell car ahead of them braked suddenly, thereby blocking the way of Bawla saheb. The screeching sound of the brakes and the wheels rubbing on the asphalt shattered the serenity of the environment.

The chauffeur of Bawla saheb was an experienced man, and somehow managed to gain control over the car. He murmured, 'That driver is probably high on something!' Bawla saheb and Mumtaz prevented injury by a timely grip on the seat before them but Mathews banged his head on the backrest in front of him.

'Where do these duffers get their driving license from?' Bawla saheb was going to say something more but he became speechless when he saw four men coming out of the Maxwell car, each of them carrying either a pistol or a *khukri*[10]. The men came forward and swung the khukri across the throat of the driver and attacked Mumtaz.

Three men, who resembled giants, tried to pull out Mumtaz from the car through the open roof without unlocking the door. When Mumtaz protested, they snapped, 'Shut up b***h, you did quite some drama!'

'Help! Help! Save me!' The divine face of Mumtaz was pale white with fear by that time, and she desperately struggled like a fish trying to get out through the net.

Bawla saheb was stunned for a moment, and then pounced on the men, trying to save his lover from their clutches. 'You scoundrel! How dare you touch my love?! Who are you people? I will—'

Before Bawla saheb could finish his statement, a bullet went through his chest. At that time, he was tightly holding the lapel of one of the men's jackets. His hands loosened instantly. In shock and pain, Bawla saheb lost consciousness.

But that didn't stop the people from what they were

---

[10]A special kind of dagger.

doing. They were goons for hire and they had chosen that profession after diligently killing their sense of ethics and humanity. They had received a hefty *supari*[11] for that job. Thus, they were not distracted by Bawla saheb being shot. Instead, they shifted their focus to the real job.

A man almost dragged Mumtaz out of the car, over the locked door, and started swinging his khukri mercilessly over the beautiful face of Mumtaz. When she tried to sit on the road, shivering with pain, the goons delivered another blow to her cheek. Mathews was frozen in fear after seeing that deadly episode unfolding in front of him. He tried to escape but fell to the ground when a small khukri came flying like a boomerang, piercing his back. The goons dragged Mumtaz towards the Maxwell car. She was in excruciating pain, and her cry for help was heard by none.

The assault was almost one-sided, when suddenly something happened. Four British military officers were returning after a game of golf at the Willingdon Club. It was almost dusk.

The car was driven by a brave officer, Lieutenant Saegert. When they came close to the site of the incident, they were horrified on seeing the scene—Mathews was crying in pain lying on the road, and the cold body of Bawla saheb was hanging over the door of his car. A little further, a man was dragging Mumtaz towards the red Maxwell car.

Lieutenant Saegert braked his car and jumped out. Along with him, the rest of the officers also came out of the car—Lieutenant Batley, Colonel Vickery and Lieutenant Stephen. Each of them was a fearless warrior but only Batley carried a gold club as a weapon. They had gone for a game and thus had not carried any weapon. However, an absence of weapon was not a reason enough to stop these brave

---

[11]The payment for an assassin to kill someone.

men from tackling the problem.

Lieutenant Saegert pounced towards a goon and punched hard the person who was dragging Mumtaz. Just then, a bullet, shot by one of the goons, pierced the wrist of Lieutenant Saegert. But it did not deter him. He continued delivering blows on the goons till the enemy was not completely subjugated. On the other side, Lieutenant Batley started swinging his golf club like a fan. Lieutenant Stevenson kicked one of the goons who was approaching Mumtaz, eventually throwing him on the ground. Colonel Vickery grabbed one of the goons by his throat with his iron grip.

The episode lasted three to four minutes and, in that short time, the goons for hire realized that these four officers were indomitable at least by them.They had started to look for a chance to escape. One of them started the engine of the Maxwell car and the rest somehow managed to jump into the car. However, one of them remained. By that time, he was about to die of suffocation in the bone-crushing grip of Colonel Vickery. Lieutenant Saegert came running and punched the goon in the abdomen, knocking him out. The police came after a while and they were handed over to the law.

What were the motives of these men? Was it a robbery? If so, then why did the men not try to steal the diamond ring on Bawla saheb's finger and the pricey necklace around Mumtaz's neck? To know the reason behind that assault, one has to jump to the past.

Let us go to the world of rulers of kingdoms in British India. They were ultimately puppets in the hands of the British, yet they believed in the power of their titles deeply. It was common for them to spend lakhs on famous dancers for a single night. Their nights were usually spent enjoying the performances of artists along with the costliest of liquor. Though the common people of the country were starving, war was tearing the country apart and the revolutionaries were struggling with all their might to free the country, these 'kings' lived in their own secluded realm, which was almost like a parallel universe.

The Maharaj of Indore, Tukajirao Holkar, ascended the throne at the young age of 21 in the year 1911. Right after that, he immersed himself in the opulence and grandeur of the royal lifestyle. He was known to be an expert of music and dance, and over that, in spite of having three beautiful wives, he spent most of his time among the singing concubines, known as *tawaif*s, spending most of his fortune in their company. It was common for famous tawaifs of Lucknow and Banaras to be invited to his courtroom to perform. He never sent anyone book with only their fee; rather, he showered them with gold, and the ones who stole his heart were imprisoned forever. They were not chained, but were offered a life they couldn't refuse, a life of grand opulence in his harem. One such tawaif was Wazir Begum.

Though by birth she was a Hindu, originally named Sowkabai Pandharinath, in those days, only Muslim tawaifs received the brightest level of limelight. Hence, she made her reputation under the name of Wazir Begum. The hypnotizing *thumri*s[12] sung in her voice were like bullets piercing right through her admirers' hearts. When she sang, the whole Holkar mansion transcended to a heavenly realm.

The Maharaj ordered her to come to Indore and stay there in lieu of a hefty monthly allowance. Wazir was elated at first, as it was better to have a permanent base instead of travelling here and there for performances. She had a

---

[12]Thumri is a vocal genre or style of Indian music.

husband, but having a husband while staying with kings was a common thing for tawaifs at that time. She also had a 10-year-old daughter, who competed with the beauty of her mother from an early age. She was none other than Mumtaz.

Everything is fated, otherwise how one can explain the sudden illness of Wazir when she was summoned to sing in front of the Maharaj's guests one day. And why would Wazir, in order to keep the honour of her master intact, say to her young daughter, 'Go child, I have taught you everything till now. Today, you will perform in my place.'

'Will I sing bhajan?' The small girl asked innocently.

'No no! You will sing the thumris that I have taught you. Make sure that the Maharaj is happy. He should not feel ashamed in front of his guests.' Wazir repeated that to her daughter multiple times.

Mumtaz was an obedient girl. She went attired in a glittering dress and sat in the mehfil after paying her respects to all the guests. The entire courtroom was shining in the glitter of that 10-year old.

Everyone started talking among themselves in a low voice, 'Is this the daughter of Wazir? She will overthrow her mother soon! What a voice and what a beauty!'

The words were no hyperbole. When the first *bol*[13] of the tabla ended and the *harkat* by the sarangi toned down, the first *aalap*[14] in her voice transported everyone to a different world, as if someone was pouring down honey through the ears. Mumtaz's voice could even wake up gods from their deep *sadhna* (meditation).

Everyone started applauding Mumtaz. '*Wah! Wah! Kya baat* (Wow! Wow! What a performance),' was heard around

---

[13]A bol is a standardized mnemonic syllable used in North Indian classical music to define the *tala* or rhythmic pattern.

[14]Musical prelude

the room. It was insulting to shower money on a performer in front of her owner, so everyone resisted that urge by showering accolades instead.

The Maharaj observed everything from his seat, higher than the rest. An orderly came with some expensive food to Mumtaz as he was instructed—strawberries, cake, Yorkshire pudding, ham and other mouth-watering delicacies. These food items were unfamiliar to the little girl. The Maharaj had returned from Britain the previous evening, and those were brought with him. It was a great gift for little Mumtaz, and as instructed by her mother, she accepted a cake and few strawberries and merrily left the room giving salaam to all.

The next morning, Wazir was summoned by the Maharaj. Her health was not good. Still, getting a summon at such an odd time instilled a certain fear in her mind. She shivered while walking but still presented herself to the Maharaj. Her only fear was whether Mumtaz had made some mistake the previous evening.

When Wazir came and stood in front of the Maharaj, he came straight to the point, 'You have never mentioned that you have such a beautiful and talented daughter!'

'*Janab*,[15] she is quite young, so—' replied Wazir but she was stopped midway.

'Young? She is not a little girl anymore,' the Maharaj said while crunching on a fresh Kashmiri apple. 'This is the right age! Listen, you are the permanent tawaif at my harem, and now your daughter will also be a permanent tawaif at my place.' A fire of hatred lit up in the eyes of Wazir for a moment but she restrained herself. Mumtaz was younger than the daughter of the Maharaj.

She gulped and said, 'But Maharaj, my daughter... actually she...'

---

[15]Janab is an Islamic honorary title, which means 'sir' in English.

Why are you stammering!' Tukajirao got agitated.

'Actually, my daughter doesn't like these kind of performances, Maharaj! She loves to sing bhajan.' Wazir knew that this was going to raise a storm, yet she gathered all the courage and said the words.

The Maharaj was now utterly dismayed and said to one of his servants, Ratanlal, 'What! The daughter of a tawaif will sing bhajan?!' He laughed and said, 'This is like a thief reciting vedas!'

Ratanlal smiled mockingly to support his master. The others in the room also started mocking Wazir: 'Huzur, the day is not far when tawaifs will demand to run the country! Ha ha ha!' Wazir kept standing with her eyes down amid the group of men laughing like they had heard the funniest joke in their lives. The Maharaj suddenly stopped laughing and said, 'Well, let two years pass and Mumtaz evolve a bit. Then she will be mine and only mine! Understood? Go, train your daughter well. Teach her how to please men.'

Wazir was becoming frailer with each day. When she thought that her daughter would have to sleep with the man whom she was forced to sleep with frequently, her eyes welled with tears. But there was nothing she could do. There was no point in fighting with the shark while swimming in the sea. There was no escape. The Maharaj couldn't even wait for two years, and Wazir Begum was forced to send Mumtaz to him.

Though Mumtaz inherited the talents and beauty of her mother, she refused to be subjugated like her. She became restless being locked in the embrace of the Maharaj. He was not very surprised by the restlessness of his latest prey. He believed that everyone struggles at first, but when they are fed with expensive jewellery and clothes, they become submissive like a pet. The Maharaj followed this formula for 10 years—from a 12-year-old Mumtaz to a 20-year-old

Mumtaz. In these 10 years, he gifted her ornaments worth 50 lakh rupees, among which there were 22 boxes of eye-dazzling bangles. However, even after all this, he didn't win the heart of Mumtaz Begum. Though Mumtaz slept with him and sang for him, she remained depressed. The Maharaj had buried her in riches, but he couldn't fathom the deepest mysteries of her heart.

The Maharaj believed that women are commodities that have a price; pay the right price and you can own one. But for the first time, his theory was proving wrong, and that annoyed him. And Mumtaz's mother was subjected to the king's wrath. 'Her mother is teaching her to remain like this! Separate Wazir from her daughter,' he ordered his servants.

The job was done. As planned, the Maharaj took both the mother and daughter, and travelled to Bombay from Indore in the month of April 1919. He checked into the Tajmahal hotel and kept the mother and daughter in a bungalow on Nepean Sea Road. Needless to say, the bungalow was heavily guarded.

In a few days, as ordered by the Maharaj, his manager Shankar Rao came to the bungalow, 'Wazir bai? Maharaj will take Mumtaz with him to the cinema; please tell her to be ready.' Wazir Begum sent her daughter as ordered. The Maharaj was not fond of the older woman anymore; she had passed her expiry date as a product of interest for the king. Shankar Rao took Mumtaz to the Maharaj but never returned.

Wazir was not a fool. She knew that the Maharaj had sent Mumtaz elsewhere to keep her away from her mother's company. However, she was afraid of something else. The Maharaj was ill-famed for his weird fetishes. Mumtaz was a young girl and, as a mother, she was unable to imagine what Mumtaz might go through in her absence. Hence, she secretly informed the police. Mumtaz was kidnapped from Bombay and she knew that Bombay was not under the area of the Maharaj's influence.

The British police arrested Shankar Rao. But Mumtaz was nowhere to be found. On top of that, Wazir lost her job at Tukajirao's harem. If the Maharaj had wanted, he could have done many other unimaginable things to Wazir just to teach the rest about the limits of a tawaif. But he chose not to create a fuss. He was already submerged in lust for young Mumtaz and took her straight to London. He even gave her a name, Kamlabai.

When Mumtaz returned from Britain to India, she was pregnant. In due time, a baby girl was born, but she died soon. Mumtaz was always against the Maharaj, but after the death of her daughter she revolted outright. 'I want to go to my mother. I do not like living in this mansion. I want to go to my mother,' she said.

Though the Maharaj was angered by Mumtaz, considering the state of mind of a mother who had recently lost her child, he said, 'How is that possible, Kamla? I love you so much. See, I have bought this diamond nose ring just for you!'

'I don't want a diamond nose ring!' Mumtaz threw away the little ornament and said, 'Release me from Indore, I want to go to my mother.'

The enraged Maharaj tried hard to stop her. However, considering everything, he decided to bring Wazir to his mansion again. He tried to calm Mumtaz down by saying that though he could not allow her to go to her mother, he could definitely allow her mother to come and stay in the mansion. But can one keep a bird caged after she had seen the open skies once?

Mumtaz became a rebel and protested with all her might If it had been any other girl, she would have been already liquidated by the Maharaj. But Mumtaz was not just any other girl. The Maharaj thought that a girl with the grace of an angel was bound to come with tantrums!

If this girl would have been just an ordinary concubine, the Maharaj would have lost interest in her long back. Two years went past like this. The act of being raped disguised as love and the act of being caged disguised as care continued for two years.

One day, Mumtaz said to her mother, 'Let us escape under the cover of night. If we can get out of Indore and into British India, then this evil Maharaj will not be able to touch us anymore. The autocracies of these kings do not hold there.

Wazir was shocked. If those words were, by any chance, heard by a faithful servant of the Maharaj, then both of them would be slaughtered under the cover of night! She said, 'Shut up! Can you even get out of this mansion, let alone escape from Indore? What is the point in dreaming about the unachievable?' Mumtaz became quiet. Meanwhile, the Maharaj never looked back at his three wives or the other concubines and tawaifs. Whether it was a hunting tour or a holiday retreat, he always took Mumtaz with him. He kept her neck deep in grandeur but never got the touch he expected.

In the beginning of the year 1921, Wazir appealed to the Maharaj, 'Mumtaz is not feeling good here, Maharaj. If you can send her to the hills for a while…' Maharaj Tukajirao was in a jolly mood that day for some reason. He called Shankar and ordered, 'Make arrangements for them to stay at the bungalow in Mussorie for a few days. And arrange for guards; make sure there are no loose ends as I won't be there.'

Opportunities do not present themselves often. The mother and daughter planned everything. If they could somehow get away from the boundaries of that Indore province into British India, then all would be well and they would live life on their own terms.

Mumtaz whispered to her mother, 'Listen maa, inform the British police about everything. When we arrive there, the Maharaj must not bring us back!'

Wazir, influenced by her daughter, informed the police commissioners of Bombay and Delhi: 'As the keepers of law of British India, I appeal for the protection of me and my daughter Mumtaz Begum. Please consider the appeal of an otherwise helpless woman.' Wazir also sent a letter to the then viceroy asking for help.

Finally, on 22 March 1921, the mother and daughter embarked on their journey for Mussorie, well-guarded by the security forces of the king of Indore. As per itinerary, they had to step down from the train in Delhi and continue the rest of the journey by car. Both of them had planned this escape earlier and they acted accordingly. They started walking away from the station; there was no way they could be taken to Mussorie.

The next things went as per plan as well. In the absence of the Maharaj, both the mother and the daughter started screaming out loud, 'Leave us! Leave us alone! Who are you? Why are you forcing us?!' Within seconds, the Delhi Police arrived at the scene. Delhi was not an area under a native prince; it lay in British India.

The men employed by Tukajirao looked on helplessly as the mother and daughter were relieved from their clutches and came out of the station, under the guard of railway policemen, without any further resistance from the king's security. Just outside the station, Mumtaz tightly hugged her mother, 'Maa! We are free! That evil king will not be able to do anything to us anymore!'

Though Wazir put on a plastic smile to keep up the jollity of her daughter, the different things that could go wrong continued to trouble her mind. Maharaj Tukajirao was not among them who gave up so easily. If his prey escaped from his cross hairs, and that too unscathed, it would definitely send him over the edge.

And that is what happened. Some incidents started happening to them that made the mother and daughter realize that the city was not safe for them anymore. Out of the fear of being caught by the Maharaj's forces, Wazir took her daughter and left for Amritsar to her native home. But the Maharaj started laying the trap even there. He wanted to set an example that a minuscule tawaif must not do such a monumental insubordination!

The first few days in the home at Amritsar went well. In the meantime, Wazir's husband also arrived there. Mumtaz started living the simple life outside the grandeur of royal amenities, but a life with a sense of freedom. Both of them, the mother and daughter, were enjoying the feeling of being free. But Wazir behind her mask of happiness, always had fear lingering in her mind. She feared that the men of Maharaj would come anytime and take her daughter away from her.

And that day came soon. A servant of the Maharaj, Ram, arrived at their home in Amritsar. That person used to talk to Wazir and Mumtaz by addressing them as 'memshaheb', but on that day, he threatened them outright, 'For the safety of you and your daughter, come back to Indore, else the consequences will be catastrophic!' Since Amritsar was not under the Maharaj's control, the servant only restricted himself to threatening them and went away.

When a person gets accustomed to oppression, a time comes when the person loses the sense of fear and it gets converted into rebellion. The same happened with the mother and daughter. They stayed back in Amritsar against all odds. Nobody knew the history of Wazir and Mumtaz there, and they were living a life of dignity.

One day, they met a young man named Biharilal, who

was famous as a social worker. The man became a close acquaintance of the mother and daughter due to his honest words and charming behaviour.

Biharilal was a trader of shawls. He had shops in Delhi, Bombay and other big cities. It became a routine for him to attend to the mother and daughter in any difficult time: to arrange for doctors and medicines in case of any illness, to bring monthly groceries and many more things. With time, he became like a son to Wazir. One day, she revealed their past to Biharilal and expressed her concern and fear for Mumtaz. She said, 'You know Bihari, I am still afraid of how Tukajirao will take his revenge on Mumtaz.'

Biharilal tried to comfort her and ease her tension, 'Maa ji, why are you so worried? This is the time of the British, and the king's atrocities will never take place here. Amritsar is a very peaceful place.'

'You don't get it, Bihari,' Wazir emphasized in a lower voice, 'We cannot live here any longer. We have to go to Bombay. The Maharaj has a lot of spies here, and I am worried about that.'

'Why Bombay?' Biharilal asked in curiosity.

Wazir first became a bit uncomfortable. If Mumtaz came to know that she had revealed everything to Biharilal, then she would be mad at her. But still she continued whispering, 'Actually I have a brother in Bombay. He managed to introduce my daughter to a businessman there, named Abdul Qadir Bawla. They both write to each other. Actually… Bawla wants to marry my daughter.'

Wazir told a story that was half true. Who will marry the daughter of a tawaif! Bawla saheb probably wanted to enjoy his days with Mumtaz, and hence, he had sent some monetary advance. But reality is always stranger than fiction. Bawla was not like other men. He really wanted to marry Mumtaz.

'Wah! That is great news!' Biharilal said, 'And you are

scared because of a native king of Indore! Listen maa ji, one of my brothers is a famous barrister in Bombay. You go there; he will take care of the rest. Higher officials of police are close friends to him. There are so many so called kings who were dragged to court and put behind bars by him!'

Everything happened as per the suggestion by Biharilal. Wazir, along with her husband and daughter, started her journey for Bombay. Biharilal's brother Bulakidas came to the Victoria Terminus (now Chhatrapati Shivaji Terminus) of Bombay to receive them. He said, 'Namaste maa ji. I have made arrangements for your stay at a place called Baseba. This is my servant Ramlal; he will always be with you. Do not worry about anything.'

Mumtaz expressed her dissatisfaction, 'Where did you bring us, maa? There is no human being around us. It is so haunting.'

'Wait for few days. Bawla saheb will return to the country after finishing his work and then my brother will take you to him. Then you will travel to so many places,' Wazir Begum tried to convince her daughter.

'God! I really hate to travel with these men all around. I do not wish to do that anymore,' Mumtaz expressed her annoyance at the proposal. 'Don't I deserve to live an independent life on my own, maa?' Wazir remained quiet.

Few days passed like this. One day, when Wazir went out to the market, she saw something that spooked her to the core. She saw that the servant provided by Bulakidas, Ramlal, and the pyada of Tukajirao, Ratan, were walking together towards her. It could be easily derived from their attitude that their friendship was an old one.

She somehow managed to hide herself from their eyes by taking refuge in a grocery shop. Suddenly, an idea came to her mind that sent a shiver down her spine—that helpful young chap Biharilal at Amritsar, his brother Bulakidas and his servant Ramlal were the men of Maharaj Tukajirao. How deep a conspiracy was that? Who was trustworthy? She had taken the pledge that she would go to the ends of the earth to save her daughter. But how?

Though Wazir was illiterate, her life experiences had taught her to be clever. She went straight to the police commissioner of Bombay. As per his suggestion, they moved to a safe house shown by the commissioner. The Maharaj had given a strict order to Biharilal, Bulakidas and Ramlal, 'Bring Mumtaz to Indore using deception, not force. If she tries to escape, then simply cut off her nose! Her adamancy comes from her beauty; that beauty should be destroyed so that no one even looks up at her. How dare a tawaif have such audacity! Make sure that you kill the mother and father by chopping them into pieces and feeding them to dogs!'

Due to the cunning mind of pervert king, Abdul Qadir Bawla ended up as collateral damage. The one goon among the four whom the British officers had managed to capture was Shafi Ahmed. If Shafi Ahmed had not been caught, then perhaps this heinous murder could have remained as a case of murder by unknown assailants in the criminal history of India.

The case was heard at the Bombay High Court on 27 April 1925. Muhammad Ali Jinnah was employed by Tukajirao Holkar as his defense lawyer. The other lawyer employed by the accused was the famous Bengali barrister Jatindra Mohan Sengupta.

At that time, Indore had been among the few revered native kingdoms. Thus, an accusation of that scale against him was a real blow to the autocracy of native kings. Besides that, it was the first time that anyone had been shot dead in Bombay. This case shook not only bthe social elite but also the entire country.

Mumtaz was also summoned as a witness. A team of experienced lawyers cross-examined her in various ways to distract her from the truth. But not being afraid by the men, she maintained her calm and described immaculately how the Maharaj of Indore, Tukajirao Holkar, kept her caged in his palace day after day; how she became a victim of the inhuman fetishes of the king from an early age; how he had deprived her and her mother of the rights of a normal human being. She did not leave any stone unturned to expose the 'revered' Maharaj in front of the court.

'My Lord! I was raped day after day. I have been running around escaping from him for the last 10 years. Don't I have the right to live my life as my own?' She broke down in tears in the witness box and continued, 'Abdul Qadir Bawla saheb loved me. I dreamt of having a family with him. That Maharaj has shattered everything! If those British officers had not arrived there at time, I would have been dead too.'

The judge was Justice Crump. The public prosecutors were the Advocate-General J.B. Kanga along with Keneth Kemp. On the other side were Jinnah and Sengupta, but later, the team grew with the addition of veteran lawmen like S.G. Velinkar.

The specialty of the Bawla Murder Case was that it was not just a murder, but had the rights of woman in a so-called civilized country also intertwined with it. It was not common in the Indian judicial system during that time to have cases where women rights were one of the central agendas. The entire incident was analysed from different perspectives, and the trial lasted days.

The chief witnesses were the four braveheart British officers, and the photographic memory of Colonel Vickery identified the six criminals. The entire episode of murder and then physical assault with a sharp instrument took place in a few minutes, but the number of people accused were high. Justice Crump started to look into every details of the case with utmost diligence and attention.

The defense lawyer Jinnah argued, 'My Lord! The deceased Abdul Qadir Bawla was carrying his own licensed revolver; it was Bawla who fired the first shot!'

'No!' Justice Crump dismissed Jinnah. 'It is true that Bawla had a license for a revolver, but let alone using it, he did not even carry the weapon on that day. And the ballistics report tells a whole different story. The empty cartridges found at the place did not match the bore of either Bawla's or Lieutent Saegert's revolvers. On the other hand, they were a perfect match for the revolvers of the accused.'

Another defense lawyer argued, 'Mumtaz Begum has obtained a lot of money and jewellery from Maharaj Tukajirao; she is nothing more than a prostitute!'

'So what?' Justice Crump looked at him with a displeased and annoyed gesture on his face. 'Does getting money and jewellery from someone makes the receiver a slave to the person who is providing wealth? Does she not have her own independence and rights? Can she be violated for not accepting the domination of her master? And in which law is it written that anything can be forced on a prostitute or tawaif? No one can be forced to have sexual intercourse without his or her consent. Any sexual act without the consent of both people involved is to be treated as nothing less than rape!'

'But My Lord, Mumtaz Begum herself wanted to go to Indore at last,' said Jinnah.

The public prosecutor Keneth Kemp said, 'That's a lie! The previous lawyer of Mumtaz Begum, Mr Nariman, has seconded her claim that Mumtaz Begum preferred drowning in the sea to going back to Indore.'

In that trial, the name of Indore's royal family came to the forefront. The entire regime of native kings and their autocracies received lot of criticism and hate after being exposed in front of the world. Though Maharaj Tukajirao tried his best to keep things in wraps by spending lakhs of rupees, eventually the cat was out of the bag. The complexity of the case grew with time, and it started creating news not just in the country but beyond the sea as well, in Britain. The Bombay Bar Association started publishing the case in episodes in its journal.

At last the trial came to an end.

Nine individuals from Indore state, namely Shafi Ahmed, Pushpashil Balwant Rao Ponde, Shyam Rao Rebhji Dighe, Bahadurshah, Akbarshah, Mumtaz Mahomed, Abdul Latif, Karamatkhan and Phanse, were tried on 13 charges. This included criminal conspiracy to kidnap Mumtaz from British India, Bawla's murder, Saegert's attempted murder, grievous hurt to Mumtaz and Mathews and unlawful assembly. Eventually seven of the nine accused were convicted, and two acquitted. Later, two of the accused were hanged to death.

Then the focus was converged on the main perpetrator of the entire conspiracy, Maharaj Tukajirao Holkar. Due to the high-profile nature of the accused, the then viceroy of India formed a five-member commission to investigate the details of all the wrong doings of the Maharaj. To make the commission unbiased, a high court judge and two native kings were also appointed as its members. The then viceroy became a member on behalf of the Queen of England. The inquiry commission started looking for worms but instead found snakes when they dug deeper.

At last, under the immense pressure of the viceroy, the autocratic Maharaj of Indore, Tukajirao Holkar, gave up his throne. He was forced to let go of the power that he used to lord over his subjects and the royal throne that allowed him to continue his autocratic atrocities. However, the Maharaj, other than resigning from his post, didn't lose much. He gave up his kingdom, married once more and went to France with his new wife. After that, he lived for more than 50 years but never returned to India. Though his honour, respect and power all turned to dust, did he really get a fair punishment for his deeds?

The centrepiece of this game of power and lust, Mumtaz, did not receive any obstruction in her way later. It is rumoured that she had been pregnant at that time and was blessed with a baby girl, a child of Bawla saheb.

In the year 1925, based on this Bawla Murder Case, a Hindi motion picture named *Kulin Kanta* was released. While writing this book, I have tried to search for the reels of that movie from many archives, but probably none survives to this day. The Bawla Murder Case became famous and thrilling because, till then, a tawaif, who was seen as the waste of society, received her due place in society. There is a reason that Eleanor Roosevelt, one of the First Ladies of USA, once said, 'A woman is like a tea bag. You never know how strong it is until it's in hot water.'[16]

---

[16]Weishan, Michael, '"A Woman Is like a Tea Bag": Eleanor Roosevelt, and Radical Women of the 20s and 30s 3-26', *The Franklin Delano Roosevelt Foundation,* 6 March 2018, http://tinyurl.com/ckcuz2te. Accessed on 28 December 2023.

Maharajadhiraj Sir Raj Rajeshwar Sawai Shri Tukojirao III Holkar XIII Bahadur GCIE

DEAR DOCTOR DEVIL: INDUMOTI PONKSHE MURDER CASE, 1959

The Grant Government Medical College, perhaps one of oldest medical colleges in South Asia, is home to only the best students in the country. The architecture of the campus resembles Victorian gothic structures with tall ceilings and huge corridors. The day was 20 November 1956—a disrobed dead body of a middle-aged lady named Indumati Ponkshe was lying on a table so that medical students could examine it.

The women of the country were still battling daily for their agency. Their lives used to start and end in the house. Indumati was one of them who passed their days with a veil on their head under a domestic ceiling. But did she ever imagine that after her death, she would be the subject of a medical study, circled by a bunch of curious minds?

At that time, there was no concept of voluntary donation of the dead body after one's death for the benefit of medical studies. If someone died in the hospital, then the body was taken by the relatives and was cremated or buried by performing all the rituals. Only the bodies that nobody claimed ended up in the morgue.

There was a soft murmur among the students. Till then, the bodies that they had dissected either belonged to some destitute beggar who had died on the streets or some accident victim, mostly insane vagabonds. The students were familiar with dirty and skinny bodies. They never thought of dissecting a body that looked more in place at a funeral rather than at the dissection table of a medical college.

The professor of anatomy arrived in due time, a serious British man, Dr Thompson. He came, glanced at the body and remembered that the body had been transferred the previous day from the morgue of JJ Hospital. He then glanced at the students and said, 'Are you all ready?'

'Yes, Sir!' the students answered back unanimously.

Dr Thompson hinted to his assistant standing beside him to hand him the scalpel. The students were sophomores. Dr Thompson usually started by showing the liver and pancreas, and he gradually moved towards the intestines. When he took the scalpel and walked forward to start dissection just above the naval, his eyes went to the throat of the lady.

Dr Thompson, a veteran surgeon, stopped immediately. He placed down the scalpel and bowed over to see the throat closely. He took another instrument to slide aside the throat to have a look at the neck.

'What happened, Sir?' A student asked.

He kept on observing the body for some minutes and then raised up his head and said to his assistant, 'Ramesh, I am not going to dissect it.'

'Why, Sir?' Ramesh was clueless. 'Look closely,' Dr Thompson pointed at the body, 'Can you spot the signs of clawing at the back of the neck?'

Hearing the words, not just Ramesh but many curious students came closer and bowed over the body to have a look. The professor was right. There were quite some clear marks of clawing in the neck.

'The principal said that the woman was admitted at the JJ Hospital, and she died there. I wondered how they missed a bloody autopsy even after seeing marks like these,' said Dr Thompson frowning at the body. 'Inform the principal that he must immediately contact the coroner at JJ Hospital; the body needs an autopsy. Something is fishy. Saying the last words, the senior professor left the hall keeping aside his apron. Ramesh stood still for a while thinking what to do, and then he ran towards the principal's office.

In any hospital, the coroner has the authority to take the final call on the body that would be used for dissection and the one that would be examined in an autopsy. The news reached the coroner of JJ Hospital by the evening.

He said, 'What! This is the same body that came from Gokuldas Tejpal Hospital. They don't have a morgue, so they sent it here.' The coroner had first refused to accept the dead body as there had been no attached death certificate with it specifying the cause of death; on top of that, there was a letter from Bombay Police requesting an autopsy of the body. But still, the autopsy didn't take place because when the coroner rang up the person responsible for that task at Gokuldas Hospital for more information, the resident medical officer (RMO) Dr Muskar promised to send a death certificate, and he did so. Remembering this fact, the coroner looked at the death certificate right away. 'Here it is, Dr Muskar has clearly stated that the cause of death is diabetic coma.'

In the meantime, a call came to the coroner from the Bombay Police. 'Hello, Sir. Professor Thompson of Grant Medical College has informed us that the body sent by your morgue for dissection did not suffer a natural death. Please perform an autopsy quickly and send us a report.'

'But…' the coroner answered, 'you already said to do an autopsy as the corpse lacked a death certificate. At that time, I called the photography cell to take some photographs before performing the autopsy. But then Dr Muskar from Gokuldas Tejpal Hospital sent the death certificate, so I…'

After examination, it was found that the clawing marks on the neck of Indumati Ponkshe were nothing more than the marks left when her dead body was transported like a jute bag from here to there. The autopsy performed after the request of Thompson that day brought to light many untold facts about this murder case of 1956. The murder was well planned and executed in phases. Many people were responsible for carrying out each of those phases.

⁂

It was 13 November 1956. The winter was just setting in, and in that cool weather of early morning, the coolies of Victoria Railway Station were sleeping on the platform, crawling and squeezing inside their makeshift blankets made of old bedsheets. The horn and bellowing steam woke them up as they saw Pune Passenger Express crawling into the platform at a slow pace.

If it had been a mail train, then there would have been a wave of activities, but this was the poor Pune Passenger Express—only train that stopped at the smallest of stations and took the whole night to cover a distance of just 75 miles.

This was an era of steam locomotives. As soon as the train slowed down to a walking pace, a middle-aged passenger rushed down from the first-class compartment. He was wearing a suit and a tie. His hair had just started to turn silvery white and the same trend was observable in his thick mustache. The man was a physician, and the stethoscope in his hand gave away his professional identity. The doctor did not pay heed to the few collies that rushed towards him. With him, were two men carrying a stretcher.

The team of coolies became attentive. 'What is the matter? Did something happen to a passenger?' They curiously made a circle around the gate of the compartment.

A lady was brought down from the compartment on the stretcher, her eyes were closed, and there was no movement in the body. A collie whispered to another fellow collie, 'What happened, *bhai*? Did she die on the train?'

The second coolie answered, 'Don't know whether she is dead or fainted, nothing can be said.'

Though a few coolies came forward, the doctor didn't pay any attention to them. He went outside with the two people of the railway staff and called a taxi. The two people of the railway staff, carrying the stretcher, peeked through the window of the cab and said, 'This lady has become sick on the train. The St George hospital is just a few kilometers away. There will be a doctor with you, don't worry.'

The lady was laid carefully on the backseat and the doctor sat on the front passenger seat. He was only carrying a small bag. He swiped his handkerchief over his sweaty forehead, and then waved at the two people from the railway staff. Then he looked at the cab driver and said, 'Be quick!'

When the taxi driver just crossed the station premises, the doctor said, 'Go to Gopaldas Tejpal Hospital instead.'

The driver asked, 'Why? That is quite far. St George will be quite near Doctor Sahab!'

It appeared that not a word of the cabbie reached the doctor, and he was looking at the lady lying in the back by then. The doctor didn't wait after reaching the hospital; he rushed to the emergency ward and brought two men with a stretcher to carry the lady inside. The doctor paid the fare to the taxi driver and followed the men.

Dr Ugel was in charge of the emergency ward at that time.

The doctor almost ran towards him. 'Namaste! I am Dr Anant Lagu. I live in Pune and I practise here.'

'Oh! Namaste!' Dr Ugel greeted back and asked, 'Is this lady some relative or...?'

'She is an old patient of mine. Her name is Indumati Ponkshe. She has hysteria. I was bringing her to Bombay to get her checked by a more experienced physician. But she suddenly fainted on the train,' said Dr Anant Lagu.

'Okay, we will handle it,' Dr Ugel became busy. It is common among doctors to feel easy when they discover that someone in the patient party is also a fellow doctor. Dr Ugel ordered the peon to bring a cup of tea for Dr Lagu and then concentrated on the patient. By that time, the lady, Indumati Ponkshe, was having seizures and tremors in her hands and feet. Dr Ugel measured the pulse and it was quite fast.

Dr Ugel observed that though the lady seemed to be like a housewife belonging to a rich family, she was lacking any ornaments on herself. At least a bunch of thin bangles were expected in the hands of a married Hindu woman at that time, but that too was not there. On the contrary, she was wearing a rather expensive saree.

Dr Ugel didn't ask Dr Lagu anything about this anomaly, and he sent Indumati Ponkshe to the female ward upstairs. Then he said to Dr Anant Lagu, 'Doctor, as you are the one who brought her here, as per protocols, can you register her name and—'

'Yes, yes, definitely! I was also an intern at a government hospital once, why are you hesitating to tell me?' Dr Lagu wrote the name and the address of the patient in the register right away:

Indumati Ponkshe
C/O Dr Anant Chintaman Lagu
20, B, Sukkarvarpet, Gali no. 12,
Pune–2

When Indumati was taken upstairs to the female ward, it was 6.00 in the morning. After doing her night shift tirelessly, the doctor in charge of the female ward, Dr Anija, was almost dozing off on her chair. She was a recent medical graduate and was still struggling to be good at being a practicing physician. When she saw that a patient was being brought on a stretcher, she shook off her slumber and ran forward.

Dr Anant Lagu was also walking along with the stretcher on which Indumati was lying. He said, 'Namaste, madam. I am the family physician of this lady. We are from Pune.' Dr Anant Lagu repeated the same story that he had told Dr Ugel to Dr Anija.

Dr Anija first injected a vial of adrenaline-thyroxin and then ordered to attach an oxygen mask to the patient, tuned at 60 per cent at 8 litres per minute. Then she injected 40 ml of insulin in a gap of a few minutes. Usually, insulin is administered to patients with significant diabetics, but did Dr Anija do a test to measure Indumati's blood glucose level? This became an important topic of debate later in the court. We will come to that in due course of time.

Even after all the attempts, Indumati remained unconscious. Dr Anija didn't take any risk, and informed her senior, Dr Saifi. Dr Saifi looked into everything and said, 'Do one thing, charge 40 ml more.'

'But I have just charged 40 ml three hours ago. Should we do it again?' asked Dr Anija.

'Yes, instructed Dr Saifi.

Everything was done as said. Injections and intra-gastric glucose drip continued for two hours. In the meantime, Indumati's urine was also tested. Soon, the clock struck 11.00 in the morning. At that time, the visiting surgeon, Dr Vabiyaba, came for his round in the female ward. When he came near Indumati's bed, Dr Vabiyaba asked about the patient's condition, to which Dr Anija replied, 'Sir, this is a case of diabetic coma. The patient is comatose due to abnormal blood sugar level.'

'Is there acetone in the urine?' asked Dr Vabiyaba.

'No, Sir, we did not do any acetone test. We just tested for blood sugar,' replied Dr Anija.

'So what if she has blood sugar? You should first see

whether there is acetone in the urine or not, and if it is there, then how much. Then you should conclude whether it is a case of diabetic coma or not! How can you guess all by yourself that the patient is in a diabetic coma?!' Dr Vabiyaba almost schooled the rookie doctor in front of everyone.

Indumati's urine sample was still on the table beside her bed. Dr Anija, on being scolded by her senior Dr Vabiyaba, rushed with the vial to get it tested. After the test, she discovered that there were traces of acetone. Dr Vabiyaba was standing till she came back. He seemed rather serious. But Dr Anija did not have to go through another schooling again. When it was 11.30 a.m., Indumati passed away.

With that, she life of a simple and rich widow came to an end. She was a victim of betrayal due to her gullible nature. The person to whom she handed over all her trust turned out to be the one who slowly pushed her towards death—a fate that Indumati probably never even imagined. But after death, the received justice, and that was the last condolence for her.

Though Indumati passed away, Dr Vabiyaba chose to remain in the ward. He said to Anija, 'Arrange for the autopsy of the body. I don't think the patient had diabetic coma at all.' Dr Vabiyaba did not wait after instructing Anija, and he left the ward while thinking about something. If someone would have minutely observed him, then they would have seen the mixed emotions of disbelief and confusion playing wildly across his face. As instructed by Dr Vabiyaba, Dr Anija wrote in the patient file, 'The patient is subject to autopsy.'

But in this whole period, where was Dr Anant Lagu? Dr Vabiyaba later gave his testimony in court that he did not notice Dr Lagu when he came to do his round in the ward. But it was proved in the investigation that on 14 November 1956, Dr Anant returned back to Pune from

Bombay. We should come back to the hospital.

Dr Anija sent the entire case file to the RMO of Gokuldas Tejpal Hospital. The RMO is the authority to send any dead body for autopsy. When Indumati's file reached Dr Muskar, the time was 1.00 p.m. He neither did anything more with the report nor arranged for the autopsy of the body. Rather, he stowed away the file in a corner of his table.

Dr Anija came at around two in the afternoon for inquiring about the situation. 'Sir, have you forwarded the file of Indumati Ponkshe for an autopsy?'

At that time, Dr Muskar was enjoying a siesta after lunch. Hearing the words from the junior doctor Anija, he said casually, 'Will do, will do! I will do everything. Is the person who brought the patient still around?'

Dr Anija shrugged her shoulders and said, 'I cannot say, Sir. I just saw him once when he came to the patient ward. I have not seen him after that.'

Dr Muskar didn't utter anything after that. He wasted some time yawning and then opened the file of Indumati Ponkshe to get the address of Dr Anant Lagu. Then he told the peon to send a telegram to the address written by Dr Anant Lagu on the file. The telegram read:

'INDUMATI IS DEAD. NEED TO
PROCESS BODY. REPLY QUICKLY.'

The day went past but nobody came or responded. Dr Anant Lagu did not come even the next day to claim Indumati's body. None of her relatives even showed up. There was no appropriate morgue in this hospital. Thus, if a corpse needed to be preserved, it was usually sent to the morgue of JJ Hospital.

When Dr Muskar was thinking about what to do with the body that was still unclaimed by anybody, a letter reached him. The letter was written by Dr Anant Lagu from Pune, which later proved to be an important piece of evidence in the court proceedings.

Dr Lagu wrote: 'Srimati Indumati Ponkshe's one and only brother Shri Gobindabaman Deshpande lives in Calcutta. I have already wired him. He will start his journey to Bombay from Calcutta and will reach JJ Hospital within two days. Thank you.' Dr Muskar understood from the letter that there is no other alternative left other than sending the body to JJ Hospital's morgue.

In the meantime, when he did not receive any reply to his previously sent telegram, Dr Muskar did something. He informed everything to the Esplaned Police Station of Bombay just as a fail-safe:

'On 13 November 1956, a 42-year-old lady by the name Indumati Ponkshe came for treatment for hysteria and was admitted to ward number 12 of Gokuldas Tejpal Hospital. She passed away at 11.30 a.m. on the same day. We have sent a wire to the address given by Dr Anant Chintaman Lagu, but no reply came. Thus, we advise transferring the dead body to the morgue of JJ Hospital, else the body will decompose and turn to carrion.' If a dead body needs to be transferred to a morgue, then, by law, a report must be sent to the local police station. Thus, Dr Muskar followed the procedure. He also sent a copy of the same letter to the coroner of JJ Hospital.

When they received the information, the police informed the coroner at JJ Hospital, 'Please accept the dead body of Indumati Ponkshe from Gokuldas Tejpal Hospital. As there is no attached death certificate with the cause of death, you must perform an autopsy on it.'

When Dr Muskar received the instructions from JJ Hospital, as told to them by the police, he didn't show any interest in an autopsy; rather, he wrote a death certificate mentioning the cause of death being diabetic coma.

Thus, the dead body of Indumati Ponkshe went to the dissection hall of Grant Medical College and Dr Thompson opposed dissecting the body.

Knowing that, the police instructed the coroner, 'Arrange for an autopsy immediately, our police surgeon will perform the task.'

Indumati died on 13 November, and 10 days later, the police surgeon Dr Jhala performed an autopsy on the dead body. After the examination, he reported that the claw marks on the neck were not premortem and happened after death due to some reason. Perhaps the undertakers handled the dead body roughly. Dr Jhala did not find any trace of poison in the stomach. But still, he sent the intestinal tissue samples for further examination by an expert.

The expert chemical examiner also did not find any trace of poison. Thus, Dr Jhala reported, 'There is no trace of poison found; diabetic coma can be a probable cause of death.'

Nothing remained to be done after that. The police sent the dead body of Indumati to the Hindu Relief Society the next day. The Hindu Relief Society performed the ritualistic funeral and cremated the body. Indumati Ponkshe turned into a heap of ash.

The coroner, Dr Thompson and everybody else gradually forgot the name of Indumati Ponkshe. Nobody cared to think about the fact that her brother Govindabaman, who, according to Dr Lagu, should have come to retrieve his sister's dead body, never actually showed up. But one person did not forget Indumati—the inspector of Esplaned Police Station of Bombay, Lakshman Sehgal. From the first day, Sehgal found the entire ordeal quite fishy.

Why did a member of a respectable family come to Bombay for treatment with the family physician? Why was she not wearing a single piece of jewellery? Why was she not carrying any money? Why did Dr Anant Lagu never show up after admitting the patient, even after being sent a telegram? He wrote in a letter that her brother would come but nobody showed up in actuality. Why? It was correct that there was nothing suspicious in the post-mortem report. There was also a valid death certificate. Still, something did not add up.

Sehgal never even dreamt that this glitch in his mind about the entire episode would be the starting point in the revelation of one of the most well-orchestrated murders in the criminal history of India, and that this case would one day fetch him the award for being the best police officer in the Bombay police force. After analysing the facts, Sehgal sent a telegram to the Pune Police after a few days requesting for information on Dr Lagu.

Getting such a telegram, the Pune police met Dr Lagu as fast as possible.

Dr Anant Lagu was present at the address he had written in the register of the hospital that night. He said to the police, 'I practise privately in Pune. I had some work on the morning of 13 November in Bombay, and hence, I boarded the Pune Passenger yesterday.'

'Why a passenger train? There are so many fast trains during the day,' asked the officer from Pune police.

'The work in Bombay was in the early morning,' said Dr Lagu, 'Usually the night train is less crowded. I thought that I would reach early morning, finish the work and come back home by the evening train—that's it.'

'Okay, then?'

'There were a few ladies in the compartment that I boarded. Among them, one was lying on the seat almost in a crouching position. I did not see her get up during the entire journey. Also, she didn't eat or drink water during the entire journey. She was lying unconscious throughout the whole night.

'When the train left Baikulla at dawn, all the passengers were preparing to deboard as Bombay was the next and last station. But the lady was still lying there without any movement. I asked the other passengers whether they knew her or not, to which no one replied. The lady had been travelling all by herself. Just after boarding the train, she had told one co-passenger that her name was Indumati Ponkshe.

'The train gradually entered Victoria Terminus Station and everyone started rushing. Still, the lady didn't move. She was still asleep, and soon it became evident that she was very sick.' Dr Lagu stopped for some breath and continued, 'Sir, I am a doctor by profession, and helping the sick is my duty. Thus, I could not just ignore the situation. I got off the train and arranged for a stretcher with two railway staff and somehow took her to Gokuldas Tejpal Hospital. Then, I finished my work and returned back to Pune on the evening train. That lady is not known to me, and I have no further responsibility regarding her. Thank you.'

Sehgal was shocked to receive the report from Pune Police. What Dr Lagu told the Gokuldas Tejpal Hospital people while admitting Indumati and what he told the officers of Pune Police had a huge discrepancy!

Sehgal didn't tell anything to anyone. He continued the investigation, without any official orders, all by himself. At first, he met the medical officer who was on the night shift that day, Dr Ugel. Dr Ugel also mentioned that Dr Lagu informed him that Indumati Ponkshe was a regular patient. Dr Lagu had brought her to Bombay for examination by a specialist.

Brilliant criminologists in the world have studied and found that whatever may be the level of intelligence of criminals and how ever meticulously they try to hide the trail, they always leave some breadcrumbs that lead to the truth. The job of a good detective is to fish out those apparently obscure clues. The same holds true for this case as well.

I just described the Bombay episode of this famous murder case in 1956. I must now shed light on the episode that took place in Pune.

❧

The year was 1922. Indumati was married to the Pune businessman Anant Karve. This was his second marriage. His first wife had died, leaving a son behind. Anant Karve was a good man, and there was no tension of any other rebellious member in the house other than his son from his first wife, Vishnu. Karve had a lot of land. Other than a two-storeyed house in Sukkarwarpeth, he also owned a successfully running business. He loved his young wife very much. He affectionately changed Indumati's name to Lakshmibai after marriage. Thus paying homage to his love, I will address Indumati as Lakhmibai henceforth.

Though Karve was a good man, it did not mean he was foolish. To avoid any conflict in the future, he secured ₹30,000 for Vishnu and established a separate business for him. He had two more sons with Lakshmibai, Ramachandra and Purushottam.

Karve willed his two-storeyed house in Sukkarwarpeth and his business to Ramachandra, but with a clause: Lakshmibai would own three rooms in the mansion till her death. Apart from that, she would receive a monthly stipend of ₹50 from the business.

Karve also ran a loan agency alongside his business. He willed all his income from the loan agency, his bank money and his post office deposits to Purushottam. In the meantime, Vishnu got married and had a son. Karve reserved some land for his grandson too.

During his lifetime, Karve gifted his wife Lakshmibai, almost a treasure trove of gold ornaments, pearls and even diamonds. After a happy married life of 23 years, on 1945, Karve succumbed to pleurisy and breathed his last. But that did not drive Lakhmibai towards poverty in any way. Rather, she received a huge sum money, as she was the nominee for Karve in his life insurance scheme. At that time, her age was 34.

Before the death of Karve, during his illness, he was treated by the local physician, Dr Anant Chintaman Lagu. Dr Lagu had a brother, B.C. Lagu, who was also a doctor by profession. The two brothers had opened a dispensary in Sukkarwarpeth.

After the death of Karve, Dr Lagu did not cease coming to the house. Rather, he spent the major portion of the day at Lakshmibai's home under the excuse of regular health checkups. Lakshmibai also thought that she had nobody of her own in that sense. Her stepson Vishnu did not take care of her. If some problem cropped up, then who would help her out? The only hope for her was the well-wishing neighbourhood doctor! His two sons were still kids at that time. But Lakshmibai never imagined that there would be a war between her elder son Ramachandra and the well-wishing Dr Lagu.

One morning, as Ramachandra prepared for school, he noticed the absence of his mother, who always helped him by ensuring nothing was overlooked and even persuading him to eat more than he would on his own.

He asked the senior domestic worker of the house, 'Where is maa?'

The domestic worker replied, 'Maiji is very sick, beta. She cannot even sit up. She is sleeping in her bed.'

Ramachandra and Purushottam both loved their mother a lot. After the death of their father, their mother was the only person whom they clung to. Ramachandra left his unfinished plate of food and ran to her mother's room upstairs. The house was like a mansion. If the domestic workers and servants were not counted, then there were only three people living in the house.

Ramachandra rushed into the room and asked, 'What happened, maa? Are you sick?'

Lakshmibai was lying on the bed with her hand over her head. She answered in a frail voice, 'My head is spinning like a top, and my chest is also aching.'

'Why didn't you call me till now?' Ramachandra walked up to his mother's bed and asked, 'You remember the way you fasted for the whole day yesterday? That's the reason why your chest is paining. Wait, I will bring the medicine.'

Ramachandra was about to turn and run for the medicine, but suddenly Lakshmibai grabbed his wrist from the back, 'Don't you worry so much! Go to school and inform the doctor once on the way.'

In a moment, Ramachandra's face changed, and he rudely snatched away his hands from his mother. He could not stand Dr Lagu for a second. Till the time his father was alive, the doctor was like a tamed cat. He just used to treat his father, respect him and then leave whenever his requirement was over.

But after his father's death, the doctor used to come regularly without any notice and sit in the drawing room for hours. Sometimes he even went straight to his mother's bedroom, without even knocking!

'What happened?' Lakshmibai shook his son, 'Why are you staring at me? What are you thinking?'

'Nothing!' Ramachandra shrugged his shoulders, 'I cannot call anyone, and I am not taking that way to school. He said those words and, without waiting to hear anything from his mother, left the room.

Lakshmibai was stunned. Dr Lagu had not visited for three to four days. Though she was not that sick, she thought of having a nice chat with the doctor when he came. After the death of her husband, it was Dr Lagu who had been protecting the huge mansion from storms like a big tree over its head. Which bank will give more interest on fixed deposits, which insurance scheme has greater returns—the doctor gave his free advice without any hesitation in all matters. He even wrote letters to banks and other places so that Lakshmibai continued receiving all the facilities. What would have happened to poor Lakshmibai if the doctor was not there! Her stepson Vishnu was not a simple person at all; perhaps he would have devoured everything by somehow tricking his younger brothers.

But it didn't matter how much Lakshmibai understood and appreciated this unwavering and selfless service of Dr Lagu, Ramachandra never liked him. The younger son Purushottam was just 12. Hence, he never got into all those matters. However, 16-year-old Ramachandra was becoming a rebel with each passing day. But what could Lakshmibai do about that? She asked Shantabai to call for the doctor. Although Shantabai was deaf and mute, she was very efficient in her tasks.

The trouble cropped up in the afternoon. It is not known whether it was planned or random, but that day, Ramachandra returned home much earlier. He walked as silently as a cat, climbed up the stairs and covertly entered his mother's bedroom. He was already disturbed and, what he saw in front of him at that moment enraged him.

Lakshmibai was lying, with her clothes off, on the huge bed inside the room. The doctor was not sitting on the chair that day. Rather, he was sitting on the bed, just beside Lakshmibai.

Ramachandra's tolerance had reached the threshold. He had informed about his dislike for the doctor to his mother earlier in various ways as well as the reasons why he did not like him, but he never imagined that things would go that far. He screamed, 'What the hell are you doing here?'

Dr Lagu was bamboozled and turned towards the door. When Lakshmibai tried to say something to his son, he stopped her, 'Don't you have any shame? Scoundrel!'

'What are you saying, Ram? I am sick, that's why doctor sahab…' Lakshmibai tried to explain in a frightened tone.

'You keep quiet!' Ramachandra shouted at his mother and then turned towards the doctor, 'I have never seen such a rascal in my life like you. The whole locality knows about your character. You had the habit of visiting the red-light district before. Most of your patients used to live there, right? I think you have gained a lot of confidence after my father's death! You cannot imagine how badly I can and will hurt you!' He continued his fiery speech for a few more seconds and left the room.

That night, Ramachandra clearly stated to his mother, 'Maa, I have seen enough. I want to tell you one thing straight and clear—if I see that rascal step into this house again, I will leave this house right then. There are thousands of doctors in the city. Your treatment will not be hampered.'

Though Ramachandra was a good human being, if he was enraged, he could not be controlled. Lakshmibai knew about this side of Ram's character, and thus she did not utter any word to further the debate. She didn't even utter the name of the doctor for the coming few days. But can Lakshmibai be fully blamed? Is it a sin for a woman to fall in love again? But, was Lakshmibai really in love with Dr Lagu?

After that incident, Lakshmibai told Dr Lagu to stop visiting, and the doctor also complied with that request for many weeks. Though Lakshmibai did not believe in the threat by Ramachandra, that he was going to leave home, she was a bit scared to bring up the topic again. Ramachandra was essentially just a 16-year-old boy, and she believed he still lacked the courage to take a bold step. Yet, she cared for her son's feelings.

Thus, two months went past like this. After that, one evening, Dr Lagu came over. Lakshmibai had a lot of words reserved for him, so she kept speaking on and on. Ramachandra was not at home for some reason and Lakshmibai was on her toes for his return. She kept on insisting the doctor to go but still he almost stretched the appointment to 9.00 in the night. When the doctor was about to leave, Ramachandra encountered him at the main door. The doctor tried to smile as a gesture of friendliness, but Ramachandra didn't reply back. He seemed very serious and just dodged the doctor to enter the house and went straight to his room.

The next day, Ramachandra started living in a different portion of the mansion and never peeked at the portion of the house where his mother lived. He cooked his own food and did not taste a morsel that came from his mother's kitchen. Sometimes, he bought food from restaurants. Though Lakshmibai was devastated by that gesture, she didn't engage with Ramachandra. This went on for a few years.

In 1952, Ramachandra got a job in the army and left home. Earlier, Lakshmibai used to get at least a glimpse of her son. But with Ramachandra's job, this too was taken away from her. Lakshmibai started living a life of grief, clinging on to her younger son Purushottam. With each passing day, she became more and more dependent on the doctor.

Ramachandra came back after a few months and married a girl of his choice without any involvement of his mother. He then took his wife to Bombay and settled there. He had severed the bond with his mother long back, and thus it was meaningless for him to stay in that mansion in Pune. In Bombay, he raised his own family.

Meanwhile, a tragedy took place. At the beginning of 1954, Purushottam, suddenly fell ill. No proper diagnosis could be made of his illness. As per advice from Dr Lagu, Lakshmibai didn't admit Purushottam to any hospital. He was treated by Dr Lagu in the mansion.

At last, on 18 January 1954, Purushottam breathed his last. In the later days, when the neighbours of Lakshmibai were called one by one for their testimonials in the murder case that ensued, they expressed their suspicion that Dr Lagu killed Purushottam by poisoning him. But why on earth would Dr Lagu do such a thing? What was his advantage in killing the younger son of Lakshmibai?

I have said before that this murder case is etched in the criminal history of India in bold letters. This was a well-planned methodical murder in phases that used medical science for achieving the end goal. Karve died in 1945. After his death, over the course of nine years, Dr Lagu laid the trap and gradually eroded away the Karve family, without even letting them notice what was happening to them, with the precision of a mastermind, cunning yet marvellous.

Ramachandra and the stepson Vishnu had carefully taken their share of the property long before. The sudden death of Purushottam meant that his enormous wealth also got added to Lakshmibai's share. At that point, Lakshmibai was completely alone in the world. There was no one alive in her father's family and she had not kept any contact with her other relatives.

For Dr Lagu, it was a golden opportunity. He took the responsibility of managing the entire wealth of Lakshmibai, and he managed every affair related to banking and business. Lakshmibai was not educated enough to understand financial and legal complexities. She trusted the doctor with her life. He single-handedly dealt with withdrawing money from the bank after getting Lakshmibai's signature and distributed the money among various business heads. He alone dealt with the loan business and other financial avenues left by the late Mr Karve.

Earlier, there had been a manager for dealing with this. 'Why spend money on an outsider for this? I am there!' the doctor had said and Lakshmibai had sacked the long-serving manager.

In the meantime, when Ramchandra became a father, after a lot of deliberation and fighting his ego, he came with his wife and son to his mother so that she could bless her grandson. But Dr Lagu prevented him from entering the house. Ramachandra also pledged to never come to the house in the future. Poor Lakshmibai was unaware of all this.

One day, the doctor was giving an injection of insulin to Lakshmibai, which was a part of the daily routine. The doctor had been giving a considerable amount of insulin to Lakshmibai daily after the death of Purushottam. Dr Lagu knew the effect of insulin on a person who was otherwise fit and healthy in the long run. He almost uttered the same words every day emotionally, 'I fear so much for you!'

'Why?' asked Lakshmibai one day, 'You forgot to give the injection yesterday but I was feeling rather well! On the other days, I feel sleepy, but yesterday it was not like that!'

'How would you feel like that?' The doctor replied in a serious tone, 'Does Shantabai ever care for you? She is deaf and mute. You must always be accompanied by a doctor for your health now; a servant is not fit for the job.'

'Where will I get a full-time doctor?' Lakshmibai thought for a while and proposed, 'You should stay with me! The entire ground floor is empty!'

'That is not possible, how can I live just like that?' the doctor replied with melancholy in his tone, 'Take a justified rent from me, then only I will stay.'

'Okay, you will pay me some rent!' Lakshmibai smiled.

Poor Lakshmibai, what she did paved her way to death.

Two months passed after the doctor shifted permanently to Lakhsmibai's house. Throughout that period, the daily dose of insulin had been eroding Lakshmibai's life like a silent virus sucking the vitality out of its host.

After two months, one day, the doctor said, 'No! I am unable to do it all by myself, Lakshmi! Your health is deteriorating day by day. If something happens, what will I say to god when I die?!'

She replied in an exhausted voice, 'What do you recommend, doctor?'

Dr Lagu said, 'Listen, I have contacted the famous Dr Sathe of Bombay. He has given an appointment in the afternoon of 13 November.'

'Bombay? Will I have to go to Bombay to get examined?'.

'Yes, what is the problem? We will board the train the night before and you will sleep in the train. Then you will freshen up in some hotel the next morning, see the doctor and then we will board the returning train in the evening.' Lakshmibai reluctantly nodded her head to give her consent.

Did she ever think that this would be her last trip?

In the later period, the testament of the deaf and mute domestic worker of Lakshmibai, Shantabai, became the most important evidence in the case. Shantabai, through her gestures, clearly stated, 'Huzur! The day they went to Bombay, the doctor injected two vials of injection to Maiji; one in the morning and one in the evening. Maiji fainted after the second injection that day. She was extremely weak.' What happened after that has been described at the beginning. Dr Lagu took Lakshmibai to Bombay but Lakshmibai never returned. By the time Dr Lagu came back to Pune, Lakshmibai was lying in the morgue.

After returning to Pune, the doctor declared in the neighbourhood, 'What a strange phenomenon! We went to

Dr Sathe and after that, we came back to the hotel. After a while, I went out to buy a stethoscope. When I returned, Lakshmibai was not in the room! The room was empty; on the other hand, it was time for the train.'

'What?' An old neighbour inquisitively asked, 'What did you do after that, Dr Lagu? You went to the police?'

'I was about to go to the police station, Chacha, but then I realized that none of Lakshmibai's luggage was in the room.' Dr Lagu made a face of sheer astonishment, 'When I asked the reception, they said that memshab boarded a taxi and left with a gentleman!'

'Gentleman?' the neighbour was shocked.

Another man gave an expert suggestion, 'Was that Ramachandra? Or maybe some brother of hers!'

'Yes! That is a high probability. I heard that Ramachandra lives in Bombay!'

The neighbours started to gossip among themselves and returned to their daily lives. Poor widow! She lost her husband at such a young age; her elder son left her, her younger son died and her stepson never talked to her. Yet, for the world, she became someone who was staying with some stranger. Seven days went past, then 15, and in this way, two months went past. But Lakshmibai never returned. However, the neighbours, strangely, started receiving letters from her!

The first letter was received by Lakshmibai's friend Yashodaben: 'I am on a pilgrimage. I am having a good time.' Another person in the locality received a letter, 'I am having a good life. No family, no responsibilities, such peace of mind!' In this way, several letters were received by many people over a month, and then, one day, another friend of hers received a letter that surprised them all: 'Gita, I am not going to return to Pune. I am in love with a person named Pawan Joshi. I have also married him. Two of us are living happily in Rathori, a town near Jaipur. I have never been so happy in my life before. Believe me, Gita, I am really happy. I do not wish to get back to my old life. Never search for me, stay well. This is my last letter.'

The neighbours, who first believed in the pilgrimage story, quite naturally, started to smell an anomaly in the matter. Meanwhile, one day, the neighbours observed that Dr Lagu was going to some place after loading all the furniture of the house in a truck.

'Where are you going with all this, Dr Lagu?' asked a neighbour named Kishan Patel.

'What to say, Patelji! Lakshmibai is living a happy life and now I am tasked with the responsibility to send all her furniture to Rathori village. What can I say after this!' the doctor replied with annoyance.

'Why are you taking all the things? Why is she not coming by herself?' asked another neighbour.

'Lakshmibai wants to forget all memories of Pune. That's why she will never come back, and I am the one who is now bearing such unnecessary duties! But what can I do, I used to be the family doctor. Hence...' Dr Lagu left without finishing.

Strangely, Kishanji received a letter two days after that, 'Namaste Kishanji. I instructed Dr Lagu to send all my belongings. Did he send the things already? Do you know anything about it? I have still not received them. Please do not search for me ever, I am happy and in peace...'

The suspicion then got promoted to gossip in the neighbourhood. Meanwhile, Dr Lagu started living in Lakshmibai's mansion. They saw a daily inflow of the latest appliances in the house. The old domestic worker Shantabai had been fired long ago.

One-and-a-half years passed like this.

A brilliant professor lived in Sukkarwarpeth, the locality

of Lakshmibai, named G.D. Bhave. With everyone's consent, he wrote a detailed letter to the erstwhile chief minister of the Bombay State. No one was able to digest the fact that a widow of a respectable family disappeared like that. However, no reply to that letter came. After that, Dr G.D. Datar, a real well-wisher, sent another letter on the same lines in February 1958. Dr Datar was a famous doctor. When the Bombay government received consecutive letters from a professor and a doctor, they took the matter seriously.

At that time, the chief minister of Bombay was Yashwant Chauhan. He instructed the deputy superintendent of Crime Investigation Department (CID), M. Dhonde, to investigate the matter. Dhonde was a brilliant officer. In just two days, he connected the dots—the main suspect of the whole ordeal, Dr Lagu, was the same person whom the Bombay Police had asked about a dead woman.

Dr Lagu; the date of disappearance; the death of the lady—everything fit the equation. But the name of the dead lady in Gokuldas Tejpal Hospital was Indumati Ponkshe, and the missing lady from Pune was named Lakshmibai Karve. Dhonde was in a fix. The day Indumati Ponkshe was travelling in the train and went to Bombay, the same day, on the same train, Lakshmibai Karve was also travelling with Dr Lagu. Indumati Ponkshe was the erstwhile name of Lakhsmibai Karve—did this simple truth never ring a bell in Dhonde's mind till then? It appears so.

With orders from the then chief minister himself, Dhonde jumped into the investigation with all his might and contacted Dr Lagu. By that time, Dr Lagu was a rich man. He had forged Lakshmibai's signature and had transferred most of her property in his name. He had also made her sign many cheques, and he used them to withdraw a large sum of money.

Dr Lagu never imagined that a police officer would

be investigating the case after so many days. There were many anomalies spotted in his testimonial. Dhonde was a veteran police officer, and it took him only a few minutes to understand that Dr Lagu was hiding something deliberately.

He said, 'Please don't leave Pune for now. If you have no option left but to travel, you must inform the police about your itinerary.' Dhonde did not waste any more time and set out for the Gokuldas Tejpal Hospital that evening itself.

After reaching Bombay, he summoned the domestic worker of Lakshmibai, Shantabai, and a few friends of hers like Yashodaben. Inspector Sehgal of the Esplaned Police Station also joined him in the investigation team. The clothes of Lakshmibai, who had died almost four years ago, had still been kept in possession of the Gokuldas Tejpal Hospital. Shantabai identified each one of them.

I mentioned at the beginning of the story that the coroner of JJ Hospital had snapped a photograph of the dead body before cremating it. Seeing that photograph, everyone recognized her in a flash: 'That is Lakshmibai!'

At last, on 12 March 1958, Dr Lagu was arrested for the murder of Indumati Ponkshe, also known as Lakshmibai Karve. And thus began one of the most sensational cases in the history of the city and the entire country. The case was heard in Pune District Court in due time. The judge presiding over the case was V.A. Nayak, who later became the judge of Mumbai High Court.

Ramachandra came to the court to give his statement, and he cried in the witness box, 'My Lord! I am the one who is guilty! If I would have controlled my ego and saved my mother from that bloodthirsty doctor, then today, such a sin would not have materialized.'

On 10 November, two days before Lakshmibai had travelled to Bombay, Lakshmibai's friend, Mrs Champutia, had come to her residence. She lived in the United States, but had flown to India to give her statement. She said, 'The last day I saw Lakshmi, she was very weak. But she was not weak enough to die in two days.'

The facts stated by Shantabai through her gestures eventually surfaced: the doctor had given two injections to Lakshmibai the day they left for Bombay.

Judge Nayak asked Dr Lagu, 'You used to keep a record of the treatments of Mrs Karve. Why is the information about these two injections missing from that?'

The public prosecutor said, 'Lakshmibai died on 13 November. But the doctor kept the record of treating her till February next year! So you can understand the trustworthiness of the so-called record!'

Everything became clear. Dr Lagu slowly poisoned Lakshmibai over days and weeks by injecting unnecessary amounts of insulin. But what was in the last two injections that killed Lakshmibai in a matter of hours and made it look like a diabetic coma? And why did the RMO of Gokuldas Tejpal Hospital write diabetic coma as the cause of death even without checking properly?

The answers were obtained soon—Dr Muskar was an oldfriend of Dr Lagu. Both of them studied at the same time and at the same college and, they used to be roommates then. They were like brothers.

Dr Anija stated, 'My senior is Dr Muskar. I started the treatment for diabetic coma under his instructions. When Dr Vabiyaba came and explained to me, only then did I test the urine. But the patient died before any action was possible.'

Dr Lagu was a cunning man. He knew that the more time passed after Lakshmibai's death, the more difficult it would be to trace the presence of poison during autopsy. Thus, he delayed the autopsy by writing a telegram about the arrival of an imaginary brother. The suspicious letters sent in the name of Lakshmibai were also collected. They were analysed and it was found that the handwriting belonged to none other than Dr Lagu!

Lakshmibai owned a hefty amount of shares of a big corporation. To transfer those shares to Dr Lagu, her presence was necessary by law. Therefore, Dr Lagu even hired a lady and disguised her as Lakshmibai in front of the magistrate. That lady also came to the court and told the truth, as she was scared by the entire situation.

The game was over at last. Dr Lagu was sentenced to death. But he did not give up. He was a rich man by then, thanks to the innocent nature of Lakshmibai. He appealed to the high court, and failing there, he ultimately appealed to the Supreme Court. However, he lost in the Supreme Court too.

There is a saying: 'Too much cunning overreaches itself.' These words were applicable for Dr Lagu. The worldly pleasures, for which he sold his soul to the devil, were taken away from him by the divine hands of justice. He was hanged even before he could enjoy the treasures for which he stooped so low.

FIRE SHOULD NOT BE PLAYED WITH: SHAMIM RAHMANI CASE, 1960

Let us travel back in time to 7 May 1966, Lucknow, Uttar Pradesh. Raja Azizur Rahmani was in severe pain, lying on the bed, in the first floor. Shamim Rahmani, the 22-year-old daughter of Rahmani sahab, leaned over her father in anxiety. Her mother was sitting beside her. Shamim looked at the grand wall clock, and with a little disappointment in her voice she said, 'Uff! Amir bhaijaan has been out for so long!'

Shamim's mother, Begum Sikandar, was also worried, but not like her daughter. Shamim loved her father beyond everything else. It was with the permission of her father that she had achieved such a feat in her life. Otherwise, it was a rare phenomenon for a Muslim girl in the '60s to be a graduate.

Begum Sikandar tried to comfort her husband by vigorously rubbing his chest and said to her daughter, 'Don't worry so much, Shamim! Amir will be here shortly with the car.'

Shamim kept nagging, 'I said that I can drive to the hospital with *abbu* but nobody listens to me!'

'It is not just about driving the car; it will be easier to get him admitted if he is taken to the hospital in an ambulance. Calm down a little, will you?' Begum Sikandar was about to tell something more but Amir Ahmed, the elder brother of Shamim, hurried into the room. The ambulance was there, and Rahmani sahab was taken to hospital. Shamim took out a car and rushed towards the hospital separately. She tried to reach there early so that there was no delay in formalities.

Azizur was the talukdar of Lakhimpur kheri. He was almost like a king without the crown and people gave him the respect befitting one. The Rahmani family of Uttar Pradesh was not just respectable, but their honour and lifestyle were both like the royals.

Rahmani sahab believed in changing with time, as he knew that one would perish if not updated with society. Unlike most families that kept their daughters locked up within the four walls of the house and married them off at an early age, Rahmani sahab thought differently about his daughter. Thus, he did not reject just the hijab tradition, he admitted her daughter in a co-educational college. A Muslim girl, without hijab, studying in a co-educational college, was nothing short of a bag of anomalies.

Rahmani sahab never stopped his daughter from doing what she wanted to do. Just before getting admitted to the master's course, she mastered shooting both rifles and pistols from an Anglo Indian.

She was also quite headstrong as a person. If she was determined to do anything, she would do it at any cost. In her early college days, she received a love letter that was sent by her classmate. In that, he addressed Shamim as 'the fiery girl'. Out of the fear of getting insulted or perhaps slapped, the author of the letter chose to remain anonymous. After all, what is the point of being a martyr in love? It was highly probable that Shamim could beat the crap out of him in front of the whole college!

Begum Sikandar had crossed 40, but no one could guess that by looking at her. Many people thought of her as Shamim's sister instead. But she was not as much of a daredevil as much of a her daughter. Though she was married to an unorthodox husband, she tried to maintain the traditions.

Let us come back to that day's incident. Though Rahmani sahab's life was saved due to the timely action of his family, the doctors at Balarampur Hospital did not rule out the probability of further complications. They constituted a medical board with a panel of subject experts, and the treatment continued as per their suggestions. Then, when the condition stabilized after a few days, Dr Hariom Gautam was tasked with continuous monitoring of Rahmani sahab.

Aged around 32, he was just an MBBS graduate. But due to his experience with people and caring nature, he was admired a lot in the city. Besides, he was good at his job and performed his duties with diligence even in pressing situations. He was also extremely handsome—tall and well-built, with a symmetric face.

But Shamim was not able to shake off her worries and, in front of Dr Gautam, she said to the superintendent of the hospital Dr Chaturvedi, 'Doctor, don't you have anyone better for monitoring my father? Someone with more specialization or medical experience?'

Dr Chaturvedi smiled a little. 'I have given the responsibility to the right person, Miss Rahmani. Please don't judge the capabilities of a doctor by his academic achievements only.'

The days went by. Shamim was in her final year of master's course. Before going to the university, she travelled to Balarampur Hospital every day and asked for the details of her father's condition from Dr Gautam. She inspected whether the nurses were treating her father properly or not, and only then she went to attend her classes.

At first, Dr Gautam did not talk too much with Shamim. He was not able to completely forget her insulting words. However, with time, the iceberg started melting. The charming beauty of Shamim, her intelligence and her disposition started attracting the doctor towards her. The flames extended uniformly in the opposite direction as well, with 22-year-old Shamim finding herself drawn to the attractive physician as well.

Though Dr Gautam proved himself as a brilliant doctor, it would be a sin to say that he was a man of unquestionable character. For him, women were nothing more than toys that should be enjoyed and then thrown away. Though he had a wife and three children at home, he used to flirt regularly with other women. It is needless to say that his flirting crossed boundaries many times. The wife of Dr Gautam was a simple lady, and she never got to see this side of her husband. When Dr Gautam saw that a brilliant and beautiful girl like Shamim was developing an attraction towards him, instead of backing off, he started moving forward into the relationship.

Shamim started frequenting the hospital more, and inspecting the well-being of her father became an excuse to meet Dr Gautam. One day, Shamim came to see her father, but he was asleep at that time. He had been given his medicines, and the nurse had also left the ward. Dr Gautam was not able to resist that day, and he grasped Shamim's hand.

When the man of her dreams grasped her hand, she could not help but feel loved, even though she didn't thow it. She somehow managed to lower her eyes, which were transfixed on the doctor's for minutes. She said in a soft voice, 'Abbu is here, I should go now. I have classes to attend.'

But Dr Gautam did not let her go. Shamim feared that if anyone saw them, there would be a scandal. The daughter of the Talukdar of Lakhimpur was already a well-discussed topic in the city for her tomboyish behavior, her education and independence. On top of that, the news of her getting into a romantic relationship with a Hindu doctor would only create further trouble.

Shamim realized that and protested, 'Please let me go! Have you gone mad?'

But Dr Gautam, expressing genuine love through his eyes, said in a romantic manner, 'All of me is yours.'

Shamim blushed a little, but realizing the risk, she ran away from the ward. There was a feeling of excitement mixed with fear in her heart. Though she had received a lot of love letters in her life, she had never felt attracted towards anybody as she did towards Dr Gautam. She sat in the classroom looking at the blackboard, but her mind wandered somewhere else. The only moment that kept hovering her mind was when Dr Gautam grasped her hand.

Three months passed by. In the month of August in 1966, the medical panel at Balarampur Hospital held a meeting regarding the condition of Rahmani sahab. After going through all the reports, everyone in the panel concurred that Rahmani sahab was not going to survive for longer than two months.The panel felt that it would be better if Rahmani sahab spent his last few days with his family members rather than in a hospital ward. Dr Chaturvedi discharged Rahmani sahab.

A doctor was assigned to the Rahmani family. After Rahmani sahab was shifted to his home, he came every day to keep a check on his health. Rahmani sahab was in agonizing pain, and to ease that for a while, the doctor used to inject painkillers or administered sleeping pills to him.

Shamim felt that the doctors were not treating him correctly. She went to her mother and demanded answers, 'Ammi, what medicines is doctor uncle giving to Abbu daily? He is becoming more and more frail every day.'

'Yes Shamim, he is being given sleeping pills,' Begum Sikandar looked at her daughter.

'Ammi, too many sleeping pills are bad for health,' Shamim frowned at her mother, 'Abbu just recovered from an illness, and on top of that, so many medicines every day… I am not feeling good about this! Dr Gautam used to take much better care of Abbu.'

The brothers of Shamim, Amir and Mohammad, due to the fiery nature of their sister, never poked their nose into anything. Shamim's cousin Iqbal already believed that as per Muslim customs, Shamim would be wedded to him. He tried to show his authority over his future wife sometimes, but Shamim never paid heed to him.

After her father was brought to home, the daily meetings with Dr Gautam ceased, and on top of that, the health of her father was also deteriorating. Thus, Shamim's suggestion of getting Dr Gautam to look after Rahmani sahab was accepted. Retiring the two-decade-old family physician, Dr Gautam was appointed in his stead. Arrangements were made for Dr Gautam to visit Rahmani sahab every day on his way back home in the evening.

Dr Gautam knew that Rahmani sahab's days were numbered. He came and said, 'Whatever medicines were prescribed will be given. Give him whatever he wishes to eat, there is no problem.'

Shamim was seeing the man of her dreams after so many days. She looked at her mother with bright eyes on hearing the words of Dr Gautam. It seemed as if she wanted to say, 'You see, Ammi! The old doctor uncle banned so many things. Abbu was becoming weak because of that, and the first thing Dr Gautam said is there are no restrictions on diet!'

She said to her mother, 'Listen, tell Murad that they should cook well for Abbu!'

Dr Gautam started visiting Mir Manzil (the name of Rahmani sahab's house) every evening. However, his main motivation was not treating or monitoring the well-being of Rahmani sahab but to meet Shamim. Rahmani sahab didn't live long. In a few days, he left his loving family and great fortunes on his journey towards *jannat* (heaven). But that didn't stop Dr Gautam from visiting. He continued coming to Shamim's house every evening.

But was the doctor simply attracted to Shamim? No! He acted as if he was in love with young Shamim on one hand, and on the other hand, his motive was to assist her mother Begum Sikandar and become close to her. Begum Sikandar was the heir to the immense wealth and opulence of Rahmani sahab after his death. If Dr Gautam could somehow trick her through his charming nature, then he would get both the queen and the princess. He did not plan to get married to either of them. He already had a wife and three kids at home, and didn't want to hamper his image in society as a righteous doctor. His only motive was to extract the maximum wealth out of the Rahmani family and than desert them.

While collecting the facts for this story, the more I learned about Dr Gautam, the more disgusted I felt with him. How can the mentality and motives of a man in a noble profession like medical science be so ugly! This reminds me of a story from the *Jataka Tales*, where the Buddha apparently found a calm, selfless and beautiful mind in a bird-hunter. Actually, the profession of a person is not a proper parameter to judge their personality; it all boils down to the mindset of that person.

With time, the frequency of Dr Gautam's visits increased. He met Shamim in the evening, and used to spend his time in Shamim's room indulging in romance and *shayeri*. Begum Sikandar used to not be at home during those hours due to work. The doctor even started coming in the morning before going to the hospital. During those hours, Shamim used to be at the university. An expert in conning women,

Dr Gautam knew that to trap Begum Sikandar, the same bait he used for Shamim won't yield any result. She was a middle-aged, revered and respected woman. He had to win her heart through diligence and decorum.

I have already mentioned that the two brothers of Shamim, Amir and Mohammad, were of simple nature. Begum Sikandar did not rely on them to run errands for the estate. By tricking her to believe that the estate manager and others were a bunch of worthless employees, Dr Gautam started to become the crownless king of Mir Manzil. He started manipulating funds worth lakhs. A storm started looming over Mir Manzil without any alarm. However, one day, everything became clear to Shamim.

A childhood friend of Shamim, Gurmeet, got a job as a nurse at the Balarampur Hospital. She belonged to a poor family and struggled very hard to earn her nursing degree and get employed. Though the financial backgrounds of the two girls were poles apart, it never hindered their friendship even once. Shamim loved Gurmeet like her own sister, and she helped her during her bad times without expecting anything in return.

There was an agreement between the two friends that Gurmeet would give her a treat if she bagged a job. Honouring the promise, she came to meet Shamim at the university, two months after joining her job. It was March 1968.

There was almost a two-hour gap between two classes for Shamim, when Gurmeet came to visit her. She hugged her tight and they both took a seat in Shamim's car. Shamim ordered the family chauffeur 'Bhaiya, take us to Aminabad.'

'Where will you get sweets in Aminabad?' Gurmeet asked curiously.

'We will enjoy the treat, but before that, we will buy bangles from Garbarjhala. Today, I am in a great mood!'

Shamim hugged her friend and answered.

Aminabad was a Mughal-era market in the city of Lucknow. The two friends did a lot of stall hopping, and then, as planned, they went to eat sweets. Though Gurmeet was a very good friend of Shamim, she had never revealed her secret love affair with Dr Gautam to anybody. She was a Muslim girl and Dr Gautam was a Hindu brahmin. Hence, she feared the consequences.

Siping on the glass of ice-cold lassi, Shamim said, 'How are you feeling in Balarampur Hospital? Abbu was admitted there.'

'Yes, I know. I went to see him, don't you remember? The "honourable" Dr Gautam used to be his doctor.' Gurmeet said while trying to lick the layer of *malai* on her upper lip.

Shamim got schocked on hearing the name, 'Honorable Dr Gautam? What do you mean? Who are you talking about?'

'That Dr Hariom Gautam! Such a shameless man! That is why we all mock him behind his back by calling him as "honorable" Dr Gautam,' replied Gurmeet.

Shamim tried hard to resist her emotions, 'What the hell are you talking about? Dr Gautam is characterless?!'

'Or what? He has three kids and a wife at home but that pervert flirts with all the nurses. He doesn't even spare his patients. If he ever encounters a beautiful female patient, he tries to touch her in multiple ways. I never talk to him!'

Shamim did not return to the university for the rest of her classes. She could not believe what she had heard. Her face was as red as a burning piece of coal. Anyone could have guessed that she was furious. She returned home like a mad bull and saw Dr Gautam sitting in front of her mother Begum Sikandar, on her bed. It was evident from their gestures that it was a regular affair for them to talk like that in private on lazy afternoons.

Her brothers were never at home during those hours.

Even Shamim usually retruned from the university late in the evening. At that time, when no one except Begum Sikandar used to be in the house, what brought the doctor to Mir Manzil?

Though Begum Sikandar was shocked momentarily on seeing Shamim, she controlled herself in a second, 'You? Now? Doctor sahab is here to get some papers of the estate signed.'

Shamim gave an electrifying look at the doctor and then walked towards her room without answering her mother. But she did not calm down on reaching her room. The man to whom she had given her mind and body had cheated on her. She realized that the doctor was having affairs with both of them.

Shamim took the stairs to the ground floor to take out the car. She knew where the doctor lived, and though she had not gone there herself, it was not too hard to find out the address of a physician working in a public hospital.

Shamim found out that Gurmeet's claim was absolutely true. Dr Gautam had a wife and three kids. She was the daughter of Rahmani sahab, and hence Dr Gautam's wife welcomed her like a celebrity. Shamim tried to control her rage and also faked a smile, had a chat, gave a short ride to the kids in her car, bought them chocolates and told them stories. The kids became elated and said, 'Didi, please come again!'

She kept quiet on returning home. When her mother came to tell her something, she didn't resist herself and asked, 'Why that doctor was there in the afternoon? Are you two planning to get married?!'

Begum Sikandar was shocked, and she shouted back, 'What are you talking? Gautam is like my brother, Shamim!'

'If he is like your brother, then why was he sitting on your bed when the house was empty, huh?'

'I already said that he came for some work. He is the one who looks after everything. Have you forgotten how to talk to your mother? Rather than talking all this nonsense, finish your studies, and I will marry you off right after!'

'Don't you even think of getting me married with that Iqbal.'

'Then whom will you marry? Iqbal is your cousin. He is the most eligible groom for you!'

'Mark my words, I will not marry that idiot even if you kill me!'

'Then listen clearly to me, there is no way that you can marry Gautam. First, he a is Hindu; second, he is married and has kids. Also, he is much older than you.'

Shamim was so infuriated that she was unable to talk anymore, and she just ran towards her room. As soon as she entered her room, she saw Iqbal sitting on her bed. She was already angry, and on seeing Iqbal, she shouted, 'You bloody scoundrel! How dare you sit on my bed!' Shamim held Iqbal by his hair and pushed him against the wall and started slapping and kicking him, 'Get out! If I see you here next time, I will beat the crap out of you!' Iqbal, discombobulated by what happened, kept rubbing his cheeks and walked away slowly.

Gautam was a clever man. Reaching home, he found out that Shamim came to visit him. He did not meet Shamim for the next few days to allow her to calm down. After a week, he waited outside the university for Shamim. Shamim's rage had really dialled down by a lot in seven days, but still she avoided him like she had not even seen him standing.

The doctor ran towards her and grabbed her hand, 'I know you are very angry with me. But instead of assuming the whole story all by yourself, let me speak my part for once. Then, whatever you will say, I will accept without any more fuss.'

Slowly, the doctor became successful in bringing Shamim under his influence. The doctor brainwashed her into believing that he got married under the pressure of circumstances, and though he got married against his will, there was no other woman in his heart other than Shamim. The doctor emphasized that in various ways.

'And the nurses at the hospital?' Shamim asked.

'That is nothing more than a conspiracy to ruin my image! There are many out there who cannot stand my achievements at such a young age, and thus they try to malign me. It is nothing but envy.'

Shamim thought that it might be true that the doctor was not able to divorce his wife due to social obligations. A letter came from the doctor after two days: 'My love, as each second passes by, it is becoming increasingly difficult to live out of your embrace. This distance is painful—I cannot bear it anymore!' Shamim was trapped in the doctor's web again. There was no secrecy this time. She was desperate and did not care about people anymore.

Soon, the news spread like wildfire in the entire city of Lucknow. What blasphemy! A Hindu man, and that too married, was roaming around openly with the daughter of late Rahmani sahab.

Gurmeet came running to her friend after getting the news, 'Have you totally lost it? Are you roaming around with that scoundrel doctor? Do you know that just after riding with you in his motorcycle that day, he took our nurse Nayna to the movie?'

'Listen, don't spread lies! Gautam is not like that, all of you just envy him!'

'Envy him?' Gurmeet answered back, 'Why the hell should we envy him?'

It didn't matter how much sense Gurmeet spoke, Shamim was blind to reason. The shroud of love blinds people from the most naked realities. Shamim was also going through that phase. She was well known for being hot-tempered, and her curt words hurt Gurmeet.

Dr Gautam's trick was going well for some time, but eventually, Shamim's was unable to tolerate his attitude. The doctor sent her love letters, and the expressions of love were prominent in his face whenever he saw her, but he never ever talked about the ultimate culmination of the relationship.

It was 11 July 1968. Shamim was not in good health. She didn't go to the university that day. Begum Sikandar was not home as she had gone to her father's place. She was supposed to return after two days. Shamim's younger brother Mohammad was studying in his own room while she was listening to old songs on her record player. Right at that time, Dr Gautam came. He asked, 'Umm, is Sikandar not home?'

Shamim got a little shocked by the untimely arrival of the doctor. She replied, 'No'.

Dr Gautam had something that had been running in his mind. Shamim's feelings toward him were a little more than he could handle and he had no attraction towards Shamim anymore. Rather, Dr Gautam had become more interested in her mother. The doctor said, 'Okay, I will see you later.'

Shamim fired up instantly. She looked at the doctor with red eyes and said in a deep voice, 'After your wife and me, is Begum Sikandar your next interest?!'

The doctor was stunned. He thought of playing other tricks. He smiled romantically, came forward and, grabbing her hand, said, 'What rubbish are you talking, darling! Who are comparing yourself to? You are my everything!'

Shamim, having the touch of her lover after so many days, became too weak to resist him. She embraced the doctor tightly and placed her head on his chest. She started crying and said, 'How long it will go on like this, Hari? You know how things are becoming complicated with every passing day!'

'Calm down, Shamim,' the doctor said and kissed her forehead.

'Tell me when we will get married. You got married under the compulsion of your family. I have accepted everything. But now you have to divorce your wife and marry me!' Shamim continued while sobbing, 'We both will go far away from here…very far.'

The doctor got annoyed. His parents had already heard the news of his affair with Shamim. They had explained clearly to him that if he left his innocent wife for Shamim, then they would no longer accept him as their son. In that case, he would be deprived of all his ancestral property. On the other hand, it seemed that the relation with Begum Sikandar would also not last long due to Shamim.

Shamim continued, 'Tell me! Tell me when will you marry me!'

The doctor said in a rough tone, 'What nonsense are you talking, huh? I have a wife and three kids, why the hell should I leave them?'

Shamim was thunderstruck. She lifted her head from his chest, and asked, 'What do you mean?'

The doctor continued in his rude tone, 'The meaning is clear. I love you, but I cannot marry you!' He pushed away Shamim and shouted, 'And why are you so shameless, getting crazy about marriage and all? I thought you have some dignity!'

Shamim was still as a stone for a while before she closed the doors of Mir Manzil for the doctor, forever.

The doctor thought that it was over at last. But had he looked deeply into Shamim's eyes when he left, he would have seen that, like a wounded tigress, her eyes were seeking revenge. It was as if all the blood in Shamim's body had been pumped to her fair face—a little knock on the head and a red fountain would spill out!

At last came the night of 11 July 1968. Dr Gautam, after returning from the hospital, went to attend a local event with his wife and kids. He was just about to leave after dinner when a chauffeur of the Rahmani family paid him a salute and delivered a note in his hand. There was no salutation in the note, nor did it have any sender's name. It was written: 'If you have loved me for real, at least once, then come right now. This will be the last time!' It was clear that the note was written by Shamim.

The doctor told his wife and kids to go home in a relative's car. He suddenly remembered that tomorrow was the last day of filling up the application form of Shamim's final year's exam. She had believed that if the doctor filled up the form with his own hand, then she would excel in the exam. Dr Gautam thought that she was calling him for that reason. He had no idea that this was going to be his last trip to Mir Manzil.

That night, Begum Sikandar was not home and her brothers went somewhere else due to some work. As soon as the doctor entered Mir Manzil, there was some quarrel and then—the bang of a firearm! Shamim's elder brother Amir came running after he got the news through some source.

When the police arrived, she said, 'I have killed him! He has cheated on me for days, and I just couldn't take it anymore! Hang me, please!'

The police searched the house meticulously till 8.30 a.m. The doctor had been shot point-blank with a double-barrel rifle. In the end, the police arrested Shamim and her elder brother.

The next morning, newspapers printed the headline on its first page, 'Government Doctor Shot Dead by Girl

Student: Assailant Arrested!' The entire country had a hot topic of debate. The daughter of an elite Muslim family had killed a doctor! In the meantime, the case of *Shamim Rahmani v. The State of Uttar Pradesh* was raised in the Lucknow District Court. Even to this date, journalists and lawyers of that time shiver on hearing the name of Shamim Rahmani.

Shamim had accepted that she had shot the doctor on the night of the incident at Kaizerbag Police Station, but later, in front of the magistrate, she said, 'Huzur, I am innocent. I don't know who killed Dr Hariom Gautam. The doctor flirted around with many women so he had a lot of enemies. Perhaps someone from them had killed him and dropped the body at Mir Manzil!'

The judge, S.N. Shukla, said, 'What was your relation with Dr Hariom Gautam?'

Shamim bit her lips and stayed silent for a while. Then, she said, 'I loved him! That's it!'

Renowned lawyers like Zafriyab Jilani and Ghulam Hussain Naqvi got involved in that case. One by one, all were summoned—from Gurmeet to the employees of Balarampur Hospital. Everyone said that Dr Gautam was a renowned casanova. After looking into every perspective, the trial was over. Judge Shukla announced that on 5 October 1969, he would give his verdict.

On the D-Day, Shamim was presented in court. Her eyes were lifeless. She was wearing a white salwar, and although knowing that thousands of pairs of eyes were glued to her, she was numb. Her elder brother Amir was also accused of making evidence disappear and misleading the police. He was charged accordingly.

The judge started reading out the verdict after the lunch break. It was a long verdict of 113 pages, and it took quite some time for him to finish. He spoke out the last line looking at the people who were present in court, 'After going through all the evidence and testimonials, Miss Shamim Rahmani, daughter of late Azizur Rahmani, is found guilty of the murder of Dr Hariom Gautam, and is sentenced to death as per Section 302 of Indian Penal Code. Mr Amir Ahmed is found guilty of disappearing evidence and hence sentenced to three years of imprisonment.' Shamim was flabbergasted on hearing the verdict; she started crying in front of everyone.

The judge looked at Shamim for a moment and said, 'But the court also severely condemns the activities of late Dr Hariom Gautam for cheating a young unmarried girl and his wife, in spite of being in a noble profession of a public physician.'

Both Shamim and Amir were not short of money. They challenged the verdict of the District Court and elevated the case to the Supreme Court of India. The news of that case started to spread like the shockwave of a nuclear bomb across the country.

The judges in the Supreme Court were N.L. Untalia and Syed M. Fazal Ali. The lawyers from both sides were the veteran advocates Yogeshwar Prasad and O.P. Rana. During that time, the descriptions of the trial were printed in almost all the newspapers of the country, and the gritty details of the legal proceedings were mixed with the gossiping love affair of Shamim–Gautam.

At last, on 28 April 1975, the Supreme Court retained the death sentence of Shamim. When the entire country was busy discussing the death sentence of such an educated girl belonging to a respectable family, the then president of India, Fakhruddin Ali Ahmed, granted mercy to the accused and applied his veto on the verdict.

Shamim was released after a couple of years. If someone was found behaving well in prison, then the term of life imprisonment was cut short—the same thing happened for her.

Later, she decided to pursue a career in Hindi movies and started a new phase in her life. Despite her aspiration to act alongside Sanjeev Kumar and Dharmendra, she didn't land a role opposite them. However, she shared the screen with Satish Kaul and Rakesh Pande, partially fulfilling her dream.

The mansion of Mir Manzil is not there anymore. Still, many people ask while walking around, 'Uhh...that Shamim Rahmani, the girl who killed the doctor, what was her address?'

Shamim Rahamani in her later years

THE WITCH AND THE DOCTOR: VIDYA JAIN MURDER CASE, 1973

Dr Jain was shivering in fear while describing the scene, 'Inspector! You will not believe it! I…I saw that my wife Vidya was lying near a drain, and her whole body was covered in blood, as if some wild animal had clawed and ripped the flesh off her face! There were also claw marks in other parts of her body as well!'

'What happened after that?' asked Fakir Chand, the famous inspector of the Delhi Police. Sub-inspector Uday Chopra was also there with him.

'Then I screamed so loudly that my servants came running out of my house. They were shocked to see everything. My manager Sukhlal said, "Mehsahab is perhaps still alive!"'

'Why did Sukhlal make that comment when you were present there? And how did he conclude that your wife was still alive?'

'Sukhlal practises Ayurveda as a hobby and he knows how to find a pulse,' Dr Jain looked with reddened eyes, 'I was not in my senses then, inspector!'

'Okay, then?'

'I didn't waste any more time. Everyone helped to lift Vidya up in the car and then we took her to Dr S.K. Sen's nursing home on Bahadur Shah Zafar Marg. But Dr Sen said that it was too late.' Dr Jain's voice got cracked at the end.

Inspector Fakir Chand frowned a bit. Many questions were bubbling up in his mind. If it was someone else, he would have fired those questions like bullets from a Gatling gun, but Dr Jain was a high-profile medical professional. Hence, he didn't pester much to avoid any complications.

Dr Narendra Singh Jain was the ophthalmologist of the president of India V.V. Giri. He was also honoured with the Padma Shri award. Dr Jain was so brilliant at his job that people often said, 'He can even make the blind see!'

Fakir Chand looked at his watch. It was 10.00 p.m. The murder had taken place around 7.15 p.m. The inspector again looked at the doctor. Despite the overwhelming devastation caused by the sudden catastrophe, a close look at Dr. Jain unveiled him as a remarkably handsome individual. His attire, including the suit, trousers, tie and wristwatch, was imported. However, the imported fabric bore splatters of congealed blood at that particular moment.

Fakir Chand said, 'Your residence and chamber are in Defense Colony. Why did you take her to Bahadur Shah Zafar Marg? As far as I know, it is at least more than 10 km away. I think the cantonment hospital was quite near. Why didn't you take her there? Also, why didn't you call the police at once?'

'Dr Sen is my friend. I was not thinking straight at that moment, and the first name that came to my mind was his. Then, Dr Sen himself informed the police.'

Half an hour passed, and Dr Jain's seat was subsequently occupied by Dr Sen. His mannerisms unmistakably revealed that he was quite angry.

'What happened? It seems that you are quite enraged?' Inspector Fakir Chand shot his first question towards Dr Sen.

'Why on earth did he get me involved in all this? His wife was dead before her body was brought to the nursing home. Instead of calling the police, he got me into all this! What harassment! My nursing home is newly established, and this incident is going to have a bad impact on it's image! He also requested me repeatedly to not call the police. Does such a naive fear of police suit a person of his calibre?'

Fakir Chand was listening very carefully. He asked, 'What did Dr Jain tell you exactly?'

'On the evening of the incident, Dr Jain and his wife were preparing to attend an event in Defense Colony, hosted by their relatives. Upon returning from his office, he instructed his wife to get ready and proceeded to his study to hastily draft an essential letter. While engrossed in his writing, he sensed Vidya passing by him on her way out. A moment later, he heard a horrific scream that prompted him to dash outdoors. He saw two men fleeing from the scene.'

Sub-inspector Uday Chopra was about to intervene with excitement, 'Sir, this is a completely different statement. He—,' but Fakir Chand stopped him midway with a gesture of his eyes.

On 4 December 1973, the horrific murder of Vidya Jain took place in the esteemed locality of Defense Colony in New Delhi. When the police had a look at the body, it was evident that the killer mutilated her in a terrible fit of rage.Who could have such a rage on a housewife from a respected high-class family? To dig deeper, we have to know the prelude of the famous Vidya Jain Murder Case of 1973.

∽

As Dr Jain was the doctor of the then President of India, he was in the elite circle of society. He was aged above 50, his elder son had already graduated as a doctor and started practising and his younger son was a medical student at that time. But even in his busy life, he had affairs with various women. He was often spotted spending his evenings with various women in various pubs and clubs around the city. Many of his friends warned him of his inappropriate behavior, especially because of the position that he held in society. But bad habits die hard.

During those days, Dr Jain was having an affair with Chandresh Sharma. We must learn a few things about Chandresh before we delve deeper into the story. There are indeed women who have been successful purely on merit, but unfortunately, there are women who climb up the ladder by being a partner in the bed of famous and rich men—Chandresh Sharma was a lady who belonged to the latter category.

She belonged to a poor family, and at an early age, she was married off to a clerk working in a financial corporation. She was never pleased with her poor husband and the normal life. She craved an elite lifestyle. Perhaps god heard the prayers of Chandresh, and when things were becoming unbearable for her in the marriage, her husband died.

Though Chandresh was in a bad fix, as both her father's family and her in-laws were financially weak, deep within, she felt relieved that her husband was no more. Being an expert in the art of seduction, she soon got hold of a rich man. It didn't matter to her that the man was middle-aged and not good-looking. She was only bothered about the wealth and the social position of that man. The man held the post of a high-ranked officer in the army.

Chandresh didn't think twice. The army officer also agreed to adopt the son Chandresh had from her previous marriage. Chadresh happily got married to him. It was all going well, till she met Dr Jain at some party held in the city. Chandresh was 26 at that time. She did not possess jaw-dropping beauty, but her personality was so mesmerizing and hypnotizing that Dr Jain couldn't prevent himself from falling into the honey jar.

One day, Chandresh came to the doctor's chamber under the pretense of an eye check-up. Both belonged to the same category—they did not like the idea of holding on to one person for a long period. Chandresh was thrilled when she understood that the prey in hand was much bigger than the army officer. The magnetism of a forbidden relationship was much more than that of a recognized one. Thus started the wild lust story between them, and soon they started spending days together.

Vidya Jain, the wife of the doctor, gave up on her husband long back. She understood the simple truth that one cannot force someone to be honest. It didn't take much time for Chandresh's husband to understand what was happening, and soon their relationship ended in a divorce. Chandresh was clear about her next step—the bank account of the army officer seemed nothing in front of the doctor's wealth.

One day, Dr Jain was getting ready to visit Bombay to deliver a plenary talk at a seminar related to ophthalmology when Chandresh said with childish gesture, 'You always go alone, you need not take me then!' Dr Jain also wanted to take Chandresh with him but one of Vidya's relatives resided in Bombay. If they were spotted together by that relative, that could lead to a problem.

Suddenly, an idea struck his brilliant mind, 'Chandra, from today, I am appointing you as my personal secretary. I will tell the organizers of the seminar to arrange for your stay. I will also pay you a reasonable salary.' The last barrier was also broken. Chandresh came running and embraced Dr Jain.

Inspector Fakir Chand jumped into the investigation with his arsenal of officers, fingerprint experts and a forensics team. It was a high-profile case indeed and the political circle was also keeping a close watch.

Fakir Chand had three doubts from the beginning of the investigation: first, Vidya Jain was wearing a lot of jewellery for the event. The murderers didn't even touch any of it, proving that the motive was not robbery. Second, according to Dr Sen, Dr Jain had been writing a letter, when he had heard Vidya screaming from outside, and by the time he had gone to her, he had seen two people running away. But Dr Jain had told to Fakir Chand that he heard a scream and when he went outside, he saw his wife's body lying near a drain. Third, there was no room for doubt that it was a pre-planned murder, but what could be the reason for the suspects to not touch Dr Jain?

Fakir Chand, on further investigation, observed that Dr Jain had withdrawn ₹10,000 from the bank just a few days before his wife was murdered. In that period, ₹10,000 was the yearly salary of a high-ranked government officer. He asked Dr Jain, 'Doctor, why did you withdraw such a large sum of money?'

'I...I donated the money to charity.'

'Donation? In cash? To which organization?'

Dr Jain was not able to give a clear answer.

Fakir Chand arrested eight people after the investigation was completed: Dr Jain; his secretary Chandresh Sharma; Chandresh's friend, Constable Rakesh Koushik; two hired goons Ujagir Singh and Kartar Singh; their associates Kalyan Gupta and Bhagirath; and a taxi driver named Ramjilal.

The investigation revealed an interesting fact. Fearing social scandal, Dr Jain had not wanted to divorce Vidya. But after the repeated requests by Chandresh to marry him, Dr Jain and Chandresh had planned that they would murder Vidya. A plan was chalked out in September, and it was executed on 4 December.

On 4 March 1974, three months after the murder, the case was heard in the New Delhi District Court. The case ran for a prolonged period of 500 days. Chandresh understood that she was trapped, and being an opportunist, the obvious choice for her was to leave the doctor at that moment.

Dr Jain returned to his home at 7.15 p.m. on 4 December. Let us see what happened three hours prior to that. Chandresh had many friends, and she used them in times of need as necessary. One of them was Constable Rakesh Kaushik. Chandresh said to Rakesh, 'We have to kill the doctor's wife now else there is no hope for me. You arrange for goons to do the job; don't worry, you will get a good payment.'

On that evening, around 4.30 p.m., in the busy area of Chandni Chowk in New Delhi, everyone, including Dr Jain, gathered at a restaurant to plan the murder. Rakesh brought his acquaintance Ramjilal and the hired goons—Ujagir Singh and Kartar Singh. For Ujagir and Kartar, killing someone was a cakewalk. Kartar said, 'This is a matter of such a prestigious family. There is a high chance of getting caught. We will do it for nothing less than ₹25,000!'

Dr Jain just nodded his head slightly, signalling that money was not a problem at all. He had already withdrawn ₹10,000 a few days before, and he gave that as an advance payment without any negotiation. 'You will get the rest after the job. Remember, if you do a smooth job, you will get some bonus!' said Dr Jain.

The two hands of death smiled. 'What are you saying, Sir! Ujagir and Kartar never leave any loose ends. Even the best of the police will roam around cluelessly.'

Chandresh said, 'Dr Jain and I will reach by 6.30 p.m. Send your associates early, and be ready!'

Ramjilal took Bhagirath and Kalyan to Dr Jain's house. As soon as they reached, they started waiting behind the house of Dr Jain to keep an eye on Vidya. Rakesh took the Singh brothers and went to Connaught Place, and then they went to a spot that was 90 m away from the doctor's house.

When Dr Jain and Chandresh returned, Dr Jain went inside his house and asked Vidya to get ready for the event they were invited for. Chandresh decided to wait in Ramjilal's taxi and watch everything unfold. When Dr Jain and Vidya came out of the house, the Singh brothers pounced on her mercilessly with two daggers. The lady started screaming, shocked by the sudden attack. But on the empty streets of the posh locality, that scream failed to reach anyone's ears. Before she could have shouted louder, a severe blow ended everything. When Vidya saw that her husband was just standing and staring at everything that was happening while she was being butchered, her eyes widened in horror, disbelief and agony. And then they closed forever. When the two killers were convinced that their prey was completely dead, they kicked the lifeless body, drenched in blood, into the drain by the side.

A moment later, Dr Jain faked a scream, and his servants came rushing out. Dr Jain staged a tragic drama before them. Before anyone could have made any sense, Dr Jain put the dead body of his wife in his car and rushed to Dr Sen's nursing home.

❧

In this case, the accused was powerful enough to influence the case. However, the elder brother of Vidya Jain was in the army, a very influential man in Delhi and a close aide of the lieutenant governor. The then lieutenant governor of Delhi gave orders for a proper investigation, so that there was no room for the criminals to escape.

Inspector Fakir Chand worked hard to wrap up the case. Two blood-stained daggers were recovered at a distance from Dyal Singh College on Lodhi Road. The forensic report stated that Vidya's blood sample matched with the blood stains on the daggers and the blood stains on Singh brothers' shirts. During that time, Ramjilal said to the police, 'Huzur, I want to be a public witness! I have not murdered anyone. I just drove the car. Please make me a public witness!' Due to that request, half of the investigation was eased for the police. Ramjilal took the investigators to the place he went and waited, and described the entire episode accurately.

After a trial of 500 days, the court gave its verdict on 6 July 1975. Every convict was awarded separate punishments. At first, as per Section 27 of the Arms Act, the Singh brothers were accused of having illegal weapons. Dr Jain, Chandresh, Rakesh, Bhagirath and Kalyan were accused of the murder of Vidya Jain and were charged under Section 120 of the IPC. The lawyers for Chandresh and Dr Jain were A.N. Mulla and B.B. Lal, respectively, and both of them tried their best to defend their client.

'My Lord! It is true that my client Chandresh Sharma had an affair with Dr Narendra Jain. But Vidya Jain was not a lady of good values. She had relations with many men.'

'That's a lie!' shouted Vidya's elder brother, 'How low a person you are to defame an honorable lady to save your client? Have you completely sacrificed your ethics?'

An astrologer was brought as a witness from Ashram Chowk, and that astrologer identified Chandresh. He said, 'A woman approached me, expressing that the person she loves has the initials "N.J." and is currently married. She asked me if there was a possibility of them getting married in the future.'

The lawyer of Chandresh, Mr Mulla said, 'My client has been in a relationship with Dr Jain for the last six years from 1967. She has not harmed Vidya Jain anytime in the past. Why would she suddenly make such a blunder?'

Can anyone predict when the devil will sit on anyone's neck? Greed is one of the seven deadly sins indeed.

Chandresh was not satisfied with the money she got from Dr Jain; she wanted social recognition and complete control. Vidya Jain was a simple and innocent lady, but she belonged to an educated family. Didn't she ever get a hint of the activities of her husband?

The neighbour of Dr Jain, Ms Sheila Khanna, told the court, 'Vidya told me that Dr Jain frequently invited his secretary to dinner, and Chandresh behaved like she was the mistress of the house. Just a few days before she was killed, Vidya had sacked Chandresh from her job.'

Chandresh had received a monthly salary of ₹300 as a secretary, but further investigation showed that Dr Jain had paid a monthly salary of ₹8,400 to Chandresh, which was equivalent to 28 months of official salary of Chandresh.

Dr Jain, Mrs Sharma and five others get life imprisonment

Lisbon junta turns over power to troika of generals

Parties plan to oppose the decision

Territory to be traded for peace only: Israel

They took it calmly

Banks to slash overtime by half

Floods cause extensive

A look at the front page of The Indian Express, published on 27 July 1975

Everyone but Ramjilal received a sentence of life imprisonment. The accused party was extremely rich, and it appealed to High Court. The fun fact is, the High Court escalated the punishment of Singh brothers from life imprisonment to capital punishment. For the others, the punishment decided by the lower court was retained.

The High Court judge said while delivering his verdict, 'The people who can mercilessly kill an innocent housewife cannot be shown any kind of mercy by the court.' The Singh brothers were hanged to death in the month of December 1983. And leaving all the fame and respect, Dr Jain went to jail with others.

Was this partiality in punishment due to the social stature of the main accused? The Singh brothers were hired goons, and they lacked backing from any influential person. But the people who planned such a horrific and shameless murder to finish off an innocent lady were actually quite respected in society. No one can deny that the real culprit was Dr Jain. This reminds me of the famous adage, 'The poor went to the gallows but the affluent survived.'

MEMORIES OF THE MALEVOLENT MISTRESS: TROILOKKYO CASE, 1876

Bengal, 1857—zamindars hailing from different regions of the state gained notoriety for exploiting their subjects. They would use extorted funds to indulge in opulent hobbies and engage in scandalous activities. On the other hand, luminaries like Vidyasagar were busy establishing schools for girls, Michael Madhusudan Dutt was giving birth to epic masterpieces and the future stars of Bengali art and culture were opening their eyes on the premises of Debendranath Tagore. The following frightening story is set in the same time period.

Women from the middle class were constrained within a toxic patriarchal society. Despite the legal abolition of the practice of Sati, it persisted in reality. Moreover, the societal expectation was to marry off girls at a very young age. If a girl surpassed the ideal marrying age without tying the knot, her parents would often be ostracized in the community. There was a prevailing belief that an educated girl would bring misfortune, even death, to her future husband. The society was immersed in a troubling mixture of superstition, casteism, illiteracy and orthodoxy, all compounded by a touch of foolishness.

This story is a tale of a girl born to an orthodox and revered brahmin family, who went on to become one of the most infamous stars in the Indian criminal history. This is the story of the supposedly first female serial killer of Bengal.

The Great Mutiny had just been over and the results

had convinced everybody that it was the end of the Mughal era and the Union Jack would be waving for times to come. The East India Company was not a company that traded spices anymore; they were the new despots of India. The last Mughal emperor, Bahadur Shah Zafar, was counting his final days. At the same time, a brahmin, somewhere in the district of Burdwan, was in a bad fix. With concern clear in his tone, the man took a deep breath and uttered to his wife, 'God knows when we will find a groom for Troilokko!'

The wife replied, 'What about that man in Katigram you told me about yesterday?'

He quickly nodded as if something blasphemous was whispered, 'That is over! The family has problems. They are not pure. I was kept in the dark.'

Troilokko was the most beautiful girl in the village. As soon as she stepped into her eighth year, proposals for marriage started coming in spades. And there were good reasons for that; after all, everybody wanted a girl who would make their neighbours envious. But her father was adamant. He wanted to marry off his princess to a family that was pure brahmin, without any history of flaws and misdeeds. Soon, the rate of proposals slowed down but the clock kept on ticking—Troilokko was ageing.

Troilokko's mother used to remain tense throughout the day. She had no idea what the future held for them and their daughter. She used to sleep on a narrow bench beside the window that opened up to the porch and stare at a small, dark and empty piece of land. Last December, Troilokko turned 13, and the ever-alert neighbourhood was already raising questions—charming girl of 13 still single? If, in the coming years, they were unable to find a groom for their girl, they were likely to be socially ostracized.

Troilokko, like the rest of budding teenagers in her village, was also illiterate. Her daily routine consisted of sleeping, eating, roaming around and waiting for the day when she would get married.

There was a small hut by their home which was home to an elderly vaishnavite woman named Tara. That hut used to be a property of Troilokko's family, but it was bought by that lady a few years back. Tara was aged around 50. She wore a necklace of tulsi beads and carried around a sack containing a small idol of Lord Krishna.

Tara poked her nose into anything and everything that went on in the village. She was the one present in all quarrels, discussions, debates and gossip. However, she also helped people in need and was the first responder in many emergencies. As expected, there were many myths around Tara: some said that she was married but her husband left her, some said that she was a widow and some guessed that her husband had been jailed abroad. There used to be a time when the vaishnavi begged around the village for a living, but later, quite astonishingly, she started living without any visible effort to earn money.

Troilokko didn't care about her origins or her source of living. To her, Tara didi was a nice person and she loved to spend time with her. Troilokko lived in a rural place without any scope of recreation or hobby. Hence, she had lots of free time. However, it was slowly getting difficult for her to find friends of her age as most of them were married. Tara didi filled this void. Though she was quite senior to her, she was her only friend. One needs a person to speak and listen to, and in absence of obvious companions, the apparently unlikely becomes the most probable. Such was the case between Tara and Troilokko.

Childhood friends of Troilokko were wives, and most of them had already experienced lovemaking. When they met Troilokko in the bathing ghat, they usually pinched her saying, 'Isn't he cute? Oh, how would our Troilokko know! She is still a child and unaware of the secrets of life!' Troilokko would be irritated by those words. 'What is it they have all gone through that is still unknown to me?' she questioned herself.

Though the reason for Troilokko to find a friend in Tara was still explainable, the reason that drove Tara to love Troilokko as her child was an illusion for many. Troilokko did not get the things she liked from her parents. After all, they were just poor brahmins saving every single penny for her dowry. But Tara took care of that. From clothes to cosmetics, Tara was the free counter of fancy commodities for Troilokko. And what more, Tara told her stories of lust, the art of seduction and the secrets of lovemaking.

At first, Troilokko got shy, her face and ears turning a rosy shade. She thought that even listening to such stories was a sin for her. But Tara insisted, 'Grow up, Tarini! What is there to be ashamed of? If you had got married at the correct time, you would have got pregnant twice by now! If you get married now, your man will expect you to know these. This is what a man expects from his woman, get it?'

Troilokko didn't think so much about it. When she heard such stories in Tara's gloomy room, lit only with a dim oil lamp, she got timid; her blood rushed through her veins and her heart beat like a drum. But she also got an undefined pleasure in hearing those stories. Her skin felt the need of touch, and she embraced herself to compensate for it. When night descended, she went back to her home and kept on imagining the scenes that were narrated to her. She wondered, 'Is it going to be great or grave?!'

At last, fortune smiled on the brahmin's fate, and he got what he was looking for. Even before Troilokko crossed the age of 14, her father found a groom who ticked all the boxes. The groom resided in eastern Bengal, had a house of his own and earned decently. He was aged around 50, but that was not a concern at all. After all, the man was a pure brahmin, and Troilokko's father felt that he was tailored to be his son-in-law.

Her mother asked, 'Isn't it better if you go to his home once? Just to be sure what he claims about his property is true!'

The irritated brahmin took no time to reply, 'She is not going to live there anyway! The man has already more than 15 wives! Troilokko is going to stay with us, he will visit us once or twice a year.' He placed his hookah on the porch and with clear vexation in his voice continued, 'Don't mess it up now. To get a pure brahmin groom when Troilokko is so old is a fortune anyway! Who marries an old girl?'

Troilokko's mother was disappointed. Though marrying off a teenage daughter seemed like good news, the option they had was not good on any scale of evaluation. She murmured, 'There are good reasons to agree to this proposal anyway. After all, who lets go of the offer to earn dowry at the age of 50! He is bound to agree to a discounted price. I just wonder whether he will continue asking money from us after getting married to Troilokko!'

Troilokko was too naive to comprehend such market dynamics. She was excited by the news that she was finally going to get married. She couldn't wait any longer to break the news to her beloved Tara didi. 'Tara didi! I am finally getting married on the next moon!'

Tara embraced Troilokko and pinched her red and soft cheeks, 'That's great news! I hope you remember the tales of love I taught you.'

Troilokko reddened a few more shades. 'Tara didi! Don't you have other things to say? I can't do all those things!'

'Now that is a shame!' Tara smiled but spoke with a tone of dismay mixed with mischief, 'All my lectures will go to waste!'

Troilokko predicted that Tara didi would start again telling the stories of lust and more. She usually got aroused listening to such stories, but that day, she was not feeling up to it. It was an auspicious day and she didn't want to pollute her day with those stories. Hence, she ran away. At last, Troilokko donned her bride's attire. Then came the moment for the ritual when the bride sees her groom for the first time peeking through a veil of betel leaves. However, the moment that was supposed to be magical became a moment of shock and misery—the man, smiling with blackened teeth in front of her, was older than her father!

❧

All of Troilokko's dreams were shattered. Her husband was a contorted man in his fifties who got out of breath while walking in the sun. She realized that her parents had sent her to hell. As expected, she was angry with her parents for sacrificing her on the altar of orthodoxy.

Troilokko's husband didn't waste time after the ceremony. His main motivation was the dowry, which he got in advance, so there was no more reason for him to stay with her anymore. After staying for a few more days with his in-laws and the newly wed teenage wife, and also grabbing a few more gifts and goods, Troilokko's husband left her. Life is quite stressful for a man with over 15 wives! After getting over the initial dejection, Troilokko moved on with her life. More appropriately, she returned to her premarital life. Her husband had left her for his other wives. She was free again, and she started spending that free time with the person she loved most, her beloved Tara didi. She convinced herself, 'I got an elderly husband. Many others share the same fate. But I am lucky to have a sister like Tara didi. I am free from serving my husband but also enjoy the status of being married. What else can I wish for! I am going to stay the way I like—free and happy!' Eventually, Troilokko started spending a major portion of the day with Tara. It became a practise for her to go home only to sleep at night; for the rest of the day, Troilokko remained in Tara didi's hut.

'Don't be sad, Tarini! Everyone does not get a husband who can fulfill her needs, but that doesn't mean you will have to kill your instincts. That doesn't mean you can't make love. That will be foolish!' said Tara.

'What?!' Troilokko was busy trying to peel some berries. She paused for a moment and stared at Tara in complete dismay, 'If I don't make love with my husband, with whom shall I? Sometime your words do not make sense at all!'

'Make love with yourself!' Tara stared at Troilokko with a smirk on her face. Her eyes suggested a lot of things without going over the details.

Those eyes amused and terrified Troilokko at the same time. The amusement was about the novelty of the proposal, and the terror was about the unknown consequences. The idea, though seemingly shocking, was so exotic that she gathered her nerve to ask, 'How?'

Tara put a paan in her mouth and started chewing. With red lips and sparse words, she continued, 'If a man cannot satisfy his wife, then the wife can satisfy herself! There is no sin in that. Got it?!'

Then Tara started to teach Troilokko how to pleasure herself. She taught her how to use her own touch to arouse herself. And the best part was, she would not need any man for that; she was enough to please herself.

The first experience was magical for Troilokko. She felt a cool gust of pleasure intertwined with warm spikes of guilt. The feeling was unexplainable, godly yet sinful, comforting yet painful and rewarding yet shameful. From that day, Troilokko visited Tara on a daily basis and tried to learn more. She was adamant to explore and exploit all the tricks she could learn.

Things were going fine for Troilokko, until the news came. Troilokko's husband was no more; after a spell of extreme sickness, he had breathed his last. The brahmin's wife started wailing for her daughter on her porch. Troilokko's mother was concerned about the perks Troilokko was going to lose, and her father was concerned about maintenance of the purity standards.

Neighbours flocked in to express their superficial concern: 'Such bad news'; 'Is this an age to be a widow?!'; 'Alas! she is never going to experience the love of her husband; 'How can god be so cruel?', were some of the statements that Troilokko's family heard.

Troilokko was stripped off the attire of a married Bengali girl. Her conch bangles were shattered, and the vermillion on her forehead was rubbed off. Troilokko started her journey as a widow amidst the bawl of her mother and neighbours.

But when everyone around was mourning the catastrophic event and expressed their disquietude with myriads of tonal variation, Troilokko seemed equanimous. She was untouched by any signs of pain or loss because one has to possess something in order to lose it. The girl had seen a man aged over 50 for literally a few moments on her wedding day. For the man, the wedding was a source of income and, thus, after he received his payment, he was least bothered about his wife. Hence, there was no reason for a 13-year-old girl to feel a string of attachment and sorrow for such a husband. Troilokko's indifference was completely logical.

After the funeral was over, Troilokko started her daily routine of spending time with Tara. After many experiences, she was now confident of the fact that the only person who listened to her, understood her and loved her was the vaishnavi. She really found peace in her company. Tara was the only person to whom she could open up without any hesitation.

Troilokko once had a childhood friend named Prafulla, who, at one point, got married and moved to a different village. Hearing the news of Troilokko's widowhood, Prafulla came to visit her friend and expressed her condolences. But Troilokko was not at all interested in being consoled. She was completely under the spell of Tara and didn't want to indulge in grief. Tara not only loved and trained her but also made sure that Troilokko was never out of stock of any daily necessities. It became a norm for Troilokko to receive all her clothes, pocket money and cosmetics from Tara.

Now, some questions are bound to arise: what was the intention of that lonely, beautiful, middle-aged vaishnavite? How could a person, who used to feed on alms, fund the essentials and desirables of a girl who was not even related to her? Was this just love and selfless compassion, or was there any other sinister motivation?

Troilokko's parents didn't like the attitude of Tara towards their daughter. No one was sure of her past. There was no explanation how the so-called poor lady was funded. The lifestyle she led raised a lot of eyebrows.

Meanwhile, Tara started helping Troilokko's entire family. The brahmin couple lost a lot of money in the wedding. Troilokko's father was getting old, and it was becoming difficult for him to make up for the lost savings. Though the couple did not like the vaishnavi and were not happy with the idea of Tara supporting them unconditionally, their hunger strangled all their doubts. The need for survival easily overrode the luxury of saintliness. The whole family came under the control of Tara, and as for Troilokko, the cozy cottage became her primary residence.

One fine noon, Tara said, 'Come on, Tarini, take a

shower and get ready. Get some good clothes on, I will do your makeup.'

Troilokko was cooking in a lazy mood in Tara's makeshift kitchen. She was quite amused by that unprecedented proposal, or rather instruction. She looked up, 'Why Tara didi? Is someone coming?'

'A brother of mine. Now go on, be quick!'

Troilokko looked up with bewildered eyes at Tara. In all these years, Tara never talked about any of her relatives. She wondered, 'Why should I get ready for her brother!' However, without futher analysis, she did as Tara said. She took a shower and draped one of the sarees Tara gifted to her. Tara then weaved her hair into a chic braid.

In a few hours came the vaishnav brother of Tara. Though he was older than Troilokko, she guessed that he must be in his twenties. He looked quite decent, was of fair complexion, had nicely done hair, was well built and had an innocent smile frozen on his lips.

She covered her hair and was about to go inside, when Tara called out, 'Where are you going? Come, sit beside him! Why are you blushing in front of my brother?!'

Troilokko was a bit uncomfortable. She was not used to the company of men other than her elders. Though some of her friends had brothers, but she was too shy to mingle with them. It was quite an odd situation for her. She felt embarrassed, and was irritated by Tara didi, 'Is she out of her mind! That man may be Tara's brother but not mine! How can she expect me to sit right beside him! The man is also weird. Why is he looking at me like that!'

He continued staring at Troilokko with that same smile stuck on his face and asked with a straight face, 'So this is the sister Tara wrote about. What's your name?' Troilokko was quite stunned. Never did she imagine that a man could speak so directly. Underneath the burning midday sun, in the small hut of Tara, Troilokko's ears became red as apple.

Tara continued, 'Her name is Troilokkotarini. She is a nice girl, but her fate is not so easy on her. She is a widow at such a tender age. Gour, she just needs love!'

Hearing this, the brother named Gour became excited. He walked up to her and stood so close that the warm gust of his breath, flavoured with the enticing smell of *jarda*, brushed over the face of Troilokko. And then he did something unexpected—he removed the veil from Troilokko's head.

Troilokko began to tremble, yet she discerned that the ticklish sensation of shame was only on the surface. In reality, she detected a profound arousal, an intense craving for touch, surpassing even the sensations she felt when engaging in self-pleasure.

After Gour left that day, Troilokko, sitting on the porch, started thinking what she shouldn't. After some time, Tara said, 'You do not need to feel embarrassed at all. Isn't Gour a nice guy?' Troilokko didn't utter a word.

At that time, a Hindu woman was expected to be benevolent, calm, abiding, helpless and dependent. On the other hand, Troilokkotarini is remembered as a person who challenged these ideals. There is perhaps no other woman in Indian history as ruthless and cunning as her.

At that time, Priyonath Mukhopadhyay used to be the head of the detective department at Lalbazar police headquarters in Calcutta. He was responsible for investigating most of the cases related to Troilokkotarini. Through his brilliantly penned chronicles titled *Darogar Daptar*, readers are able to imagine the precision and panache with which the cunning lady committed her villainous endeavours.

At the same time, another serial killer became quite well known in England. He was named 'Jack the Ripper'; the name spiced up news and sold more papers. Around 1888, his merciless murders in and around the poverty-stricken area of Whitechapel in London became the talk of the town. Everyone in London feared the unpredictable death blade of the 'Leather Apron', another fancy name awarded by journalists. Though most of his targets were sex workers, there were exceptions too. And here, in another corner of the world, the method and targets of Troilokkotarini were so similar that it was almost baffling. Troilokkotarini's primary targets were sex workers and their pervert customers. The similarity was so striking that many addressed her as 'Jack the Ripper of India'.

But what were the conditions that led to this? A package of orthodox protocols, superstitions, socio-economic taboos, betrayals and latent malversations led to this unhappy metamorphosis of Troilokko.

∽

Troilokko's prediction turned out right. Gour started visiting her sister quite frequently. Though the primary excuse was paying a visit to his vaishnavi sister, he was mostly accompanied by gifts for Troilokko.

Troilokko had also eased up quite a bit. She awaited Gour's arrival almost impatiently; she awaited the moment when he would come with the bouquet of prezzies for her; she awaited that risqué smile, post which he would untangle her hair carefully braided for him.

Though Troilokko's parents lived just a few yards away, they were unaware of this ongoing game, thanks to the shrewdness and alertness of Tara. But even if they smelt something fishy, they would most likely say nothing as their means of survival depended on the vaishnavi.

By now it must be clear that Tara was a seasoned pimp, who was trying her best to recruit Troilokko into prostitution with carefully measured steps. She did not want to hurry for such a prized commodity, and she had laid out the plan in such a manner that Troilokko would give in herself and nobody would resist or even bat an eye! It can also be assumed that Gour was not her brother but rather an agent from Calcutta's infamous red-light district, Sonagachi. Perhaps he had a deal with Tara.

It is not known what was the expected timeline of Tara to complete the process of selling off Troilokko, but Tara fell ill, and before she could reap the benefits of such an aggrandizing project, she died due to absence of treatment.

At first Troilokko cried a lot, even her parents, who were unaware of the recent developments, shed the tears for the poor lady. They were the only family in the entire village who had a strong bonding with the lonely Tara, and so they inherited whatever assets she possessed after her demise.

But the real nuisance started after that. Gour's frequency of meeting Troilokko increased with time. His aggression had also grown in the absence of Tara.

On a blazing summer day, in the cozy room of Tara, Gour finally got intimate with Troilokko. Tara was a master at keeping secrets. For so many days, she kept the relationship between Troilokko and Gour a secret. Nobody got a hint of what was going on in the gloomy hut of the vaishnavi. But as Tara was no more, the scandalous affair of Troilokko spread like wildfire in every home of the village. Eventually, the news reached her parents.

Troilokko was unaware of all this. One evening, she was busy with Gour in the desolated hut that Tara had left. For her, making love with Gour became a usual affair. However, that evening, Troilokko's mother, along with some other ladies from the village, barged into the room out of nowhere.

'What a shame! A widow in such…Disgusting! Disgusting!' the moral keepers of the village shouted. At first, Troilokko was stunned by the suddenness of their arrival. She started covering herself up as quickly as possible. Gour was a clever person. Before people could have got the chance to recognize him, he jumped out and dissolved in the darkness.

Troilokko's mother grabbed a lock of her hair and pulled her out of the hut, 'Bloody whore! Just see what I do when we get home! I will poison you right now!'

Such an incident, at that time, was bound to be criticized by everyone in the strongest possible manner, and the expected happened. There was no place in the village where people were not talking about that issue. Every nook and corner of the settlement was reverberating with words of disgust and anger. It became almost impossible for Troilokko's father to hold his head high while going out, and, more importantly, it hampered his professional goodwill as well.

One night, with tears in her eyes, Troilokko's mother asked her husband, 'Shall I poison her with berries? I think it will be painless. It is better to be without a child than having such a disgrace. At least we can live in the village normally like before!'

Troilokko's father was clueless. He didn't know what to say in a situation like this. Above all the dogma and strict measures he had taken to ensure her daughters dignity in society, he was her father. He was now the rope in a tug of war where the participants were fatherly affection and societal morality. He was sick of hearing theories about his daughter in every corner of the street, and that constant tussle of feelings made him insentient. He replied, 'Do as you wish!'

Troilokko's mother convinced herself that it was much better to live with the grief of losing their child than to live with the shame of being the parents of such an ignominious girl. However, she was saved from murdering her child when one night, Troilokko absconded with Gour. It is not known for sure whether she took that step after getting wind of her mother's plot.

Troilokko had no idea about Gour's family, but she left all of her family and friends for an unknown future with strong belief in just one man. She boarded the train from Burdwan, and upon reaching Howrah, she was awestruck with the wave of people.

'So many people! Where are they going? You never said that Calcutta is such a crowded place!' said a spelbound Troilokko while grabbing Gour's arm as tightly as she could.

'They are going in search of work, my dear!' Gour dragged her along and called a carriage, 'Oi! Come here!'

Troilokko climbed on the carriage, and after settling herself, she murmured, 'Have you told your family that I am a widow?' She dialled down her tone as she thought that if the coachman discovered such a blasphemous fact, he would most likely throw her out of his carriage.

But Gour told her that she was in Calcutta, a city which was not like her orthodox village. Also, he told her that people fought a lot to demolish the taboo that widows cannot remarry. He shook her and said, 'Tarini, how can being a widow be a sin in the city of Vidyasagar—even he also fought so that widows could remarry.'

Troilokko whispered, 'Can you take me to that Sagar babu once before we get married? Please!'

'Sagar babu?!' Gour sounded astonished. He was chewing a paan right from the time when he deboarded the train. He spat it out of the carriage window and continued with a tone of concern and suspicion, 'Who the hell is Sagar babu?!'

Troilokko got surprised. The Gour he knew used to bring gifts for her, and talked to her in a voice filled with love and compassion. The sudden change in Gour's tone made him quite a different person for Troilokko. She struggled to believe that this was the same person she made love to.

But still, she gathered courage and said, 'I am talking about Vidyasagar. You said that he convinced the sahibs to make a law so that we widows can get married...'

'Okay!' Gour realized that there was no reason to fear, 'You mean Vidyasagar! But what will you say to him? You don't even know how to read. Do you have any idea how great a scholar he is! You will not be able to speak in front of him.'

'I will not say anything,' Troilokko replied, 'I will just see him once to pay my respects, that too from a far!'

Gour painted the clean road with his red gob one more time and replied, 'We will see!'

He paused for a few moments and finally said, 'Now we will go to our house. Stay there for a few days, and then we will start preparing for our wedding.'

'What are you talking about? Wouldn't it be a sin if I stay with you without being married to you? What will your family think about me? Whatever happened back in the village is past, I can't continue those here. I thought...' Troilokko stopped suddenly.

By then their carriage stopped in front of a two storeyed villa. Gour got down, paid the fare and then extended his hand towards Troilokko, 'Come down.'

'What is the name of this place? This is your house?' Troilokko entered the building with her veil pulled over her head, 'You live in such a big house?!'

Troilokko was a rural girl. She was habituated to interpret the word 'house' as a shabby place where few people lived in uninhabitable conditions accepting the fact that it was her fate. But the house before her was enormous and the place was bustling with many people. She estimated that there were at least 17 rooms distributed between the two floors, and women were either coming out or going inside the rooms. The women, she saw, bore no resemblance to the women she was accustomed to seeing in her village. Those women neither knew how to dress decently nor did they have a sense of compunction.

Some men were also loitering around, but by their attire and attitude, Troilokko guessed that they must be servants. She realized that the house was controlled by women. That was not uncommon for her as she had seen many such homes in her village where the wives enjoyed uncontested authority, but here things seemed weird.

Gour came in after Troilokko, and with a grin mixed with playful eyes, he said, 'This place is called Sonagachi, and this is going to be your new house! Got it, sweety?'

What is the origin of the name Sonagachi? In Bengali, *'gach'* means tree and *'sona'* means gold. There is a tree that sheds golden leaves in winter, known as Sonajhuri. So, does the name come from that tree or does it just mean a golden tree? Neither of them was the answer.

Sonagachi was actually named Sonagazi. According to the famous 'barefoot historian' P. T. Nair, who has dedicated his life to mine the history of Calcutta's nooks and corners, the name of the place, also dubbed as the biggest marketplace for sex workers in Asia, has a quite holy origin.

Long ago, an infamous dacoit by the name of Sanaullah used to live in that place with his mother. According to a famous legend, after the death of Sanaullah, his grieving mother heard a voice from his room: *'Ammajan, aap mat royiye! Intekam ke baad allah ne mujhe gazi ka naam diya hain! Aap mat royiye!* (Mother, don't cry! After seeking revenge, Allah has bestowed upon me the title of a gazi! Don't cry!)' When Sanaullah's mother described the incident to her neighbours, people started flocking to the room and prayed for their well-being. Whatever were their prayers about, it is rumoured that all were granted eventually. The room of Sanaullah Gazi became a place of worship.

'Gazi' means a saint or a preacher in Islam, and should not be confused with the Arabic term *'ghazi'*, which means warrior. Many of us might have heard of Ghazi Pir, a Muslim saint who lived around twelfth to thirteenth century, in and around the Ganges delta. According to legends, Gazi Pir had the ability to use magical powers over animals, especially tigers in the Sundarban area, and locals still worship him to keep themselves safe from tigers.

According to P.T. Nair, following that incident, Sanaullah's mother erected a sizable mosque at the site, leading to the area being named Sonagazi. Over time, this name evolved into Sonaghazi mosque. Eventually, the locality came to be known as Sonagachi, aligning more closely with the linguistic nuances of the local Bengalis during that period. Though any physical evidence of the mosque does not exist today, the Masjidbari Street gives an idea about the existence of a mosque at some point in time.

Troilokko understood what Gour meant when he said that those people were her in-laws. She might be a child by age, but she was smart enough to understand that the house was anything but a normal domestic Bengali family home. Here, every room had a female owner. No woman was doing her own chores. Nobody cared about anybody. Gour took Troilokko with him and allocated a room for her, 'Go, get yourself cleaned up. You also seem tired after such a long journey. Go, get some rest. I will go out and get some groceries.'

Troilokko made a quick and thorough survey of the new environment, and with tears in her eyes, she grabbed Gour's hand and pleaded, 'Please don't leave me alone.'

'Have you gone mad! Who is leaving you?' Gour seemed terribly annoyed, 'I have to buy you things. You said that you were not able to bring anything when you left home. You look like a homeless beggar! Let me get some proper clothes and cosmetics for you. Now leave me and freshen up. I will be back in no time!'

After Gour left, Troilokko stood by the four-poster holding one of the posts and started sobbing. She realized that her life, from that moment, had changed completely. Suddenly, she had recalled the face of her friend Prafulla. She recalled the scenes of her village: the green paddy fields waving in the wind, the sparkling waters of Damodar, the reaping season, the sweet smell of jaggery, the sound of the lonely *baul* singer and many more. The scenes made her eyes wet and her heart heavy.

'Look at her! This girl is going to bring a flood of tears, I guess.' Troilokko quickly turned around and saw a middle aged, fair, heavily built lady standing near the door and uttering those words. She was wearing a white saree in a peculiar fashion, had loads of gold jewellery on herself and had a tilak on her forehead. In a bittersweet voice, she called out, 'Where are you from, sweetheart? Let me introduce myself, I am the landlady of this place.'

Troilokko, on seeing the tilak, guessed that she might be a vaishnavi like her beloved Tara didi. She tried to speak after wiping her tears, but was unable to articulate her thoughts. By that time, other women had gathered around the landlady. Some of them were looking at her like they were seeing a girl for the first time.

A fair and young lady came to the front with her bangles making a sweet sound. She asked, 'Are you married or widowed? Is the man who came with you your boyfriend?' The reason for this question was that Troilokko was wearing a coloured saree, and by Hindu customs, a widow should only dress herself in white. Troilokko answered in an almost unperceivable voice, 'Widow!'

'So sad!' somebody started expressing her sympathy, 'You made the right decision by coming here! Here, you will live a good life. Just sleep and eat as you wish, and nobody will command you!'

Gour came back. He was accompanied by a porter carrying a huge load on his head. Meanwhile, Troilokko had already taken a shower and got freshened up. Gour said, 'Just brought all your goods. You have your bedding, your trunk, your utensils…arrange them as you want. And if you need anything, just instruct this boy. He is your personal servant from now. Got it?'

Troilokko belonged to a poor rural family. She not only had to do her own chores but also did other jobs for her family. Other than her clothes, she never had anything personal. This sudden upgrade appeared as a shock to her. She also could not believe that she was going to have her own servant. This meant that she could order whatever she wanted and the boy would do that for her—just like the zamindars in their village. This felt like a dream to Troilokko.

However, the enormous house started to change as the sky turned dark. The house, initially perceived by Troilokko as an exclusively female community, began to welcome men of various backgrounds into its premises. Additionally, the women of the house began grooming themselves. They stood in the balconies, by the windows and at the door. Songs were heard various rooms, accompanied by the distinct jingling of ghungru. Laughter, and sounds of discomfort resonated loudly from certain quarters Troilokko remained confined within her room, disturbed by everything that was happening around her.

Among all this incertitude about the upcoming life, one thing became very clear to her. She was going to live an independent life. This was a thing that she had never experienced up till then. The fact that a woman could also command and have a room all to herself started seeming sweeter than everything else. While making love to her, Gour had once said, 'You are my little queen!' Troilokko realized that from that day onwards, she would really live like a queen.

Almost three months passed since the night when Troilokko became a resident of the pleasure district. Now, she was active in the trade of pleasure. After learning the styles and acts of the other ladies of the house, she was an expert in all of those. She always enjoyed a long queue of men waiting desperately to spend time with her.

The role of Gour in her life changed rapidly. When he brought her there, he was the man of Troilokko's dreams. But soon, for her, he became just a pimp, and Troilokko treated him as one of his servants. Gour never felt strongly about this demotion. He used to be a part-time pimp in Sonagachi, but when Troilokko came into business, he had permanent employment. As days went by, the reputation of Troilokko spread far and wide, and soon she became one of the most coveted sex workers in the entire market.

Kaliprasanna Singha, an eminent poet of that time, gave Calcutta the title, 'The City of Hookers'. He wrote, 'There is almost no locality in Calcutta anymore which does not have at least ten prostitutes. Every year this number is increasing and if this continues like this then will anybody be left with a reason to be proud of this city?'

Actually, that was not an exaggeration at all. During the middle of the nineteenth century, the number of sex workers in Calcutta reached such an alarming number that, on 11 March 1857, the Bengali daily *Sambad Prabhakar* stated that normal women were then getting lost among prostitutes, and it was getting increasingly difficult to separate homes from brothels.

A few years later, Troilokko bought a three-storeyed house in Sonagachi. The grandeur of the house was enough to unhinge one's jaw. Other than that, gatekeepers, servants, cooks and others made the place a micro queendom with Troilokko as the sole authoritarian figure.

Troilokko was completely transformed. She always remained in a state of high temperament; a little error in anything and the whole house started rumbling with her rage. Everybody tried to keep her pleased as much as possible. She was no more that weak and thin rural girl. Now, she was bold and daring. She chewed paan and sang obscene songs to attract customers.

There were also some songs that she composed herself. This was not unique to Troilokko. Many sex workers of Sonagachi used to compose original numbers. Later, a collection of those lyrics were published under the title of *Bessasangit* (Songs of Whores). The funny thing was that the book also contained love songs written by eminent personalities like Bankimchandra Chattopadhyay, Girish Ghosh and Dwijendralal Roy along with numerous songs by unnamed sex workers!

Troilokko had a sense of music right from her childhood. Before dedicating herself completely to the business of sex work, she had trained in music under a tutor. She learnt the various genres of Hindustani classical music like thumri, ghazal and kirtan. Along with that, she was also into dancing. A divine lady with a voice like a nightingale—the description was enough to sell the unexplored markets. The name of Troilokko soon featured among the top few premium escorts of Sonagachi.

With each passing day, Troilokko's fame continued to

soar to new heights. Meanwhile, Gour succumbed to cholera, leaving Troilokko with a profound sense of loss. Although she had never truly loved Gour, his death severed her last tie to her birthplace, Burdwan.

Troilokko experienced a deep sense of loneliness, feeling as though she had lost not only Gour but also all her ties to her past. Despite her wealth and fame, she found herself unhappy, haunted by the melancholy of solitude that echoed in her mind like a turbulent storm, shattering her inner peace completely.

Time passed by, and soon, Troilokko met a man whom she could describe as the real love of her life. And that was the man who led Troilokko into the dark realm of serial killing.

Kali babu, a financially struggling man, duped people during the day and made money as a pimp at night. After a day of duping people, he frequented budget-friendly brothels. One day, he encountered Troilokko while accompanying a wealthy client of hers. At the first sight of her, he was captivated by her celestial beauty.

Troilokko, too, fell in love at first sight. She longed for a person whom she could call her own. Kali babu was broke, but he was undoubtedly a handsome man and also treated Troilokko well. In a few months, the relationship evolved to such a level that they started living together. Kali babu shifted into the princely palace of Troilokko.

Her love for him was so intense that if Kali babu remained outside for a couple of hours, Troilokko became tensed. 'I told you so many times not to leave me alone!' one day Troilokko said when Kali babu returned late.

'Dear, if I don't go out for work, who is going to send money to my home? My family will die starving! My boy is just a year old!' said Kali babu while embracing Troilokko tightly in his arms.

Troilokko hit him softly on his chest, and said with mixed feelings of annoyance and romance. 'Stop joking! I told you so many times to leave your job. I will provide you with whatever you need. But you never listen to me, do you?' said Troilokko as she locked him tightly.

'Okay ma'am, your wish is my command!' Kali babu smiled at her, and as Troilokko slowly closed her eyes, he started kissing her lips.

Eventually, the time came when Kali babu took control of Troilokko's life. He started supervising her income, expenses and assets. He took control of the keys to her locker and over the daily menu. In short, he took control of Troilokko.

It caused a catastrophic downfall of Troilokko. The news became public that Troilokko was the mistress of Kali babu, which meant that he enjoyed exclusivity over her. As the meteoric rise of Troilokko, her fall was also breakneck. Soon, a time came when Troilokko had to spend her savings to run the house. However, Troilokko continued to send money to Kali babu's family. She spent money on the luxury commute of Kali babu, and his acts of pleasure and recreation. By that time, Kali babu's monthly budget for liquor had also doubled.

The savings of Troilokko became almost zero within four to five years. Troilokko understood everything. Still, an indomitable weakness towards Kali babu prevented her from saying anything. She never wanted Kali babu to feel insulted by her words and leave her.

One day, Troilokko observed that Kali babu was sitting with a gloomy face, with a letter in his hand. 'What happened? Whose letter is that?' Troilokko asked.

Kali babu exhaled a deep breath and said, 'From my home. My family is about to die! They wrote me to go visit them once.'

Though Troilokko was obsessed with Kali babu, she still

was a kind person. She said, 'You must go! Try to catch the evening train. I will tell Kartik to take the bags and see you off at the station. Take my coach!'

'I will not!' Kali babu started nodding his head vigorously, 'I can't leave you, sweetheart!'

'Stop being a child!' said Troilokko while putting an end of her *pallu* on lips which were smiling with pride, 'Am I going to die! I will be there for you, waiting. Your wife is ill and you are saying you won't go? That is not fair. You should also go and see your newborn boy for once!'

'That's okay. It can be ignored!' Kali babu suddenly pulled Troilokko onto his lap. While holding her hand and playing with her fingers, he looked up at Troilokko with a romantic gaze, 'How can I leave my lovely darling all alone?'

Whether Kali babu was actually going to miss his 'darling' or whether he was going to miss the life of grandeur he lived on her funds was hard to tell. After all, he lived the life of a king without actually doing anything to deserve it. Whatever might be the reason, that time, Troilokko almost forced him to board the train from Howrah Station. She arranged for a carriage to take him there, and then she bought the ticket for him. She had no way to know what exactly was the condition at Kali babu's home, so she imagined the worst and gave him some money for any unforeseen situation that he might encounter.

Love is a strange thing. As long as Kali babu was contemplating visiting his home, Troilokko was hell bent on sending him. But when she saw the face of her lover disappearing into the horizon, peeping out from the compartment window of the train, a sudden sense of emptiness engulfed Troilokko. Nobody realizes how valuable one is until the person is not there anymore. It is in the absence that someone values the presence.

She suddenly felt a shock. Her Kali babu was really gone!

In the last few years, she had never let him out of her sight for even a single day. But now he was gone. Was he going to return? What if the thought of living with his wife and children hit him all of a sudden? What if he changed his mind to leave the companionship of a whore like Troilokko, and instead chose to live a normal family life? Was she going to die alone then? Troilokko's mind was troubled by a series of what ifs.

What if he didn't return? Whenever Troilokko thought of that possible future, a chill went down her spine. In those 35 years of her life, though she had earned a lot of money, owned a lot of jewellery and commanded a lot of men, but it was only Kali babu who comforted her without any lust.

However, contrary to what Troilokko thought, after five days, Kali babu returned to Calcutta. Other than Troilokko, nobody else could perceive what she went through in those five days. She almost forgot to eat and sleep. Her days started with gazing out of the window and ended the same way. Everytime somebody tried to talk to her or tried to feed her, the reactions they got in return were harsh and bitter.

Though Kali babu returned, he was not alone. He was accompanied by a baby boy, probably aged around five. He said, 'Pratima is no more. She was suffering from jaundice. She was just surviving to see me one last time. She really loved me a lot. All she knew in the world was me!'

Kali babu continued in a sobbing voice, 'We have no close relatives there. That's why I thought of bringing my son Hari with me.'

'Great!' Troilokko ran towards him and picked up Hari in her arms. He had curly brown hair, and had a fair complexion. His curls framed his face, and his eyes weren't entirely black.

'What a lovely boy!' Troilokko left no space on Hari's face that was not wet with her kisses, 'And what a beautiful name, Hari!'

As Troilokko felt like a querida in Kali babu's proximity, the only man who truly loved her irrespective of anything else, she now revelled in the joy of motherhood with the arrival of Hari. She realized how it felt to have a child whom she could call her son. Soon, all household chores was administered by Kali babu, and Troilokko spent all of her time looking after Hari. From bathing him to feeding him, from playing with him to singing him lullabies, Trolikko felt that she had ultimately fulfilled her dream to be a mother. It did not matter that she was his stepmother, Troilokko loved Hari perhaps more than the woman who carried him for nine months. She felt that the missing bead in her chain of happiness was ultimately found.

However, with the arrival of the child, Troilokko and Kali babu were financially crippled. Since Troilokko now had a family, it became increasingly difficult for her to get customers. One by one, the servants left as they suffered paycuts. Eventually, the last piece of luxury that Troilokko owned, her black berline, was also sold off by Kali babu.

And the inevitable happened. Kali babu started taking loans, mortgaging Troilokko's jewellery as mortgage. Soon, seeing all the doors closing upon them, Kali babu tried to revoke his old profession, brokery. But any profession needed practice, and in the lap of extravagant luxury, he had forgotten the tricks of the trade. Hence, that didn't work out. Suddenly, one day, Kali babu said, 'It seems we have nothing left to sell or mortgage anymore. I have an idea, Troilokko!'

Troilokko was busy feeding Hari. For the last few days, the rations had been dwindling. Apart from Hari, both Kali babu and Troilokko were almost starving. She suddenly lifted her face and asked, 'What idea? Are you thinking of renting our house to other whores?'

'No, no! Those hookers will bring drunk men and make

the house dirty. And when the time for paying will come, everyone will act as they were living on air! I don't want such a fuss. I have a better idea. Listen...'

The next day, as per plan, Kali babu went to mingle with the young brats who were looking for some good time in the street. In those times, the streets of Sonagachi were abuzz with boys who just crossed the age of 15 and were eager to spend their pocket money on buying pleasure.

Kali babu wanted to exploit these people. His method was simple: to start a conversation by sharing a smoke and then advertising Troilokko as if she was the best doxy in the neighbourhood that money could not buy. Then he convinced them to follow him to his house.

Troilokko usually started by inviting them and arranging drinks and smokes. As the conversations got dirty, Kali babu would light a cigar and request the client to smoke and drink. Usually the clients asked him to join. But he said, 'I don't drink and smoke, but that should not stop you from enjoying!' Then he used to call for a servant and commanded, 'Make sure that our guest's glass is never empty.'

Troilokko would distract the target and Kali babu would secretly mix the ashes of the cigar in their glass. Only a few are aware that the cocktail of tobacco ash and liquor is a deadly combination. Soon, the client would faint. And then started the real deal.

Troilokko and Kali babu started by taking off the gold ornaments, the watches, the wallets and, at last, the costly attire that the clients wore. Then they dumped the client in a nearby drain. In Sonagachi, sights of people sleeping half drunk in the dirty waters were not uncommon in those days. The clients usually spent their nights half conscious, lying in the drain. The police patrolled the lanes in the morning, and then they would take them to the nearby police station. Usually, those clients were spoiled of famous families who had a revered position in the society. They were usually people who were new in the lanes of lust. Thus, they refrained from telling the truth that they were looted by a whore, as they were not supposed to be there. Hence, they never lodged a complaint. This was the new idea that Kali babu thought of, and it started paying the bills for Troilokko and him for quite some time without any hassle.

But no shrewd idea lasts long. The tricked young babus might refrain from lodging a police complaint fearing a loss of prestige, but that was not stopping them from spreading the news among their fellow mates. Within a few months, the deeds of Troilokko and Kali babu were out in the market. Though that didn't stop the influx of clients, the clients did become more alert.

Thus, Troilokko and Kali babu were back to square one. On the other hand, Hari was growing up and his needs and requirements were becoming expensive. Kali babu immersed himself in the stockpile of liquor in order to find relief from the agony of poverty. Troilokko had lost all her jewellery, and her house was the only property she was left with. Once it was gone, they would be on the streets.

One day, Troilokko was just stepping out of the bath, still rinsing her hair with a *gamcha*,[17] when Kali babu came almost running to her and said, 'See whom I have brought with me!'

---

[17]Gamcha is a rectangular piece of traditional coarse cotton cloth, sometimes with a chequered design, worn as a traditional headdress by men in the Indian subcontinent, mainly in eastern India (including Assam), Bangladesh, as well as in eastern Terai of Nepal.

'Oh maa! Ganesh babu! Long time! It has been decades since this house had the opportunity to serve you. How are you doing?' Troilokko said with an amused tone.

Troilokko had first met Ganesh babu when she had encountered Kali babu for the first time. He had introduced Ganesh babu as his good friend with a strong foothold in the brokerage industry. Ganesh babu pulled up a wide grin across his face, 'I am fine.'

Kali babu almost pulled Ganesh towards the drawing room and said to Troilokko, 'Come fast, dear, I have great news for you!'

When Troilokko arrived in the room a few moments later, the two men seemed immersed in a serious discussion. Kali babu had a glass of wine in his hand and was saying, 'You said that you do not have any acquaintance with *Borokorta* (big brother), will he believe your words? Remember, he is nothing more than than an old illiterate rural coot.'

'Aha! You are not getting the point, Kali babu,' Ganesh babu protested. 'It is true that I have never met Borokorta but the man whom I have taken in confidence lives in Calcutta. His ancestral home is in the village, and he is a distant relative of Borokorta. He will be the one proposing the idea to him, not I. Got it?'

'So you are saying that this man of yours living in Calcutta is aware of our plan?' Kali babu seemed worried and sceptical.

Ganesh smiled and said, 'He is a good man. You have nothing to worry about. I just need a young girl, that's it!'

Since Troilokko was clueless about the topic, she turned towards Kali babu and said, 'I have no idea what you two are talking about!'

'Sit darling, let me tell you the whole story,' Kali babu took a sip from his glass and pulled Troilokko on his lap,

'Ganesh and I have a plan. Have you heard the name of *kshatriya* brahmins?'

Though she originally belonged from a *kulin* brahmin family, but she had never heard about kshatriya brahmins. She said, 'Who are they?'

'It's obvious, there are only a few of them in Bengal,' Kali babu smiled at Troilokko, 'Among these brahmins, the price of a girl is huge! Their customs are quite opposite to us. In their community, it is the groom who gives the dowry to the bride's family! Got it? Other than that, they do not marry any girl outside their caste. Ganesh has brought the news of such a kshatriya brahmin man who is searching for a bride. They live in a remote village in Birbhum.

'Why?' Troilokko stuffed a sweet paan inside her mouth and started chewing, 'Why is he not getting a girl? Is he blind or deaf?'

'None of them!' Kali babu nodded his head, 'He is over 40 and almost broke. Apart from that. the groom is completely illiterate. He doesn't even know how to sign his name. In such a closed community, who would like to give their girl to such a man? Other than that, the number of unmarried girls in the community is so low these days that one has to pay a dowry in the range of four to five thousand to get a bride. And that excludes the jewellery and other gifts. There is no way that this man is going to get such a huge sum of money. He is the only son of an old widow.'

'But I am still confused about your plan. Neither you nor I am from that community, so why are we talking about this?' Troilokko was still clueless.

Kali babu then smirked and said, 'Yes, that is true. But who is stopping us from being so? Listen carefully, get hold of a young whore. That groom is desperately looking for a young bride whose family would settle for a dowry of five or six hundred. They are just trying to save the bloodline, but they cannot afford more than this.'

'Let's say I find a girl. What happens after that?' Troilokko had no idea how Kali babu planned to get rid of the groom after marriage. A whore was not going to stay as a bride somewhere for a long time.

'Then we will get her married,' Kali babu gulped the last drop of the wine in a single shot, 'The girl will go to her in-laws after the wedding, and when the time is good, she will run away. In the meantime, all the dowry and jewellery are ours. How is the plan?'

Now Ganesh babu said a few words, 'I have almost convinced the groom's family in Calcutta. I said to them, "The girl is a bit old, like fifteen or sixteen, and is the only daughter of a widow. They are not well off, but still they have agreed for such a small sum of dowry as the girl is overage. Right now, the girl is living with her uncle. He is the one who is looking after them. They are ready to give cash and jewellery worth ₹500. But they are not in a position to cater a huge amount of guests. Hence, that cost has to be borne by the groom's side. But that is not a huge sum anyway." Hearing this offer, that fool was jumping in happiness. What an idiot!'

Kali babu also boarded the laughter train and said, 'They have no idea that this entire episode is just a farce,' he kept the glass on the table beside him and continued, 'Ganesh! Don't be late. We are almost penniless. Tell them to come the next week to fix the wedding and bless the bride.'

Ganesh said, 'Don't worry. But where is the bride?' He then turned towards Troilokko and asked, 'Can you get hold of someone?'

Troilokko understood the concern and said confidently, 'Invite them the next week. I will get a girl by then!'

After Ganesh departed, Troilokko and Kali babu didn't

discuss the plan anymore. Troilokko finished her daily routine of feeding Hari, and then she sat on the porch to dry her hair. Kali babu said to Troilokko, 'You promised Ganesh a girl so easily, but how do you plan to get her so quickly? And most of the girls here have a guardian. Who will let their daughter get involved in such a con without some gain?'

Troilokko seemed completely at peace, as if she had planned everything already. She continued combing her hair for some time and then pointed towards some slum tents at a distant corner, 'Can you see those tents?'

'Yes, I am not blind. As far as I know, some old whores live there. They have been out of the business for a long time. They now earn their living by serving as domestic workers around the area.'

Then Troilokko pulled Kali babu down to sit beside her and said, 'An old lady lives there. Her name is Digambari. I heard stories that she used to be from a rich family, but after arriving here, she started her business as a *kayashtha.* But that doesn't matter. What matters is that some years ago, she bought a baby girl from a poor old whore, and she brought her up as her own daughter.'

'Is that so?' Kali babu frowned at her, 'You live in a palace far away from them. How did you get to know so much?'

'At that time, Digambari used to work in our locality as a domestic worker. I still remember she borrowed ₹3 from me to buy that girl Bidhi. She must be around 14 or 15 by now. She has just opened shop but still she is not a regular player. I think if I propose this offer to Digambari, she will not have any second thoughts,' Troilokko spoke almost in a single breath.

'Hmm!' Kali babu seemed convinced about the plan. 'Sounds good!'

Digambari almost got the key to a gold mine with

the offer. Her days of glory were gone, and she had been struggling to survive. In such a time, an offer of few hundred rupees was nothing less than a lottery. But she had one condition—she would take half the share as her daughter was the key to the whole plan. With no other option in hand, Troilokko and Kali babu agreed to that. Even if they end up getting ₹500, they would have peace of mind at least for a few months. After all, it was impossible to get another girl who fit the plan so perfectly.

Ganesh was a man of his words. In a few days, he arranged for a house on rent in a posh locality near Sonagachi.

'But without any guarantee, how did you manage to get a house on rent for just a month in such a locality?' Troilokko asked Ganesh babu, almost amused by his skills.

'This is Calcutta, my lady! You can get tiger's milk if you have the money, so what's a house! As soon as he got the rent in advance, he handed over the keys without uttering a single word,' Ganesh seemed to enjoy the way Troilokko was impressed by him.

They didn't waste any more time. On the evening of that day, Troilokko and Kali babu took Bidhi and settled themselves into the new house. Troilokko took the role of the widowed mother and Kali babu got ready to play the role of her brother, their only guardian. As planned, the groom's family came to see the bride. Troilokko made Bidhi wear a simple saree and groomed her to look like a girl belonging to a normal Bengali family. She also trained her on how to behave in front of the guests. Bidhi was a quick learner. In such a short time, she overcame her bohemian behaviour and impressed the guests with a shy and humble attitude.

The groom's family agreed to the wedding in no time. After such a long search, they had ultimately got the perfect bride. An uncle of the groom finalized the marriage after a month with a gold coin.

The groom was a little gloomy as he was almost spending his entire wealth on the wedding. But as soon as he saw Bidhi, he felt that everything was worth it. After the guests left the house, everyone had a good laugh about the upcoming con game. It was not easy to get such sheep those days. In the meantime, Kali babu sold off the gold coin to a jeweller in Sonagachi to fund their needs for the time being.

All the arrangements were being made for the wedding as the date arrived closer. Meanwhile, Ganesh babu had collected a sum of ₹200 from the groom's family to spend on the arrangements. Hundred rupees were divided among the masterminds of the plan, and the rest was spent towards the cheapest possible options to complete the hogwash.

'Everything is almost done as per plan. But what about the guests from our side?' said Troilokko, 'The *barjatri*[18] is definitely going to be suspicious about that. Who would be the people from the bride's side?'

'No one will suspect anything,' Ganesh seemed to be in a high mood, 'I have discussed this with around 20 to 25 prostitutes in the area. They will be present on the wedding day.'

'But none of them behaves like women from respectable families. Will that not affect our plan?' asked a sceptical Kali babu.

'I have arranged everything,' Ganesh babu assured his friend. 'I have trained them to act like the ladies belonging to normal household.'

The wedding gifts, along with sacred bowl of turmeric and oil, arrived from the groom's family three days before the wedding as per the customs of kshatriya brahmins.

---

[18]Guests from the groom's side.

According to protocols, the bride had to frill herself with that before bathing, but in reality, nothing like that happened. Rather, Bidhi spent her night before the wedding with one of her customers.

The wedding needed a purohit and a barber. The skillful conman Ganesh babu also arranged for them. Getting a barber was not a big deal, but one has to appreciate the skills of a man who even convinced a brahmin purohit to marry off a sex worker as a brahmin girl. Money speaks above all indeed! It can even make a man, who is supposed to go by the rules of Vedas and be the purest in the society, indulge in such blatant chicanery.

As per schedule, the groom arrived in the traditional wedding attire. It was evident that he tried to make himself look as young as possible with as many tricks as few bucks could buy. Right from the *chandan* on his forehead, to the fine dhoti he was wearing, it showed how excited he was about the marriage. He also seemed a bit tense as he was wiping his face with his silk handkerchief almost once every minute.

As per the plan of Ganesh babu, the false guests from the bride's end started acting in front of the guests from the groom's side. But Ganesh and Kali babu missed out on a minute detail. Usually a wedding is kept jovial with some playful kids. It was almost impossible that none of the guests had any children. The anomaly was evident, and on top of that, though they were supposed to act friendly with the groom, their behaviour was not just friendly; it was rather a little perverted.

One of the old men who arrived as a guest from the barjatri whispered to another old man, 'Don't you feel that something is not right?'

The man, to whom it was spoken, was busy sipping the cold sherbet served by the concubines and was ogling at them. He replied without turning his eyes 'Why? I am feeling great actually!' Then he turned towards the man and said, 'Don't confuse them with the women you see in your village. This is Calcutta, here women dress and behave like this only. They are not like our illiterate and shy housewives.'

But that old man did not give up that easily. He said, 'I am not just talking about the women. Have you observed that other than the uncle of the bride and the man who came with the proposal, there is no single man around from the bride's side! I am not feeling good. I often hear news of so many scams happening in Calcutta and—'

The happy old man stopped him midway, 'You are now overthinking, moshai. The man who brought the proposal, Ganesh, is a trusted marital agent. I have never heard of any such thing about him. You have grown very finicky with age. Now rest that big brain of yours and cool yourself with this magnificent sherbet!'

The man was about to say something when the uncle of the groom arrived before them and said in a hurry, 'Please come, the bride's uncle, her only guardian, is saying to wrap up the money-related affairs before the rituals. I also agree with him. Let us finish the deal, and then we will enjoy the wedding peacefully.'

As per the terms, some cash was handed over to Kali babu in a few moments. He didn't waste time and commanded to bring the bride to the wedding stage, 'Bring her, the *lagna* is about to get over now!'

Some of the guests from the groom's side were growing a little sceptical about everything, but as soon as Bidhi arrived, dressed in the attire of a Bengali bride with red veil and chandan makeup, everyone was too amazed to suspect anything anymore. 'The fact that our boy got such a girl at such an amount is nothing short of a miracle!' said one person from the groom's side.

Eventually, the rituals and customs of the wedding started. First the *stree-aachar* or the rituals of the women; then *subhodristi,* the moment when the bride and the groom see each other through a veil of betle leaves; then the seven rounds of promises around the holy fire; and at last, the *sindur-daan,* the custom of applying vermillion on the bride's hair parting by the groom. Everything happened as planned. The fun-filled night after the wedding, when the guests tease the newly weds, also went smoothly. Ganesh chose three girls, who could keep check on their behaviour, to spend the night. They were introduced as distant sisters of the bride, and they played their role quite well, chatting with the friends of the groom throughout the night.

The name of the groom was Madhusudan. He was not much involved in the games; rather he was waiting to get his alluring new wife all by himself in private. That night of closeness, the *suhag-raat,* or as it is known in Bengali, the *ful-sojja,* was supposed to happen on the third night after the wedding. But it seemed that Madhusudan was almost restless for that moment. He tried hard to hold himself together but then, involuntarily, his eyes turned towards the white feet of Bidhi decorated with *aalta*[19].

'I must say my friend, your wife looks like an angel. But there is something I need to ask. Did you observe the sisters of your wife? I know that the women in Calcutta are educated and frank, but they were behaving weirdly, didn't you see? One of them was touching me frequently for no reason. And the way they were sitting, seemed as if they were trying to seduce us!' Madhusudan's close friend Nitai said to him. However, the groom was so smitten by Bidhi that he ended up saying, 'Stop thinking so much, Nitai.'

---

[19]Aalta is a red dye that is applied to the hands and feet of women, mainly in the Indian subcontinent.

On the next morning, as commanded by Kali babu, Bidhi wore the jewellery that the groom had brought with him. Adorned with jewellery and the attire of a newly wed bride, the rising sex worker of Sonagachi, Bidhi, got ready for her journey to her in-laws' home. And she was accompanied by Kali babu and Digambari, who were playing the roles of uncle and domestic worker, respectively.

Ten days after the drama, Kali babu, Bidhi, Digambari and Ganesh returned to Troilokko's place. Madhusudan was also supposed to come. But instead of worrying about his absence, Troilokko busied herself with removing all the jewellery from Bidhi. She had previously talked to a jeweller in the vicinity, and within an hour, all the jewellery was sold to him. But the man also took advantage of the situation, and thus, the team made a loss. The jewellery, that was worth a little above ₹500, only fetched about ₹350.

'There is nothing to be done,' Troilokko arrived at her home after the transaction. 'This jeweller is familiar to me. He will not expose us to anyone.'

'What you did is completely right,' Kali babu said while counting the notes and distributing them among the perpetrators. 'When you are accomplishing something big, you should not think of petty losses, what do you say, Ganesh babu?' Then Kali babu looked at Ganesh with a mischievous grin and asked, 'Did you tell Troilokko about the kind of reception you received at Bidhi's in-laws' home?'

Ganesh was smiling shamelessly, 'That needs a special mention! In the last few days, the food that I ate is more than I eat in a year!'

'But what happened after you people arrived there?' Troilokko was unable to contain her curiosity anymore.

'Whatever was bound to happen!' Ganesh pulled Bidhi

on his lap, and squeezing her lips he said, 'Our Bidhi cooked rice for *boubhat* (bride feast), and everyone enjoyed the meal. Everyone was so innocent.'

'Oh maa!' Troilokko's eyes opened wide with a gasp, 'They ate the food cooked by a prostitute? Everyone lost their honour, then! But why did Madhusudan stay back? Didn't he want to come? Strange!'

'Who said he didn't want to come! That fellow was not letting his wife out of his sight for a second,' Kali babu burped and then continued, 'That man is like a leech. He was not letting Bidhi go anywhere without him for a moment. Hence, when we reached the station, I asked him to buy some sweets for Bidhi, telling that she is hungry. The moment he became a little inattentive, we sprinted from there!'

Everyone was almost rolling on the floor laughing hysterically. Troilokko, although participating in the laughter riot, didn't feel too good about everything. Though her situation had made her a crook, she was still a woman with sympathy and conscience. Even after getting so much money after such a bunco, she felt bad about the old widow who spent all her belongings and brought a girl home for her son. The family was punished without doing anything wrong.

'What happened to you?' Kali babu noticed the silence of Troilokko. He grabbed her arm and embraced her saying, 'Now we will live in luxury. Come close, my darling, I haven't seen your face for such a long time!'

Troilokko tried hard but was unable to smile. She kept on thinking about that old widow and her son. Thinking about their state of mind, she felt remorseful and inconsolable. But Kali babu thought that Troilokko had not been smiling because he had not been here for the last few days. After looking straight into her eyes for few seconds, he started singing a sweet song for her. Trolikko finally smiled and threw herself in the arms of Kali babu.

Six months passed after that episode. Troilokko and Kali babu had been living a peaceful life. Meanwhile, Bidhi had become a professional sex worker, and Hari was already a boy of six who roamed around the alleys of Sonagachi for the whole day and spent his time mingling around with the boys on the street. Needless to say, there was no concept of studying or anything similar for him. One fine morning, out of nowhere, few men barged into Troilokko's house, 'There! There he is! My wife's uncle, grab him! He was the one who ran away with my wife!'

Kali babu was about to leave for something when that incident happened. But he did not lose his cool. He knew how to handle situations like these. With an expression of genuine surprise on his face, he curiously looked at the men and said, 'Who are you people? I don't remember ever seeing you!'

'Is that so? You haven't met us? How will you remember. After all, the money and the jewellery are gone, right!' One of the men almost grabbed Kali babu by the collar, 'Return everything right now or we will go to the police!'

'Okay, go ahead!' Kali babu replied in a cold tone while smiling, 'But before that, won't you see the girl who was married into your family?'

Bidhi's husband for a week, Madhusudan, was at the end of the crowd. In the past few months, he was not only financially destroyed but his mental peace was also ruined completely. He was not willing to come, but his uncles almost forced him to come and see the end of it.

Despite all that happened, Madhusudan was not enraged, or maybe he was too numb to express any feelings. Inertly, he asked, 'Oh yes…my wife…where is she? Can you please call her once?'

Kali babu said in a mocking tone, 'Sure, son! You see those rooms right on the street? There is your wife! Come on, go ahead, and see with your own eyes!'

The group of men was not ready for such a turn of events. They had assumed that the uncle of the bride was the chief antagonist, and they planned to get Bidhi out of there. But after hearing Kali babu, they proceeded towards the place where Bidhi lived.

Before leaving, the leader of the group did not forget to threaten Kali babu, 'If we do not find her there, then we will drag you to the police station!'

'Sure, sure! I am going nowhere,' Kali babu's grin was almost upto his ears.

When the squad crossed the road, Troilokko walked up to Kali babu and said, 'When they discover that she is a prostitute, won't they turn wild and attack us?'

'That is why I sent them there!' Kali babu said with that grin still on his face, 'Do you think when they discover that the bride, who had cooked for the entire family and villagers, is a prostitute, will they dare report that to the police? Impossible! That would ruin their honour. They would rather leave Calcutta without even talking among themselves.'

But Troilokko was still not convinced, 'I don't have a good feeling about this.'

'There is nothing to be scared of. As long as I am here, you need not fear anything,' Kali babu assured her as if nothing had happened. His prophesy came true. After the team went towards Digambari's room in high spirits and rage, nobody saw Madhusudan's family around Sonagachi after that. After a while, they got the news from somewhere that the men went back to their village, and in order to hide their grave mistake of believing these people, they spread the news that the newly wed bride had passed away due to cholera.

It was a time of celebration for Kali babu. Ganesh sponsored the bottles of liquor, and Bidhi danced lasciviously. They celebrated not getting caught even after such a big scam. This made them all quite fearless. After that, they scammed five to six families in similar manner. Every time, the cast was almost same, and every time the ending was the same too.

This continued for some years. Troilokko and Kali babu almost never faced any financial difficulties. And Hari earned the name as one of the most despicable, sloshed, egregious and feckless boy in the area. And this plummet was made smooth by the constant supply of pocket money from Troilokko.

However, the steady strategy of frauds eventually hit a ceiling. Bidhi had grown quite old by then, and there was no way that she was eligible for marriage anymore. In that time, a bachelor girl who was aged more than 20 was a myth, even among the educated elites. And they were unable to find any substitute for her.

Kali babu asked the same question to Troilokko every day, 'Did you get someone new?'

'No!' Troilokko said every time. 'The mother of all the teenagers around here have become very cautious. They say that they are happy with whatever their daughter earns by performing and sleeping with men. They do not wish to earn more by endangering themselves by becoming involved in any dubious activities.'

'Cowards!' Kali babu said with clear repugnance. 'But what shall we do now! Soon we will be out of business!' However, by the time the business shut down, Kali babu had devised another innovative and scandalous plan.

During that period in Calcutta, the occurrence of children being kidnapped, especially those adorned with ornament was not uncommon. However, the approach adopted by Kali babu was truly sinister. Young girls began to disappear from the streets of Calcutta regardless of whether they were adorned with ornaments or not. The girls ended up in Troilokko's house, and she raised them she was like their mother. Then, when they were old enough, they were married off to distant villages as brahmins, *kayasthas* and *baniks*. Troilokko used to play the role of mother and Kali babu played the role of a father. They used to choose the groom in such a manner that they would bear all the costs as Troilokko and Kali babu pretended to be penniless. The girls were usually aged between five and six. They were still not mature enough to understand their own safety and well-being, so they never caused any trouble. And after spending few days at the in-laws, the girls used to run away with Kali babu with all the jewellery and money they could carry. Kali babu trained the girls to approach the situation like it was a game. Then they were reused as long as possible, thus ensuring a constant flow of money.

But that new path also hit a dead end. Due to the rising reports of missing girls in Calcutta, the police became a lot more vigilant and aggressive. In 1868, British civil servant Sir Stuart Saunders Hogg CIE had established an investigation department in Calcutta Police. Mr Idnan became the superintendent and Mr Lamb was the first-class inspector. These three men took the pledge to hunt the gang that was responsible for these crimes.

They pushed their subordinate Indian police officers to get to the bottom of these criminal activities at any cost. In the drive to save their jobs, almost everyone in Calcutta Police became alert and started to dig into the matters with highest possible diligence. Sonagachi was already famous as of the hub of all illegal activities in the city. On top of that, most of the missing reports were filed around this. Thus, the detectives zeroed in on the red-light district and started combing the area.

Troilokko was never fully confident about the plan to kidnap young girls but went along with the conviction of Kali babu. However, as time passed, even Kali babu started doubting his plan. Right from the time when he used to rob the spoiled brats by intoxicating them, Troilokko earned the reputation of being a pernicious woman. Also, after Bidhi's first heist, Troilokko used to hire some girls in the area to act as guests from the bride's side. It was a possibility that under the pressure of police interrogation, some of those girls might reveal the details of the felony. If that happened, the detectives would keep a strict watch on the house to apprehend them red-handed.

A tense Kali babu said, 'We should stop this method of earning now.'

Troilokko looked up at him and said in a feeble tone, 'Have you thought of something else?'

Yes, Kali babu did think of something, but that eased his way to the gallows in just a couple of years.

Troilokko failed to save her love with all means possible—money, sex, etc. She tried everything. It must be said here that she also followed the footsteps of her husband in the next couple of years.

❧

During the time when the British moored their anchor on the banks of Hugli River, the most prosperous among the residents of the Sutanuti area were the Seths and the Basaks. Though the British administration did not leave any stone unturned to cease the production of various raw materials so that they could economically cripple India and easily reign over the country, the axe did not come down in the same way on all. There were many cunning Indian businessmen at that time who kept good ties with the Raj, often acting against their own countrymen, and became millionaires in that period.

As the majority of Indians started their dive into the deep, dark well of poverty, people like Janardan Seth and Sobharam Basak dealt in gold coins by just exporting raw materials for textiles from the port at Sutanuti. The market of Sutanati expanded with time and eventually covered an area of around 500 acres. The size of the market gave it its name, 'Bara Bazaar', which means 'big market'. Though the pioneers of befriending the ruling outsiders and securing oneself were the Seths and Basaks, with time, the Mullicks and Marwaris also joined the league. In a span of around 50 years, the area became the financial district of eastern India. Gaining or losing a fortune there was a matter of days, and only the bravest and smartest survived the market. It was a place where one could get anything and everything with money. One of the busiest jewellery shops in that area was Chandra Golds and Jewelleries. The proprietor of the store, Satish Chandra, was a man aged around 50.

Be it a gentle businessman, a poor father trying to marry off his daughter or some impecunious widow who kept her jewellery as mortage, Satish babu didn't show mercy to anyone when it came down to extracting the proper amount under any circumstances. He lived in a three-storeyed house at Chitpur and had a flourishing family comprising his wife and children. Apart from that, he was also having an affair with a woman named Kamala. He had kept her in a separate house in Bagbazar, with all the required amenities for her care. During the weekends, or whenever he felt low, he would visit there to have a happy time. People often said that even the smartest could not trick him—until one day.

That day, there were around five to six customers at the front counters of his shop, and he was busy with some accounts mismatch from the previous night. Around 10.30 a.m., a huge clarence stopped in front of his store. The two white horses pulling the carriage groaned and started hitting the road when their reins were pulled.

A richly dressed gentleman deboarded the carriage. He was wearing an expensive silk kurta with a red *pagdi* on his head. His huge moustache and beard made him stand out from the crowd. He had a chandan tika on his forehead and was holding a walking stick with an ivory headcap.

Satish babu pulled up his attention from the ledger and observed that even the *nagra* shoes worn by the gentleman did not cost less than a thousand rupees. The man gazed at the signboard of the shop for a while and then approached the main entrance.

'Fatik! Fatik!' Satish babu shouted at one of his servants. Fatik was a young salesperson who sat at the counters. He was busy negotiating with an old man about the rates of making some new jewellery from some old ones. Hearing the call of his master, he almost ran towards him with his palms joined.

'Did you call me, babu?' He asked with a gentle smile.

Satish babu was not happy about the fact that his words were lost in the noise. He shouted at Fatik, 'I told you a thousand times to manage your time based on the customers. What are you doing with that old beggar! Leave him and attend the babu who just stepped in!'

'But babu, that old man's daughter is getting married, and he is really struggling with the funds. He was just asking for the least possible rate—' Fatik knew he was going to be scolded, but he tried his best to justify his act.

'Stop being a monk! You are just a salesman! Hence, do your job and get rid of that old man. A rich babu just entered the shop. Go, attend to him!' Satish babu pointed at the door, 'See what he wants and be sure not to appear silly!'

By that time, the princely man had almost made his way to Satish babu, who suddenly changed his facial expressions from an oppressive master to a benign servant, 'Yes babu, how may I help you?'

The man greeted Satish babu and spoke in fluent Hindi, '*Namaste babu, main Saraikela estate ka raja, His Highness Kunwar Chadradhar Singh ka mulazim hu. Naachiz ka naam Shatrugna Pande.* (Namaste babu, I am a member of King Kunwar Chadradhar Singh. My name is Shatrugna Pande.)'

'Nomoste Nomoste!' Satish babu spoke Hindi like it was spoken by most of the Bengalis. He almost exposed all his teeth and asked, 'Tell me, how I can serve you?'

Pande understood the reason for Satish babu's behaviour and said, 'Actually, Satish babu, in the past few days, our king has heard a lot of praise about your shop. His daughter's wedding is scheduled for the upcoming month. His command is that all the arrangements for the wedding should be made from your shop. That's why he has sent his special person, me, here. Do you understand?' Satish babu realized that a lottery ticket had landed in his lap out of the blue, and he thanked the lord a couple of times.

Satish babu started helping Pande in the selection of jewellery. Within an hour or so, Shatrughna Pande selected three *sitahaar*, along with some *ratnachur, mantasa,* kamarbandh, *kaanbali, jhumka and haatpadma.* Apart from normal bangles, he also selected few fish-mouthed bracelets.

Then he thought for some time and asked Satish babu, 'Can you suggest me more designs?'

The choice and taste of the royal manager had already blown Satish babu out of his mind. In a short calculation, he estimated that he usually sold less jewellery in a whole month than what he had sold just in an hour!

'Babu,' Pande snapped Satish babu out of his trance, 'Can you hear me?'

'No worries, everything is fine,' Satish babu snapped out of the daydream and showed him more designs. After the selection was over, the bill crossed ₹2,000. The transaction amount made him so joyous that he wished to run to Kamala right then and make love to her to cool down his excitement.

Pande stood up and said, 'Thank you! Can you kindly send a trustworthy person of yours with me? I haven't brought much money with me. Right now, we are staying in a rented house in Barabazar. It is very close from here. Please send someone who will take the necessary items and bring the money back while returning. Is it acceptable?'

'Why not!' Satish babu called Fatik and ordered, 'Go with babu and return carefully.'

But Fatik never returned.

Shatrughna Pande was none other than Kali babu, who had pulled an excellent act. As soon as Fatik entered Troilokko's house, both of them pounced on him, and Troilokko committed her first murder.

In a fainted voice she asked, 'Wh—where will you dispose the body? I—I am very scared!'

Kali babu was panting after the quick and heavy exercise. He said, 'There is nothing to fear. Everything is sorted.Don't worry, I will bury him near the pond at midnight.'

Troilokko tried hard to calm down but she couldn't. Sitting by the side of the dead body, she shivered constantly.

In the middle of her empty mansion, the lifeless body of Fatik was left alone.

ꟹ

Despite being accountable for numerous crimes, Kali babu seemed to have a guardian angel safeguarding him, offering repeated opportunities for redemption. However, with each chance, Kali babu had escalated his criminal endeavours from iniquitous to outright nefarious. Through strokes of luck, he managed to elude justice every time. Nevertheless, even divine forgiveness has its limits. Ultimately, Kali babu couldn't evade the clutches of the law and received capital punishment for the murder.

And the police officer, whose sharp intelligence and tireless efforts brought Kali babu to justice, was Priyonath Mukhopadhyay.

Priyonath Mukhopadhyay was an efficient policeman. From Satish babu's shop, he had traced the clarence, and from the coachman of the clarence, he traced the Sonagachi area. He did not waste much time in fishing out the address of Troilokko by interrogating the locals in the area. While conversing with many people, he also discovered the past frauds by Troilokko and Kali babu that made his suspicion more rigid.

Satish babu's men identified Kali babu even without the makeup and dress, and in a few days, police arrested the latter. Nobody from the shop had seen Troilokko, and there was no evidence to prove her involvement in the murder. Thus, apart from interrogation, the police were unable to do anything against her. Meanwhile, Troilokko was shattered. Kali babu, the man whom she never let out of her sight for more than a few days, and for whom she left her profitable profession of sex work, was behind bars. Troilokko became almost numb, and she spent her days gazing at the sky without anything else going on in her mind. She tried to chastise herself in various ways to feel the kind of agony that Kali babu was going through in the lock-up. She even tried to kill herself.

We have already witnessed her sacrifices for Kali babu. In the next few episodes of her life, we will see her ruthless side. But along with that, we will also observe her protective attitude towards her stepson Hari.

Troilokko began spending all her savings on the lawyer appointed to defend Kali babu. She not only sold the last bit of her jewellery but also ended up in selling her huge mansion that she had bought all by herself. She was not satisfied with having only one lawyer and appointed few more to try their best in order to get Kali babu out of jail.

For the lawyers, this opportunity was a gold mine. They knew Troilokko was not literate, so it became easy for them to fool her and extort as much money as possible. Meanwhile, nothing seemed to make real progress in saving Kali babu. There were too many pieces of evidence against him and, thus, the jury members of the Calcutta High Court unanimously agreed that capital punishment was the only verdict for him. But Troilokko still tried with all her might. After selling the house, she rented a room in the locality where Digambari and Bidhi used to live. Her daily routine was to visit the police station to convince them either by begging for mercy or by other means.

The woman who used to own a huge mansion and employed several servants, for whom many men used to come with expensive offerings, was reduced to a helpless, middle-aged lady, who had neither money nor beauty. The only things that Troilokko possessed then were the memories of a relatively simple and happy past and the agonies of losing her near and dear ones. Her days passed in roaming through the corridors of court and police station, and at night, she just stared out the window of her rented house, like a stone with a beating heart.

On the other hand, though Troilokko escaped justice due to the lack of evidence, Priyonath always suspected that Fatik was murdered by two people. Hence, he started to interrogate Troilokko in various ways to extract her confession. When Troilokko understood that buying the loyalty of an inspector was not an easy job, she tried her once adored skills in order to attract some lower ranked policemen. But she failed in that attempt too. Nobody showed any affinity towards a woman who had lost her glamour and sensuousness.

Ever after several days of hardship, Troilokko failed to save Kali babu from getting hanged. As per his last wish, Kali babu held Troilokko's hand one last time and whispered in her ear, 'Never ever confess anything. Goodbye, my love.'

But Troilokko kept weeping and said, 'I want to confess, Kali babu! Without you, how will I live? What will be the meaning of this life!'

'Think of Hari, Troilokko. Who will take care of him? You need to be strong.' Hari was the only reason Troilokko had remained quiet in front of the police. After the death of Kali babu, Troilokko became almost insane for a few days. Hari was quite scared to see his mother like that. One day, he asked, 'Maa! What happened to you? You sit like a stone in the house for the whole day. You should go out and walk a little!' But Troilokko never answered back. She and Hari soon moved outside Sonagachi and relocated to a place where the police wouldn't be able to sniff her out. In that new locality, nobody knew about her past life. Hence, nobody disturbed her.

There is a saying that time heals everything. But in this case, Troilokko was not able to forget the loss of her beloved Kali babu. However, she gradually returned to the main stream of life for the sake of Hari.

But it soon became unfeasible for her to manage expenses for two. A time arrived when she only had a single meal a day in order to feed Hari properly. There was no source of income. With rising prices, it also became almost impossible for her to serve Hari proper meals. When Troilokko got up every morning, the first thing that would trouble her mind was, 'What will I feed Hari today?'

She felt as if Kali babu was looking at her from the heavens with disgust in his eyes and saying, 'I left my son in your hands, and you are not able to even feed him properly? Would it have been the same if Hari was your own blood?' Soon, to sustain the two of them, Troilokko started sleeping with men from the lowest sections of the society.

She roamed around a little during the afternoon just to get some air. She felt that her room was like a prison and felt suffocating. But she didn't know anyone in the new locality. So she started to visit her old neighbourhood, Sonagachi. Some of her friends were still there. She started to have a chat with them almost daily, about life and philosophy, just to relieve her from the hell she went through every night.

On the other hand, Hari grew up to be a disgusting human being. At the age of 18, there was no misdemeanour left in which he had no experience. He used to spend his time committing petty crimes and in the rooms of young concubines. He never paid heed to any requests by Troilokko. For him, Troilokko was just a machine that gave him money when he needed it.

Due to the rising demands of Hari, Troilokko started facing financial scarcity. But he knew how to exploit his mother emotionally. Everytime Troilokko tried to be strict, he threatened, 'Give me the money at once or I will never return home. Never!'

One afternoon, Troilokko was strolling in the lanes of Sonagachi, when someone said, 'Troilokko di? How are you?'

Troilokko looked up and saw that a woman was smiling and waving at her. The woman said, 'What are you gawking at? Have you lost your eyesight with age! You do not remember me? I am Kusum! Come up, the stairs are on that side.'

Finally, Troilokko recognized her. When she had first arrived at Sonagachi with Gour, there had been another tenant in the house—Kusum. Back then, she had been a lean, dark girl, but she had put on quite some weight in all these years. That's why Troilokko didn't recognize her at first. The only memories of Kusum in her mind were of a young and happy girl who always behaved very nicely.

Troilokko advanced towards the stairs with a smile on her face. It had been a long time since she had met an old friend. Her mood was jovial. They spent a lot of time talking to each other that evening. Although Kusum was not going through the level of financial turmoil that Troilokko experienced every day, her business was also not minting money like it used to during its heyday.

Troilokko came back to her home with a sense of satisfaction after a long time. After that day, it became a routine for Troilokko to visit Kusum's place. In the vast, cruel world, at last she had found a person to whom she could pour her heart out. Kusum also enjoyed Troilokko's company.

Meanwhile, Hari's demands kept on increasing, and a time came when Troilokko failed to satisfy his needs even with all her might. Slowly, Hari started becoming aggressive towards his mother, and soon, he started beating her when his demands were not met.

One day, when Troilokko returned after a bath, Hari stormed into the house, almost giving her a heart attack. He was seldom in the house during the day and usually returned around early morning, stewed to the gills. Then he would leave the house again after having some food. But that day, his eyes were red, and his spit, dyed red with paan, was trickling down from the corner of his mouth. It was evident that he was too drunk to stand on his own, and he was tripping on every step he took. And there was a young girl standing right beside him, holding his shoulders. In that condition, he was trying to sing a song, humming without any words clear.

Troilokko was horrified. This was the first time that he had come home with a sex worker. The girl's disposition could not dodge Troilokko's experienced eyes. She was a greenhorn and really struggling to smile in front of her client, Hari.

Without any further talk, he came to the point right away. He pointed towards Troilokko and barked, 'Give me my money!'

Troilokko answered back, 'What money?'

'What money? You fucking whore! The money you earn every night, that money!' Hari said. 'Okay, keep your money bitch! Just give me the money that my father gave to you!'

Hearing this kind of language from Hari was not new for her. But she felt insulted to be showered with those words from her son in front of a young girl. She tried to keep her anger in control and replied, 'What has your father left, huh? All the money is earned by me. It is my money!'

'Shut up!' Hari shouted at the top of his voice and pounced on his mother. He grabbed Troilokko by her hair and started shaking her head vigorously, 'Give me my fucking money, you slut! Or else I will fucking slit your throat right now!'

After showing her how capable a 'man' he had become, Hari became exhausted and sat in the middle of the room. Then, panting like a dog, he growled, 'Listen carefully! I am now going to fuck this girl, her name…yeah, Ratanmani. I will return tomorrow morning. I should get ₹100 by that time, otherwise I will beat the crap out of you.' Troilokko was lying on the floor groaning in pain. Hari had kicked her in the belly and slammed her hard against the wall. She asked herself, 'Is this karma? The punishment of all her sins?'

Next day, though Troilokko roamed around the streets of Sonagachi, her mind was somewhere else. Hari had been missing since last night after the incident took place when he had threatened Troilokko that if he didn't get ₹100 by next day, she would witness his wrath. Troilokko did not care for her life anymore. But she thought that if she gave up on Hari, then Kali babu would never forgive her. So, the only thought in her mind was how to gather the money.

❧

Troilokko was stressed about ways to arrange the money. She thought of visiting Kusum's home to have a little chat to relax her mind and soul. As soon as she reached Kusum's home, Kusum said in a calm manner, 'Come in, didi'. Her eyes were wet, and that did not escape Troilokko's eyes. She asked,'Why are you crying?'

'No...nothing. I will go and fetch something for us to eat.' Kusum quickly turned around and rushed inside the kitchen.

In no time, she brought a big bowl and kept it between them, 'Here you go! There was is batasha at home, so I mixed some coconut and puffed rice.'

Troilokko kept the bowl aside and said, 'We will eat

later. First tell me, what is the matter? I can clearly see that something is wrong.' Kusum made no, sound for a while but soon, tears started rolling down her cheek. Then she suddenly spoke out in a quavering voice, 'I am in big trouble, Troilokko didi, and I am responsible for it! But now I am clueless about what to do!'

'What happened? Tell me.' Troilokko, who had come to have a chat and be comforted comforted Kusum by slowly rubbing her back. Kusum gathered herself, cleared her throat and said, 'I was the mistress of a customer named Nilmadhab babu. He was the one who had been paying my rent for the last four years. I have made a terrible mistake, didi! I have kicked out that good man. I am a sinner!'

'Why? If he was a good babu then why did you do so?'

'Out of greed, didi!' Kusum said while weeping. She continued. 'A new boy came for a few days to me. On getting influenced by him, I bit the hand that fed me. I thought that it was much rewarding to be the mistress of this young chap rather than that old man. That young guy used to shower notes on me like they were nothing to him. But what a fate I have! Right after I chucked out Nilmadhab babu, that young rascal stopped coming here. Today, I got the news that he had taken another woman as his mistress.'

'Then go and beg in front of Nilmadhab babu.' Troilokko gave her opinion on the matter, and after taking a spoonful of puffed rice mixed with finely diced coconut, she said, 'This kind of kicking and cursing happens a lot. This is nothing to worry about!'

'No didi, I have hammered the final nail in my coffin myself!' Kusum again started crying loudly. She said, 'The friends of Nilmadhab babu were forcing him to leave me for quite some time. I got the news that he had found a new admirer named Rupchand Pakshi. I tried to beg him to take me back, but he didn't even look at me. He said that he had no more interest in prostitutes anymore. What will I do, didi? I will starve to death!'

Then she lowered her voice and said, 'The only thing that I have with me now is a bit of jewellery gifted by Nilmadhab babu. But now, I think I have to mortgage them one by one.'

'What else will you do?' Troilokko said while she was thinking how she could arrange the money for Hari.

'Didi, tell me something.' Kusum again shook Troilokko by her shoulders, 'How can I win back the heart of Nilmadhab babu? If I can't bring him back from that woman, I will die of hunger, didi.'

Troilokko was looking at Kusum somewhat differently. There was an unknown emotion in her gaze.

'Troilokko didi!' Kusum almost shouted at her, 'Are you even listening or am I just blabbering alone!'

Troilokko then smiled and folded her lips in. Then she said, 'What a fool you are, Kusum!'

'Why?'

'If you would have told me this before, then your old babu would not have left you, and neither your new boyfriend would have gone away. Rather, your jewellery, money and everything would have doubled!'

'What do you mean!' Kusum stared at Troilokko, flabbergasted on hearing a scheme that sounded too good to be true.

'I'll explain,' Troilokko continued in a confident and soothing voice. 'I know a gurudev. He not only fulfils the wishes of his bhakts but also doubles their possessions by magic spells. If you had told me of your troubles, I would have taken you to him!'

'Is it true?' Kusum grabbed Troilokko's hands in excitement. She was too gullible to think rationally.

'Why should I joke, huh?' Troilokko continued. 'I still remember, the previous year, I took two girls to my gurudev.

He mostly roams around in the Himalayas, and rarely comes here. Luckily, he was there at that time. And then he just casted his spell. And now, they now have their own house and car and what not!'

'But,' Kusum seemed agitated, 'Will he be available now? Can you take me to him once?'

Troilokko nodded. 'Yes, he is around for some days, but he does not meet any strangers just like that. He is a yogi after all. There are lots of protocols.'

'I beg of you, didi, please take me to him once,' Kusum suddenly lay down on the floor touching her head on Troilokko's feet, 'Otherwise I will be finished!'

'He is now residing in a secluded garden. You will have to go there with all your jewellery. He will bless you at first and, then, if he is in the mood, he will double your belongings.'

Just after saying that, she paused for a bit thinking about something, and said, 'Can you come to Maniktala bridge around 4.00 in the morning? Beware, you will have to come alone. If Baba gets the hint that someone is with you, he will vanish in thin air!'

'I will come alone!' an elated Kusum promised.

∽

The sun was yet to rise, but the crimson hues had already adorned the high clouds. The darkness was gradually fading as time passed. Troilokko was walking fast towards the Maniktala bridge. She left home early in the morning when it was still dark. After climbing on the bridge and walking a few steps, she was able to spot Kusum through the thin fog. She was standing with a bag in her hand and was dressed in a good quality saree.

Troilokko went in front of Kusum and inspected her for a moment. She then said, 'Why is none of your jewellery on you? I told you to...'

'I have brought everything!' Kusum rolled her eyes towards the bag she was holding, 'I came alone walking through the empty streets, so I was not able to muster the courage to wear it. But I have brought everything with me.'

'Bravo! Now let us go, Baba does not meet people after the sun is up in the sky.' Both of them chatted a lot while walking. Kusum was a very innocent and simple girl, and she talked about her past, how many babus had slept with her, how many houses had she changed, etc.

After a while, she said, 'Where are you taking me, Troilokko di? This seems like a jungle!' After crossing the paved roads of the city and then walking through mud roads around its fringe, they had reached a jungle after a trek of two hours. Though it was around six in the morning, the place was devoid of much light. There was a strong aroma of leaves, which was quite unpleasant.

Troilokko was looking around carefully. She was coming to that area after almost two years, but it was highly improbable that she lost her way.'There, there it is, the big iron gate covered in vines!' Troilokko said to herself. She still remembers that one of her clients had brought her here to enjoy her for a night. It had been a long time since someone had stepped through the gate as the house was famous for being haunted. Troilokko spoke in a suppressed voice, 'We are here! You see that gate? We will go towards it. Come, follow me!'

Kusum followed her with a little fear in her heart.

It was evident that nobody lived around there. The big iron gate was almost indiscernible due to the big trunk of banyan tree that had grown around it. Troilokko pushed hard to open the rusty gate. After succeding, she called out Kusum, 'Come inside!'

Kusum was stunned as she entered the gate; a huge mansion occluded the sky like a dark cloud.

The mansion was so ancient and gargantuous that its sight was nothing to enjoy; rather, it invoked a sense of dread in the viewer. It was evident that in the last few decades, it had not recieved the footsteps of any living soul.

There was a time when the mansion had been snow white in color, but now the marbles were covered with reddish sediments due to rain. Two statue of lions facing each other on the roof were still partly recognizable. Every door and window in the mansion was closed. There was a time when there used to be a huge garden in front of the house. The pond on the other side was also still as dead.

Kusum asked Troilokko, 'Your gurudev lives here, Troilokko di? I...I am really scared!'

'If you are so scared then let us go back!' Troilokko seemed annoyed and agitated, 'I am here not for me but for you! If you are so spooked out, it is better that we return to Sonagachi.'

'No, no! When did I say so?' Kusum shook herself out of the fear that had encompassed her. She spoke in a confident voice, 'We will enter the mansion, right?'

'Wait!' Troilokko said in a serious tone, 'We just can't enter like that. He is a sadhu from the Himalayas. We can't just go and present ourselves in front of him! We will first have to bathe in that pond to wash off our sins, and then we will meet him while our clothes are still wet!'

Troilokko hurried towards the broken stairs on the pond's bank and said 'Come, keep your bag and your clothes here, then take a dip and pray to god so that your sins are washed off!'

Kusum took off her clothes and put them and her bag on the stairs in a hesitant manner. Then she started immersing herself in the water. When she was immersed till her knees, she called out, 'What about you, Troilokko di? Won't you wash off your sins?'

'What an idiot!' Troilokko suddenly mocked Kusum, 'Is it me whose jewellery are going to get doubled? You need the help. Hence, you take the dip.'

Kusum became attentive and serious again, and she immersed herself deeper in the pond. Troilokko silently scanned the surroundings. It was not dawn anymore. The sunlight was quite bright then. But there seemed to be nobody else around that place. The only sound coming was from a jungle babbler somewhere in the bushes.

Troilokko again recalled that devilish look on Hari's face and remembered his words, 'If I don't get ₹100 rupees by tomorrow, I will beat the crap out of you!' The words rang in her ears again and again.

Like a cat, she silently tiptoed towards Kusum. After she immersed herself upto her waist and got close to Kusum, she said, 'Issh! There is so much dirt on your back! Come here, I will clean it.'

'I cannot reach those areas all by myself didi, I…' Kusum was about to finish the sentence when Troilokko grabbed her neck and pushed Kusum inside the water. It didn't matter how desperately Kusum tried to beg for life, Troilokko seemed still as stone. After a couple of minutes, everything became as still as it was before.

After a while, Troilokko escaped with the bag full of jewellery that Kusum brought. And inside the pond, the lifeless body of Kusum floated upside down.

❧

When somebody sins for the first time, there is always a tussle between one's compunction and the will to sin. After the tussle is over and the devil in us wins, the person can do wrong things as easily as a weathered convict. They throw out words like ethics, morals and humanity out of their mind. With passing time, when that person becomes more habituated with crime, the sense of compassion vanishes completely.

The same happened with Troilokko. Soon, she started committing murders like it was her job. She became desperate, partly due to the fear of losing Hari and partly due to the fear for her own life. She found a confidant in Khungi, a woman who had come to her asking for a job as a domestic worker. Khungi was an example of how cruel and cunning a woman could be. With each passing day, she became the main partner of Troilokko in her devilish endeavours.

Nothing happened for about five days after Kusum went missing. Then, the other tenants and neighbours became curious about her. Troilokko acted her part of being a well-wisher and visited Kusum's place for quite a few times as if she was dying to know what happened to Kusum. The landlady was unhappy, not due to the absence of Kusum but the potential loss of dues that she owed her. Troilokko tried to sooth her as much as she could. Then, after a while, everybody forgot about a missing, old and broke sex worker.

After 10 or 12 days, the news came out in the local daily: a half-rotten, swollen corpse of a middle aged woman had been recovered from the swamp of an old, abandoned mansion, few miles from Maniktala. Someone passing by the mansion had discovered her body, when the grotty smell of decomposed flesh hit his nose. Everyone assumed that the woman committed suicide for some personal reasons.

The demands of Hari also started rising exponentially, and to meet Hari's demands, Troilokko's fearlessness also increased. Khungi started luring illiterate and innocent girls like Kusum with the promise of doubling their jewellery. And Troilokko lured them to the same abandoned ruins one at a time and drowned them in the pond. Then she grabbed their bijouterie and travelled back to her home without any signs of excitement.

In this way, within three years, five women met the same fate. The financial condition of Troilokko also became stable. Even after fulfilling Hari's ultimatums, there were still enough funds in her hand to live a decent life. But with the increased flow of money, her morality decreased.

Meanwhile, the police began suspecting foul play. After the autopsy of every body that was discovered, the cause of death was common—asphyxiation due to blockage of windpipe by water.

Troilokko took a woman named Angurbala, a retired sex worker, to that mansion with the same plan in mind. She was her sixth victim. When Troilokko pushed her into the water, the sound of the tussle caught the attention of two men who were passing by at that time. They witnessed the whole incident.

After witnessing such an act, they froze for a while but then came running to save the drowning lady and grabbed Troilokko. To maintain the secrecy of the place, Troilokko didn't even bring Khungi with her. Troilokko tried hard to escape from the men but she failed to get out of their grasp. They dragged Troilokko to the nearest police station.

At first, Troilokko behaved like a lioness caged against her will. She roared in a voice that could have made any single person pee in fear, 'Leave me! Let me go! You don't know who I am! I am Troilokko, the queen of Sonagachi! I will slit your throats. I am warning you people, leave me!' But when she realized that this attitude was not helping her, she became silent and started groaning. The officer-in-charge was not there in the police outpost at that time. There was just an old constable sitting outside. His name was Bipul Bihari Das. Though he had crossed the age of retirement about two years ago, still he was on service due to the forged dates in his documents.

Bipul Bihari used to be a regular customer of the red- light district. His perverted interests had not die down. The men who brought Troilokko to the police station were mostly illiterate, poor villagers. The leader among them said, 'Daroga babu, this woman was drowning another woman near a mansion.'

'Is that so?' Bipul Bihari observed Troilokko through his thick glasses. He did not fail to recognize Troilokko, the once famed star of Sonagachi. He had once visited Troilokko for a night. That scintillating experience suddenly flashed in his mind when he saw her.

Bipul Bihari asked in a casual way, 'Who was drowning whom?'

Another man came forward and said, 'She is the one behind the deaths we are reading about in the newspaper.'

'Is that so?' Bipul Bihari almost closed his eyes and yawned. He struggled to get up from his half-laid pose and suddenly made an angry face, 'Were you there when the rest of the murders happened? Joking with the police, huh? I will get all of you locked up!'

The men were very poor. They feared the police more than they expected help from them. Naturally, surprised by the unexpected behaviour of the Bipul Bihari, the men stared at each other. The matter of serial murders had already made itself a serious concern in the locality. When they ultimately caught the killer, they expected a welcoming gesture from the police. But they ended up getting the threat of being locked up!

Nobody dared to speak anymore.They knew about the hospitality police offered, and they were not keen to receive it. Bipul Bihari also blew away the matter as if nothing had happened. He politely said to Troilokko, 'Madam, please go home. If there is any need, we will contact you!' After getting such an easy escape from the point where she thought everything was finished, Troilokko was jaunty and exhilarated. She returned back to her home in a cheerful mood.

Khungi asked her, 'Why are you so late? I was quite worried!'

Troilokko didn't answer the question. She just said, 'An about-to-die old maggot will come. Even if I am not home, treat him nicely.'

Those men had also helped Angurbala reach her home that day. Right after she recovered, she informed her friends and relatives about Troilokko and her evil plans. She also contacted the police. The responsibility of investigating the matter was given to Priyonath Mukhopadhyay. The old enemies were brought in the ring by fate again.

Priyonath was always confident about the criminal nature of Troilokko. He was unable to catch her once due to dearth of evidence. Now, he began his investigation with full attention and care. On the first day of visiting the scene of crime, he found out the group of men who had apprehended Troilokko that day. And on the basis of information from the eyewitnesses and the victim Angurbala, he arrested Troilokko.

Troilokko was produced in court when the date of trial came. With her, the constable Bipul Bihari was also summoned. Everyone grilled him and demanded the explanation for releasing Troilokko on that day, in spite of complaints by direct eyewitnesses. Bipul Bihari was suspended from the job and arrested on the grounds of abetting a crime. His trial also continued in parallel with Troilokko's case. The case was promoted to Alipore district and session court.

Priyonath made sure that Troilokko did not escape this time. He did all he could in his power to ensure that. But by the weird justice of the God, gliding through the various loopholes of the British Acts, the veteran lawyer of Bipul Bihari pulled both of them out of the apparently unescapable whirlpool of Priyonath. They bribed all the first-hand witnesses on that day to give false statements.

As there was no evidence against Troilokko and Bipul Bihari, the court didn't give a verdict against them. She became free to kill—and she killed more.

❧

After the episode of court and trials, though Troilokko escaped the clutches of law, it became impossible for her to live in her locality anymore.

She changed her home to a smaller one in the lanes of Panchu Dhopani in Chitpur. Hari, the worthless son, accompanied her. That house, where the final chapters of Troilokko were written, still carries a bad reputation in present-day Kolkata.

The lane of Panchu Dhopani was filled with many tenants who were former sex workers. During the first few days in the new locality, Troilokko didn't go out much, but gradually, she started making friends with rest of the women there. The residents had no idea about her recent achievements and their spine-chilling details.

Troilokko rented a room on the first floor and her immediate neighbour was a woman named Priyobala. Troilokko developed a friendly relationship with her in a couple of days. Apart from that, there were other women named Kanakchapa and Labanya, who also resided in the first floor. Among the residents, there was also a woman named Rajkumari. Though she lived on the same floor, she was different from the rest. There was a time when she used to be the companion of a nawab and that earned her a lot of gold jewellery and precious gems. She was Troilokko's last victim.

In my analysis of her character, I understood that though she got caught in the circle of criminal activities due to her poor financial conditions, the influence of Kali babu, and the compulsion of Hari during her later days, crime became an enjoyable hobby for her instead of just need. Perhaps her insatiable greed changed her.

One day, while in conversation with Troilokko, Priyobala mentioned, 'Have you seen the attitude of Rajkumari? She always keeps herself locked in her room and never speaks to anyone. She behaves in a way as if she is a queen!'

'Yes, I have felt that too,' Troilokko replied. 'She doesn't even reply properly when I call her, as if it is really hard for her to smile. What's the reason behind her attitude, huh? She looks like a witch, with spots of pox all over and an ugly complexion.'

'It doesn't matter, she was a queen of seduction! Once, she had a client…' Priyobala suddenly lowered her voice. 'That babu was some nawab. He kept her in a three-storeyed home in Ahiritola. He kept her sunk in expensive clothes and jewellery! Then that babu closed his eyes and his sons threw out Rajkumari from the house. Rajkumari left her palace crying, with all her belongings, and then took a room here. That's her story!'

Troilokko tried to jovially wave off the seriousness in Priyobala's tone, 'Shut up! Haha! I have seen a lot of so called babus like that! If you would have seen my fanbase during my heyday, there was no shortage of kings and nawabs!'

'I know that, didi!' Priyo tried to please Troilokko, 'When I was at Jaanbazaar, I heard you name. Many babus came to me singing your praise. They all lauded your voice and dance.' Suddenly the warmth and appreciation in Priyobala's tone simmered down, and she returned back to her whispering mode, 'But Rajkumari still has a lot of jewellery, didi! You know Bidhi? That domestic worker on the groundfloor. She has seen it with her own eyes. She was the one who told me.'

'What did she see, huh?' Troilokko paused at once, and she recalled the days when she also used to have a chest full of jewellery in her house in Sonagachi.

So many years had passed since Kali babu had passed away. Troilokko regretted her decision of selling all her jewellery and property for the sake of her love. She regretted that Kali babu had not loved her. Rather, he had just used her for his needs.

But what did she get in return? She just increased her crimes to sustain herself and Hari, and all these sacrifices for what? Just to please a man who probably never loved her the way she did.

'There is a ton of gold in Rajkumari's room! That is why she always keeps herself locked inside her room and never invites anybody.'

❧

The year when this was happening was 1884. The then viceroy of India, Lord Ripon, proposed the Ilbert Bill, leading to a revolt by the entire white community. Before the Indian Civil Service Act of 1861, the entire State machinery of colonial India was solely in the hands of the British. When the law was passed in 1861, Anglo-Indians were also given some rights in the administration of the country. The amendment in 1897 made the ground for Indians in the administration of the country more solid.

By 1880, many learned Indians, especially Bengalis, were appointed to high-profile roles in the Raj government. With time, they were promoted to the posts of district magistrates, session judges and other esteemed positions. Although Indians were promoted to higher ranks in the judicial system, the power to judge a white person was not in the hands of Indians at that time. Only white judges could award any sentence to white convicts. It should also be mentioned that the salary and power of such Indian officers were far less than the white people.

To eliminate this racial discrepancy, the Viceroy Lord Ripon, famously known as an India sympathizer, ordered Councillor Ilbert to draft a Bill that would give equal judicial power to Indian judges. The Bill was to be drafted to bring in equal pay for them, apart from the power of judging white convicts.

As soon as this draft was released, there was a terrible repercussion throughout the entire white community. Their pride in being the superior race was clearly challenged by the possibility that Indians would be awarding them sentences for their crimes. They tried their best to resist the passing of the Bill in British Parliament.

On the other hand, eminent Indians like Surendranath Bandopadhyay started to raise awareness in favour of the Bill by holding public meetings across various parts of Calcutta. Needless to say, in this scenario, the police force of Calcutta was having a hard time maintaining law and order.

Daroga Priyonath also got busy during that time due to this reason. However, he heard the news that on the morning of 9 August 1884, a woman was murdered in the lane of Panchu Dhopani. It had been a while but the police were still nowhere near solving the case. Priyonath had some time after his outstation assignment, so he paid a visit to the crime scene. He observed that many of his collegues were roaming around the area.

'What is the matter with you, moshai?' an officer frowned at Priyonath and asked, 'A murder like this took place in the city and you were nowhere to be found!'

Priyonath smiled back. 'I was on deputation to a different

department, you know…for that Ilbert Bill. I just came here to see what's the progress. Who is killed?'

'The victim is an old prostitute,' the officer lowered his tone, 'Rajkumari. The preliminary estimated motive is her stock of jewellery and ornaments.'

'How did she die?'

'She was strangled to death. Police surgeon Dr S.C. Mackenzie has performed an autopsy; someone climbed onto her chest and strangled her. Many small bones of the ribcage were broken. Perhaps it was some unhappy customer. He not only killed her but also ran away with her jewellery.'

Priyonath was scanning through the entire scene minutely. The house was very shabby, and it was evident that the residents of that area were anything but reputable. There were an array of rooms right after the main door, and the next floor was structured in the same way.

Priyonath asked, 'Did the killer come from outside?'

'That is still not clear,' replied the officer. 'A domestic worker named Bidhi opened the main door every morning when we came to investigate. But she was not able to say anything clearly. One time, she said that she saw the door wide open when she got up in the morning, and the next time, she said that it was perhaps closed! A bunch of idiots!'

'Can you give me the interrogation report? I just want to go through it once,' Priyonath continued while smiling, 'I am on leave today, and reading an interrogation report would be a good way to kill time.'

'The body of the victim Rajkumari was discovered in her own room on the morning of 9 August 1884. The incident was first discovered by a domestic worker named Bidhi who resided on the same address. The door was closed but not bolted. After knocking several times, when there was no response, she barged into the room. She found that the dead body was lying on the floor. Upon finding it, she immediately informed the rest of the residents, and everyone agreed to first inform the landlord. The landlord informed his neighbour, and from him, the news reached the police.

'The police discovered that the door was closed and the dead body was lying over a straw mat on the floor. There were no visible signs of assault on the body, but fingerprints were clear on her throat. There were also signs of nails gouging the skin. After the autopsy of the body, the police surgeon Dr Mackinzie reported that someone sat on the chest of the deceased and strangled her to death.

'There was nothing else in the room apart from common furniture. There were two brass bowls by the side of the bed. There were traces of curd and flattened rice on them. The assumption is that two persons ate the dinner the previous night and one of them was the victim, as traces of the same food was found in her stomach. Thus, the primary assumption is that the second individual might be the killer.'

While reading the report, Priyonath thought for a while, 'The door was closed and the dinner was had together. It points to the fact that the killer was someone known to the victim.'

He resumed reading:

'All the jewellery boxes and chests of the victim were in a broken state. There was nothing expensive inside, but it was reported by the other residents that she used to possess a lot of jewellery and ornaments. A list of her jewellery was also prepared after interrogation of the other residents.

'Whether any man came to visit her, just before the night of murder, that is, on the night of 8 August, is still not certain from the interrogations. But it was reported that two residents of the first floor came to her that night for casual chatting. This is reported by the domestic worker Bidhi.

The next morning, Bidhi found that the door was closed, but there are still doubts over her statement as she does not appear mentally sound. According to her description, there is no logical way for the murderer to escape.'

Priyonath raised his gaze up from the pages.

Later, when he met his colleague, he asked, 'Have you considered the possibility that the murderer might have sought somewhere in the house throughout the night, and when Bidhi opened the main door in the morning, they made a run for it?'

'No, moshai!' replied the other officer. 'Along with Bidhi, the two ladies who went to the victim's room the previous night were also on the porch when she opened the main door. They also did not see anyone running out.'

'What is the name of those two ladies?'

'Priyobala and Troilokkotarini. Both of them are helping a lot in the investigation, especially Troilokkotarini. In these four days, she has aided us while searching through the entire house.'

Priyonath was horrified. 'Are you sure that the name is Troilokkotarini?'

'Yes, moshai!' the other officer said and poured in a paan in his mouth.

'Her son's name is Hari, right?' Priyonath asked with eyes wide open.

The other officer, who was pleasantly chewing the paan, suddenly stopped and said, 'Yes, you are right! Do you know him?'

Priyonath seemed visibly excited, 'This the same Troilokko who was caught few years back and her trial went on in the Alipore district and session court. She was accused of killing five women in a deserted house near Maniktala. She had a narrow escape at that time due to lack of evidence and testimonials. You are a part of the Calcutta Police and you have not heard the name Troilokkotarini before! The women who should be in the crosshairs is rather serving you paan!'

The officer had stopped chewing long before. He was discombobulated for a while and then snapped back, 'Huh? Then what shall we do? Should we arrest her?'

'What will you achieve by arresting her?' said Priyonath, 'You don't know Troilokko. There is no criminal act that she cannot accomplish. This path is not going to work. We have to think differently. We have to lay a trap so that she herself admits to all her crimes.'

Then all of the policemen discussed something among themselves. All the other residents of the house except Troilokko were called individually. Priyonath wanted to talk to them personally.

On the same evening, Priyonath again visited the crime scene at Panchudhopani lane, and Troilokko was directly brought in front of Priyonath for questioning. A policeman said, 'Priyonath babu, you have been interrogating many people. But we have information that there are many accusations of murder against this Troilokkotarini before this incident. What do you think? Is she the one who have killed Rajkumari?'

Priyonath was sitting in a chair. He rose up, observed Troilokko carefully, and said, 'You made me interrogate everyone in the area. If you would not have allowed me to do that, I would have assumed that Troilokko is the killer. But now I am sure that she is completely innocent. I am going to shred Troilokko's previous reports, as everyone has described a different scenario this time. I am sure of the fact that Troilokko has no involvement in this murder!' Troilokko kept staring at Priyonath cluelessly. Disbelief was visible on her face. She was unable to believe her ears.

'But how are you so sure that she is not involved in this murder?' asked another officer.

'Because I am sure about who the real culprit is!' Priyonath said the words and signalled the other officer, 'Let Troilokko go.'

At first, Troilokko was completely silent in awe. Then she almost jumped to the feet of Priyonath, 'How can I thank you, babu! Finally, I am relieved from such a great disaster!'

'Don't worry,' Priyonath stepped back hesitatingly and ordered a constable standing near him. 'Call everyone in the area. Everyone deserves to know who the real killer is!'

Troilokko stood up and sat in a corner in a very relaxed mood. She still could not believe that Priyonath himself released her this time. But then, who was the suspected killer? Troilokko was now curious. In a few minutes, Bidhi, Kamini, Labanya, Priyobala and the rest of the residents came. Hari also stumbled in.

At first, Priyonath called Kamini, and he started grilling her mercilessly. In a few minutes, she revealed, 'Babu, I woke up very late in the night once and then I saw that Hari, the son of Troilokko didi, was approaching the room of Rajkumari as silently as a cat.'

Troilokko was stunned by the words, and Hari was dumbstruck.

Priyonath said, 'Is that so? Then why didn't you call the rest of the people?'

'But Sir, why shall I wake up the others? Hari often visits the room of Rajkumari in the night. Both of them drink together and make love till the morning!'

'What the hell are you talking, Kamini?' Troilokko couldn't control keep anymore. 'Hari was like a son to Rajkumari, and you are saying they made love to each other every night! How can you lie so blatantly!' Then she turned towards Priyonath and said, 'Huzur, please don't believe a word of this witch. She is lying!'

Priyonath stopped Troilokko's speech by raising his

hand. Then he continued interrogating Kamini and all the descriptions clearly pointed towards Hari as the killer.

Then came Bidhi. She scratched her hair and said, 'When I opened the door in the morning, Hari pushed me away and ran off. I saw him running out of Rajkumari didi's room!'

'Lie...lie!' Troilokko shouted at the top of her voice, 'Scoundrel girl! The maggots will eat you alive! You are lying so casually about my son! You will not even get a place in hell!'

After that came Labanya, Kanakchapa and the rest. Everyone agreed that there was a secret affair between Hari and Rajkumari. Hari already earned a fame as a regular visitor of Sonagachi and a miserable drunkard, and everyone repeated that Hari used to visit Rajkumari every night. They also said that on the night of the murder, there was a fight between Hari and Rajkumari.

Priyonath ordered the other policemen, 'Arrest Hari right now! I will get the warrant.'

At first Troilokko was dumbstruck for a moment. Then she cried out loud, grabbed Priyonath by his feet and howled, 'Huzur! I can swear by god that Hari is innocent. He is not a boy like that. Believe me, everyone is lying about him!'

Priyonath didn't pay much heed to her. He continued to note down the report of the interrogation in his diary. She grabbed Hari tightly and said in a choked voice, 'Hari! My son! Don't leave me! I will give whatever you want! Priyonath babu, please don't take him away from me!'

Hari was almost stoned. The abruptness of the entire episode had hit him so hard that he even forgot to cry. Troilokko and Hari could not believe that in a fraction of an hour, everyone unanimously told a concrete lie to frame him as the killer. The police van arrived in a few minutes. Hari was bound in cuffs and dragged to the van, but Troilokko clinged on to him. She held him almost like an iron shackle, impossible to pull apart. Like a deranged person, she continued howling, 'I will not let him go! I will not let him go! He is innocent! Why are you taking him? How will I live without him? I will not let him go!'

Priyonath ordered the officers to separate the mother and son. He smiled calmly and said, 'I am really feeling sorry for you. Troilokko That babu of yours…what was his name? Kali! He was hanged and you couldn't do anything. Now your son will share the same fate as his father, and you will have to see that with your own eyes! Don't be sad, this is just the game of fate.'

Troilokko suddenly stopped crying and looked at Priyonath with a gaze that was enough to vaporize cities. There was a peculiar insanity, rage and helplessness in her tone when she said, 'Hanged?! Hari will be hanged?!'

'He has committed murder, what do you expect? Will we treat him like a god?!' A policeman said with a mocking tone.

Troilokko was cold as ice for some moments. Then, in a roaring voice, she shouted, 'Daroga babu! Hari didn't kill anyone! I am the killer! In the name of Maa Kali, I am speaking the truth. I killed Rajkumari!'

'That is not true, Troilokko,' Priyonath said. 'Now you are just trying to take the blame to save your son. Everyone can understand that!'

'No!' Troilokko shouted, 'I …I am speaking the truth. I, along with Priyobala, have killed Rajkumari! All her jewels are with me!' Hearing this, Priyobala, who was standing at a distance, became white with terror.

'How is that possible? We have searched your room thoroughly and there is nothing there!' said another police officer.

'It is there!' Troilokko kept shouting, 'There is a secret

locker in my almirah, all the jewellery is there. Come with me, I will show it to you!'

'Is that so?' Priyonath acted like he was literally surprised with the new revelation, 'How did you kill Rajkumari? And why did you kill her?'

Troilokko closed her eyes and simmered down her voice, 'I, along with Priyo, planned to steal the jewellery of Rajkumari by making her unconscious. To do that, I arranged some seeds of *dhutro* and crushed them. Dhutro seeds are very poisonous!'

'How did you get them?'

'From a far away forest. I mixed a little bit of that powder with some sweets,' Troilokko bit her lips. 'On that evening, I and Priyobala went to Rajkumari's room. She didn't invite us, but we insisted. She was not very happy, but we still carried on chatting. When it was around 11.30 p.m., Priyo said, "Let us go, Troilokko didi, it seems Rajkumari di will not offer us anything to eat! I am feeling hungry. Let us go."'

'Then?' asked Priyonath.

'Then, to save herself from being shamed, Rajkumari asked us to sit and brought sweet curd mixed with flattened rice for us. I took some in my mouth and said that it was not sweet at all. Then Priyobala said that she will bring sweets from her room, and she brought the poisoned sweets. We gave the poisoned ones to Rajkumari.'

Troilokko paused for a breath, and then she continued, 'But she insisted on not taking the sweets. After a lot of requests, she took one, but she was completely alright after eating that. Then I asked Priyobala to bring some tobacco for the hookah. I had told her about the back-up plan and beforehand, as instructed, she brought the tobacco laced with that poisonous powder. But even after that, Rajkumari was not fully unconscious, though she was a little intoxicated. It was already too late. So, we didn't wait anymore.'

'Then what did you do?'

Troilokko took a deep breath and replied, 'Then I was left with no other option but to kill her. I ordered Priyobala to grab her feet. I climbed on her chest and choked her with my hands. Rajkumari struggled a lot, but she was not able to keep up with me. Then she stopped moving altogether and never waked up!' Troilokko covered her face with her hands.

After a long time and a eerie silence, she removed her hands from her face and spoke in a tired voice, 'Please hang me! But let Hari go. He is innocent.'

'But why shall we trust you? You may be just telling a story,' Priyonath started playing around, 'Do you have any evidence to support your claim?'

'Yes,' Troilokko replied. 'In that secret locker, beside the jewellery, you will also find more of those poisonous sweets. I had hidden them so that Hari does not consume them accidentally. You will also find the poisoned tobacco there. And for the rest, you may interrogate Priyo.'

Eventually, the jewellery of Rajkumari, the poison-laced sweets and the tobacco were recovered from that secret locker in Troilokko's room. Priyobala also gave in and told the truth. Finally, Troilokko was arrested.

But she was not devastated on her arrest. Before embarking on her journey towards the police van, she embraced Hari tightly and said, 'Be good, my child! Don't worry about me, be good!'

Though Priyonath failed to get Troilokko punished for first two murders, he understood one simple truth. However cruel and cunning Troilokko was, when it came to Hari, she loved him more than anything else. There was no impurity in her love towards her stepson. That is why Priyonath made Hari his trump card to extract the truth and the evidence from Troilokko herself. He had planned the whole game with the other residents to reach that point.

In a few days time, the sensational case *The Empress vs Troylucko Raur* got its date in the court. This time, Priyonath didn't leave any stone unturned. The nail marks on the throat of the victim matched those of Troilokko. The fingerprint on the brass bowls matched with Troilokko's. From the intoxicated sweets to the stolen jewellery found in her secret locker, everything was presented as solid evidence against her in the court.

The coroner who did the autopsy Dr Mackinzie, the domestic worker Bidhi, Kamini, Kanakchapa and everyone else in the house except Priyobala were presented as witneses. Even the testimonials of the women from Sonagachi were also recorded, which revealed the past series of crimes commited by Troilokko. And Angurbala, the woman who cheated death by a hair's breadth, was also called in to give her testimonial against Troilokko.

After some hearings, Troilokko was sentenced to death on 3 September 1884. Though Priyonath was lauded for his efforts in winning the case, somewhere deep inside him, Troilokko's maternal instinct left an unerasable impression. He also visited Troilokko in the jail to meet her. For a few days, just before her hanging, Troilokko was calm and quiet.

The day he visited her, Troilokko said to him, 'Daroga babu, I understood that you were extracting the truth from me using Hari as bait. I am not angry about that. But I have two requests for you. Will you please fulfil them?'

Priyonath asked, 'What requests?'

Troilokko looked through the grills of the high window in her cell. In a broken voice, she said, 'Right from the day I first came to this city, I had only one dream to—witness Vidyasagar babu with my own eyes. I thought I will pay my respect to him even from a distance. He is the one who has erased the sorrows of widows. I am a sinner, but if things had gone well for me, I would have had a family even after being widowed!' Troilokko sobbed as she told, 'Can you… can you please pay my respect to him once, Daroga babu?'

Priyonath was taken aback. It was really unexpected to hear the name of a luminary like Vidyasagar from the mouth of a convict sentenced to death.

But he didn't express his emotions. He just nodded his head and said, 'Okay, I will covey this wish of yours to him. The next one?'

Troilokko then took a few seconds, and said in a low voice, 'Daroga babu, will you please check up on Hari sometimes in a while? He is a bit stubborn. Everyone thinks that he is a drunkard and spends money on girls. But he is really a good boy at his core.' Troilokko started crying incessantly while saying, 'Who will look after him in my absence, Darogababu? I beg of you, please promise me that you will look after him!'

Priyonath had expected to see a dark realm, but what he was confronted with left him speechless.

Everyone has forgotten Troilokko, who once ruled Sonagachi. Everyone has forgotten that girl who trusted her love and followed him to the city of Calcutta only to be pushed into hell. Perhaps everyone still remembers her deeds as the earliest acts of serial killing in India. But perhaps it was only Priyonath who recognized Troilokko as a mother who loved her child above everything else.

BIBLIOGRAPHY

Anand, Pinky, and Gauri Goburdhun, 'From the Case Books of Hired Assassins: How an Eye-Doctor's Wife Was Murdered', *Scroll.In*, 21 December 2017, http://tinyurl.com/3p7t29pm. Accessed on 31 December 2023.

Anant Chintaman Lagu vs The State of Bombay, 14 December 1959, 1960 AIR 500, 1960 SCR (2) 460, http://tinyurl.com/2u9tsz5x. Accessed on 31 December 2023.

Bandyopadhyay, Aparna, 'Violence and Love in Late Colonial Bengal', *Journal of Social Sciences*, Lady Brabourne College, Kolkata, 2016.

Chakraborty, Yajnaseni, '"Khoka" Then and Now, Kolkata's Notorious Pagla Murder Case', *Get Bengal*, 20 May 2021, http://tinyurl.com/42eravsp. Accessed on 31 December 2023.

Dalvi, Prastut, and Vidhi Thaker, 'Historical Series: The Malabar Hill Murder Trial of 1925', *The Leaflet*, 20 September 2020, http://tinyurl.com/3nx7ppen. Accessed on 31 December 2023.

Dash, Etishree, 'The Contract Killing of Mrs Vidya Jain', *Lawminds*, http://tinyurl.com/5n8r6d8t. Accessed on 31 December 2023.

Forbes, Geraldine, 'In Search of Elokeshi: The Death of Young Wife in Colonial India', *Readings in Bengali History: Identity Formation and Colonial Legacy*, Asha Islam Nayeem and Aksadul Alam (eds.), Bangladesh History Association, 1 January 2017, pp. 139-162.

Garg, Jaanvi, 'Tarakeswar Affair', *Legal-lore*, 25 August 2022, http://tinyurl.com/bdzy54nj. Accessed on 31 December 2023.

Gauba, Khalid Latif, *The Shamim Rahmani Case and Other Famous Trials*, Hind Pocket Books, 1971.

Ghosh, Deepanjan, 'Sex Worker, Con-Woman, Serial Murderess: The Story of Troilokya, Who Terrorised Calcutta in 1800s', *Scroll.In*, 26 November 2018, http://tinyurl.com/2vv23ab8, Accessed on 31 December 2023.

Ghosal, P.N., 'Pagla Murder Case', *Calcutta Police Journal*, Vol. 1 No. 1, 1939.

Kapoor, Abeer, 'A Decade after the Nanavati Case, Another Crime of Passion Jolted and Fascinated India', *Scroll.In*, 4 June 2018, http://

PB-3551 8

tinyurl.com/38htvpvt. Accessed on 31 December 2023.

Kulkarni, Dhaval, *The Bawla Murder Case: Love, Lust and Crime in Colonial India.* HarperCollins Publishers, 2021.

Mukhopadhyay, Priyanath, 'Darogar Daptar No. 78', *Darogar Daptar No. 73-84,* Baninath Nandi, Kolkata, 1898.

N.S. Jain vs The State, 29 September 1977, ILR 1978 Delhi 327, 1978 RLR 442, http://tinyurl.com/ynjrua9d. Accessed on 31 December 2023.

Nair, Thankappan P, *History of Calcutta's Streets,* Punthi Pustak.

Sarkar, Tanika, *Hindu Wife, Hindu Nation Community: Community, Religion, and Cultural Nationalism,* Indiana University Press, 2001.

Shamim Rahmani Etc vs State Of U.P., 28 April 1975, 1975 AIR 1883, 1975 SCR 315, http://tinyurl.com/yckah2tj. Accessed on 31 December 2023.

Shriyanshi, 'Bawla Murder Case 1925', *Legal Vidhiya,* 7 April 2023, http://tinyurl.com/2y2rrhkd. Accessed on 31 December 2023.

Sir Tukojirao Holkar vs Sowkabai Pandharinath, 1929, 31 BOMLR 7, 117 Ind Cas 424, http://tinyurl.com/2vw2hhjb. Accessed on 31 December 2023

The Empress vs Troyluckho Nath Chowdhry And Ors, 12 November 1878, (1879) ILR 4 Cal 366, http://tinyurl.com/585cncu6. Accessed on 31 December 2023.